CAPTURED

GATEKEEPERS OF THE GODS

JENNIFER CHANCE

OLIVERHEBERBOOKS

Cover design by Dar Albert

0 9 8 7 6 5 4 3 2 1

 Created with Vellum

For Misti
Run with the stars, beautiful girl.

Prologue

A bright, bold moon lit up Timiménos, capital city of Oûros, and Dimitri Korba could still hear the far-off sounds of the street parties. It seemed like the whole country was celebrating the recent engagement of the crown prince—and so they should. It was a welcome piece of good news for a royal family, who'd had to endure far too much tragedy this past year.

But deep in the forest that bordered the royal palace, all was still and dark. Any Oûrois native knew the trees in this hidden vale could conspire to block out intruding light whenever privacy was required. Tonight was apparently one of those nights. Most likely, a chatter of nymphs had decided to throw a pool party in one of the forest's enchanted grottos, and guests were decidedly unwelcome.

Dimitri typically made it his policy to avoid the forest when any minor deities of Olympus snuck out to breathe in real, mortal air. He didn't have anything against nymphs, of course. They, like he, were consecrated to Zeus, which automatically elevated them in his opinion. Unlike him, they were also gener-ally content to stay well within the borders of Oûros, frequenting only the specially consecrated grounds of the country's forested, remote countryside.

There were several such spaces within the country of Oûros, designated earthbound playgrounds for when the minor gods tired of Olympus. Which was often.

Dimitri couldn't blame them for that, either. From everything he'd heard, Olympus was filled with way too much drama. If the nymphs had sought out a quiet retreat to let their hair down and laugh with their sisters, they undoubtedly needed it.

Tonight, however, the wind had carried a terrified cry to his ears as he'd stood on the back balcony of the royal palace, and he hadn't hesitated. He'd dropped over the wall to the manicured lawn and taken off at a run. Within moments, he'd entered the forest, senses prickling with apprehension. Nymphs didn't cry out. They never needed to, especially in the modern era when they were no longer hunted by humans or gods for entertainment. These days, they enjoyed both Earth and Olympus freely and joyfully, never having to cower in fear.

But the cry he'd heard had definitely been one of fear.

He crept closer, noting that there was no sound of birds or wild creatures in the trees. That also wasn't right. When the nymphs came to play, all of creation played with them. He also couldn't hear any splashing and laughter that should have been coming from the nearest pool. Someone or some*thing* had chased most of the nymphs into hiding, perhaps all the way back to Olympus. All except the one whose cry was close and real.

"No!"

This time, the word was a little more than a gasp. Dimitri froze for half a beat, then pivoted slowly forty-five degrees to the north, his sharp gaze piercing the darkened forest. He set off again, treading softer now, lighter, using the skills that he'd learned in the Oûros National Security Force, as well as through all his years of active combat duty serving crown, country, and occasionally, god. Zeus was the patron of all nymphs, regardless of their parentage. Dimitri could do no less than ensure their safety.

As he drew closer, a new sound broke through the stillness. Muffled sobbing. Then another harsher, darker, more guttural voice murmured, "*Yes.*"

A male, but not a man, Dimitri knew immediately. First, no mortal would dare trespass into the royal forest, not if they valued their life. Secondly, the gods of Olympus didn't speak quite the same as humans. Their voices contained a resonance, a strange timbre that jolted mortal bones, as readily identifiable as fingerprints.

It wasn't a major god who'd trapped the nymph, he didn't think. They constrained their activities to where no one could stop them. For a minor deity though, the playgrounds of Earth gave them more freedom to be assholes.

Not tonight, though.

The nymph cried out again, more urgently, the sound cut off as if her mouth had been quickly and brutally covered. Dimitri moved forward, unerringly homing in on the location of the sound. Within only a few moments he was right up on the couple, their fervent whispers echoing over the surface of one of the Pools of Timelessness that linked Olympus and Oûros.

Then he heard a sound that stopped him short. The hiss of snakes.

His brows shot up. Snakes meant Typhon, one of the biggest assholes of the Greek pantheon, but Dimitri didn't think the monster god was stupid enough to breach the gates of Olympus. It was one thing for his minions to slink out and attempt to wreak havoc in the world, but not a primary god, or as primary as that slithering eel could ever be after Zeus dropped a mountain on him back in the good old days.

Then again... there'd been some talk of Typhon stirring up

mortals of late, sneaking into their dreams in Morpheus's shadow, whispering tales of riches and power. If this minor asshole deity was in service to the monster god, it'd be interesting to capture and interrogate him. The gods might be getting twitchy, especially with Oûros attracting international attention with the royal engagement. Perhaps, Dimitri thought, he should watch, wait, and make his move after the two minor deities split up.

"Please... *no*." The broken, desperate cry of the nymph settled it for him.

He crashed through the remaining trees, surging out into a surprisingly bright grotto, the pool beyond gleaming with the light of the full moon. In one smooth motion, he leaned down, scooped up both deities, and vaulted with them into the deep water of the pool—the nymph's natural habitat and usually a source of strength for her kind.

True to form, the moment she hit the pool, the nymph somersaulted away. She transformed into a streak of light as she shot deeper into the pool, back to where the water disappeared into a heavily shadowed cave. Dimitri's focus on her safety nearly was his undoing, though, as he turned back just in time to duck beneath a punch from the monstrous creature that rose up from the surface of the water. The minor god roared and dove for him, but Dimitri flipped backward and kicked away toward the edge of the pool, his powerful legs driving him out of reach. He hauled himself out of the water as a crack of lightning split the night sky far above, and whirled back to get a good look at his adversary

"You dare!" The first impression Dimitri got of the guy was snakes—lots of snakes, streaming out from his head like he was some drag queen Medusa, writhing off his shoulders and down his legs. All of them hissed and snapped, venom dripping from their teeth, as their keeper staggered out of the water. "You have no authority here."

"Go home, wormboy." Dimitri squared himself even with the minor god, balancing on his toes. "And don't let me catch you pulling that shit again. Things have changed, and you know it. Even in Olympus, no means no."

"You're nothing but a rejected changeling. When the true power of the gods rises, you'll regret ever attempting to control us—any of us."

"I'm sure I will." Once again, Dimitri knew he should trap the god, use him. Something about the smug, shifty-eyed creep dripping in snakes hit him the wrong way, setting aside the stench of rot that wafted off him. "In the meantime, keep your slimy hands off Zeus's daughters. Go fuck some pond scum if you're feeling lonely."

The god's snakes hissed wildly as he bristled, his meaty fists balling up. "I should kill you right now."

Dimitri grinned. "Try it and die. And sure, you'll just wake up in the underworld, but even Hades knows dogshit when he sees it. I'm thinking you won't be getting out to see the sunlight for oh, another thousand years, but go ahead. Take your best shot."

The monster god roared in outrage just as Dimitri's pocket vibrated with a quick, staccato urgency. *Shit.* A text from Prince Kristos. No other communications could override his phone's automatic notifications freeze when he was getting his demigod on.

Still, he had a few minutes. "Here we go, wormboy."

Dimitri bolted forward, fists clenched, arms pumping. Another bolt of lightning ripped through the night sky, and Dimitri roared with wild, ecstatic joy. He was made for battle, he was made for storms. He was made to kick this asshole straight onto Hades' trash heap.

If he struck the monster god before the asshole poofed, it meant the deity consented to do battle, which further meant he was free game. But the minor god's eyes widened with legit terror as Dimitri pounded toward him, and Dimitri knew it was because he'd guessed right: wormboy had undoubtedly pissed off the god of the underworld at some point in the last three thousand years, and Hades wasn't great at forgetting. If he could just—get—to him—

Dimitri lunged the last few feet, arms outstretched—

And soared into open space. He tucked and rolled, well used to chasing the gods back to Olympus. He came up to his feet again just a few feet shy of the water's edge. Wormboy was nowhere to be seen.

Dimitri's phone buzzed again.

"I hear you," he muttered, pulling the waterproof unit free from his pants. He stared down at the screen and scowled.

"You've got to be shitting me." The entitled blonde ice princess hadn't been back in Oûros for five hours, and already she was causing problems? This night was getting better and better. Still, he punched back a quick response.

He'd find Lauren Grant and get her back to the castle, then head to his office and do some research on the current crop of Typhon fanatics worldwide. If wormboy's little dig meant there was a bunch of the monster god's fanboys about to stage a convention, the Crown needed to know about it. More likely, though, it was empty threats from an idiot with snakes for brains.

He turned away from the pool when a splash caught his attention. He glanced up, then shook his head with a smile.

Two dozen nymphs now floated at the far end of the pool, their collective glow rising at his attention, lighting them up like Disney fairies. "Thank you..." Their whispers flowed across the pool toward him, though they were too timid to come closer.

"Yeah, yeah." He lifted his hand, waving them back to their party. He didn't have to warn them to be more careful next time. The nymphs also didn't forget, and were smart enough not to make the same mistake twice.

The blonde he was about to go babysit was another story.

Shaking his head, Dimitri set out again toward the bright lights and music of the city.

One

Tonight wasn't about doing everything perfectly. Tonight was about letting go.

Flipping the *tsipouro* glass over with a flourish and smacking it down onto the table, Lauren Grant smiled with the first surge of honest pleasure she'd felt in weeks. After a whirlwind tour of Europe, she and her friends had returned to Oûros today, reuniting with the last of their group—who was also the soon-to-be newest member of the Oûros royal family.

Lauren loved Emmaline like a sister, but she'd only been trapped behind the palace walls for a few hours before she'd started getting antsy, too jittery in her own skin. She'd had to work way too hard to find this dive bar in the seaside paradise of Timiménos, and harder still to ditch her friends and the persistent tagalongs from the palace security. But it was worth it.

She'd spent most of her life under the careful watch of others, and that hadn't kept her safe. For safety, she'd had to rely on herself. Same for having fun.

Two men and one woman were left facing her across the table. The woman listed to the side, supported by her husband, who kept shaking his head and grinning. The pile of cash in the center of the table was barely enough to buy a pair of shoes, but cash was never the goal anyway. It was simply a way to keep score.

The goal was to be the last woman standing.

"Another!" Lauren called out, and a cheer went up from the crowd circling the tiny table, along with laughter and catcalls, the usual fare of late-night drinking contests. The waitress moved forward, a new round of *tsipouro* at the ready, but the husband waved her off as his wife slumped fully against him.

That left two.

Lauren smiled saucily at the duo. She was almost certain they were brothers, which didn't bode well for her. They were big men, swarthy, their Greek heritage not a distant echo but evident in every line of their sun-worn faces and thick, dark hair. These were the true backbone of the Mediterranean, not the people living in the vaunted castle on the hill, where her dear friend Emmaline was being courted by an actual prince. Hell, not even courted. She was going to marry the guy. And that was cause for celebration.

"*Yamas!*" She raised her glass with the word to another round of applause. Close enough to the Oûrois equivalent of "cheers," her lapse into Greek made her competitors eye each other smugly. The three of them tilted the *tsipouro* back, and the potent grape liquor washed down Lauren's throat in a fiery line of absolution. The distilled spirits might have been made of the dregs of the wine-making process, but it definitely packed a punch.

As she crashed her glass down on the table and more money changed hands, she saw him.

It didn't take much. A shift of the crowd in exactly the right way, the right-dodging face that should have dodged left. She didn't squint into the gloom surrounding their table to make sure, because she didn't have to. The man was Dimitri Korba, ranking captain of the Oûros National Security Force. Kind of a high-rent shadow, but that didn't improve her mood.

Dimitri Korba was everything Lauren didn't need right now, here in this tiny little bar in the seaside capital city of Oûros on the one occasion in days she'd been able to escape her carefully cultivated world.

Granted, the man was mouthwateringly gorgeous in a big, iron-fisted kind of way. Six foot four if he was an inch, he wasn't built like the guys she knew back at home, their lean muscles and sinewy bodies honed with miles on the bike and the tread-mill. Dimitri Korba was a giant. Heavily muscled legs, powerful arms, granite-set jaw beneath his dark, flashing eyes. Everything about him angled dark, from his richly tanned skin to his black hair to his obstinate scowl. He was the quintessential bull, deter-mined to tromp into any china shop in his way if it blocked him from his goal.

But in the end, he was simply another babysitter.

And Lauren knew how to handle those.

Swiveling around, she waved for the waitress, not missing the fact that the arc of her swing was a little too wide, a little too sloppy. Finally, the drink was taking effect. Finally, for at least a little while, the game was changing. She wouldn't have to think for a while, wouldn't have to think about anything but the next hour or how she was going to get herself home. Tomorrow, there would be consequences. There would always be consequences. But in this moment, she didn't need to worry about—

"Miss Grant." Strong hands caught her as she canted dangerously to the right. The right? Hadn't she been moving to the left? She blinked up into the impossibly hard planes and harsh, dark-eyed stare of the man looming over her. Because that was what Dimitri Korba did best. He loomed.

"I thought that was you back there," she said archly. She could always do "arch," even drunk off her ass. She'd be able to do "arch" when she was ten years dead, she suspected. "Stand aside. I have a wager with these men." She turned around, but her drinking mates were gone from the table, standing at a distance. They looked at her reproachfully, their gaze ricocheting in a triangle between her, Dimitri, and the small pile of euros between them. She could tell immediately that the game had soured, and anger blossomed within her, thick and hot. "Oh, great. Look what you've done."

She spoke in Oûrois as a matter of course, though the desire to slip into a flow of utterly American curses was almost impossible to beat down. She shoved Dimitri away, and he stepped back easily, fluidly, with the movements of a born fighter. Then she stood, proud that she didn't falter, and held herself precisely in check to ensure her center of gravity was stable. She inclined her head with all the grace born of twenty-three years of Grant family training and control. Lifting her chin again, she smiled at the two men and gestured to the cash.

"I default by cause of this ox beside me," she said, her words ringing out loudly in the now preternaturally quiet bar. She had a feeling Dimitri did that a lot, intimidated others merely by standing near them. "The money is yours, with my thanks. And here." She reached for her purse, startled when Dimitri's large, bronzed hand shot out to cover hers.

For a moment, she stared at it. His hand looked overlarge, almost cartoonish against hers. She was no simpering pale flower, but her light golden tan couldn't compare to his skin tone, weathered almost to burnt sienna with the work he must do in the sun all the time. The sun, the wind, the rain, the—

Focus. She was losing control here, the *tsipouro* hitting her too hard after barely seeming to affect her for the past hour. It had been that way last time, but she'd been building up a tolerance since then, she'd thought. The same way she'd been building up a tolerance to Dimitri Korba.

Neither of those was working out too well right now.

"Let go of me," she said curtly.

He smirked but obligingly dropped her hand. "Your wish is my command, princess."

"Remember that." She flipped her purse open, dipping in for the money clip she'd always intended to go for at the end of this night. It wasn't a lot of cash, merely a fraction of the amount on the table. But it was a gesture, and gestures mattered to proud people.

"My thanks for a good evening, and for your company." Lauren flipped the clip on the table to the cheer of the drunken Oûrois around her, then scowled again at Dimitri. "Get out of my way."

He continued to fall back, but not nearly fast enough or far enough, and another flare of anger bit through her, clearing away some of the alcohol-induced fog. She knew she was being unreasonable. She knew she was probably being borderline stupid. Somewhere in the sane part of her brain, she realized that Dimitri Korba hadn't been sent here by King Jasen or Queen Catherine, her hosts at the palace of Oûros.

No, he'd most likely been sent by her friends—probably Emmaline, who worried constantly about everyone, or maybe by Fran or Nicki. They'd all known her since college and understood her moods. She'd been cooped up too long, first in a series of hotels across Europe, and now back here in royal confinement, since Emmaline's engagement to Prince Kristos...

Even *thinking* those words seemed absolutely ridiculous. Nevertheless, that was exactly what had happened a few short weeks ago. They'd landed in an honest-to-God Greek myth of a fairytale kingdom, and damned if Emmaline hadn't caught the eye of her own Prince Charming.

Which Emmaline should. She deserved it.

While Lauren deserved to be babysat by Megatron behind her.

Stifling a giggle, Lauren pushed her way through the crowd, knowing Dimitri would be on her heels. The hulking bodyguard would ordinarily be someone she appreciated, at least for eye candy. She'd never seen him naked, but she'd seen enough of his muscles to turn her own tennis and Pilates-strengthened body completely weak. She got the feeling he didn't build all those cuts and curves on a pink mat somewhere.

Stop thinking about him.

She pressed out through the bar until she finally burst forth like a buoy clearing the surface of the ocean, gasping at the sudden fresh air. It was June and another cloudless night in Oûros, and the sky was an excessively beautiful canopy of stars. The capital city of this idyllic nation had no appreciation for light pollution, and Lauren almost felt oppressed by the stars shining down over her. They were so close. So amazingly, stunningly close—

"You are drunk. And foolish."

Dimitri's rebuke pulled her back with the viciousness of a slap. "Don't talk to me. Don't even come near me," she said, turning sharply around.

Well, perhaps not so sharply as that. Her arms went out a little too far to steady herself, and she knew exactly what she looked like. But she'd practiced this. She'd practiced everything. She knew what she needed to do. Slowly, carefully, Lauren straightened, locking down her core and keeping her weight evenly balanced on her toes. She needed to get away from Dimitri Korba. Far away.

Suddenly, it seemed the smartest way to accomplish that was through him.

"You're not allowed to order me around, you know. You barely *know* me," she snapped, though she knew she sounded fourteen and not twenty-three. She pointed her elegantly mani-cured finger into the rough cotton shirt stretched tight across Dimitri's *exceptionally* broad pecs. Without realizing it, she flat-tened her hand on that chest, feeling the powerful muscles contract, the heart beneath thud against her palm. She scowled up into the man's angry, uncompromising face as the wave of his disdain crashed over her.

Disdain and...something else. Something that was more familiar, that thrilled through her like a siren song. This she understood, this she could work with. This was a barrier she could throw up to protect her from everything else.

But first, she had to be sure...

She knotted her hand in Dimitri's shirt and sagged forward.

Instinctively, Dimitri's arms went around the American woman, tightening his control on his own body as he gathered up hers, trying to keep her on her feet. Even drunk—hell, *especially* drunk—Lauren Grant was beautiful, with her normally restrained hair now tied into some sort of loose, low bun, her elegant features soft and easy, not held tightly in a coy smile or coolly sophisticated smirk. When she wobbled, he firmed his hold on her, scowling down the street toward the castle.

He needed to get her back there. It was late, and the streets were dark, but she was a guest of the royal family.

And he had a job to do.

"Mm. You're so warm." Instead of fainting as he expected, the American pressed forward, angling her soft curves along every plane and ridge of his ever-more-hardening body. Her face was buried in his chest, her breath hot and wet against his shirt, and her arms shifted to encircle his waist, hands moving down to palm his ass.

His gods-damned eyes almost crossed as she wiggled forward.

"That's not something you want to do, princess," he growled, stepping away from her. She seemed alternately too alert and too sloppy, but *tsipouro* could do that to a woman. It could do that to a full-grown man, and Lauren weighed barely enough to strain his arms as he steadied her again.

"What if I do want to do it?" she whispered, swaying close. Her lips parted and her eyes were wide and clear, and she looked so beautiful standing there in the starlight that he nearly groaned, though he knew what she was doing, could sense the cunning and intelligence wafting off her as easily as her expensive perfume and the cheap *tsipouro*.

She'd correctly figured out he was getting hard over her, but he'd have to be dead not to want that piece of ass. However, she'd incorrectly decided that he was going to do anything about it.

That wasn't his assignment. And he'd be damned if someone as brittle as this uptight American ice pick would make him go back on his assignment.

He'd known she was trouble the first time he'd seen her, striding up the beach like she'd owned the entire country, wearing nothing but a see-through cover-up over her tiny bikini, which did nothing to shield her and everything to thrust her assets into the face of anyone with eyeballs to see. She'd spoken Oûrois with a native's ease—a native royal, anyway, her consonants crisp and her syllables short and precise. And she'd tossed her blonde hair and ignored him as if he was some sort of foot soldier, when in fact he commanded his own company in the ONSF, he served the crown at the highest levels of Oûros's military...and he wasn't even fully human, for fuck's sake.

None of that mattered to this woman, though. She'd assessed and catalogued him in one swift glance—then charged forward.

He got the feeling she did that a lot.

"You don't like me very much, do you?"

Somehow the American had moved closer again, leaning into him so that her full lips, parting on her words, rested below his mouth. Since she'd shown up in his country less than a week ago, that mouth had been the subject of way too many fantasies and irritating daydreams, all of them ending badly for him. But the near-term ride was almost always worth it in his mind.

But that was his *mind*. This was reality, and he had to get the obnoxious woman back to her quarters. He sure as hell couldn't let her make her own way, not with her about to get hit with the full brunt of *tsipouro*.

"Dimitri." The sound of his name startled him, and he glanced down—a mistake, but a reasonable one, given the fact that Lauren Grant was a refined American heiress with a million years of finishing schools and private tutors and expensive colleges...and yet she spoke his name like she wanted nothing more from him than his mouth and his body.

Lauren pressed up toward him, her lips brushing his.

Need rocketed through Dimitri hot enough to burn. He let her nuzzle his mouth once, twice, until his sight dimmed to a pinpoint and his muscles were clenched so tight, he practically spasmed. She wasn't his to play with. She was part of the group of friends of Prince Kristos's new fiancée, a woman he did admire, unlike this unholy hellcat who darted out her tongue to taste his mouth, turning him inside out, and—

With a surprising amount of strength, Lauren drove her heel into his instep.

The move was remarkably effective, given that he wasn't wearing his usual ONSF boots but the soft-soled shoes that had made tracking her child's play tonight, and he flinched away from the blow while trying not to hurt her. Unfortunately, that provided the blonde with all the distraction she needed. She slipped out of her light sweater and left it hanging in his grasp.

Then she was off through the darkness, running faster than he would have given her credit for.

Dimitri hopped once on his foot, allowing her enough time to feel safe, then he set out after her. He should let her go, he knew. She was running back toward the castle, back toward safety. He could simply track her and make sure she made it, then vanish into the night. Easy and done, mission accomplished.

Besides, if she believed that she'd given him the slip, what harm would it cause? She'd feel good about herself, as if she'd won some kind of battle. He would have done what he'd been ordered to do, to get her home safely. Everyone would sleep better in the end—except maybe him, his cock now hard enough to pound nails and his body so ready for sex he was about to burst.

Dimitri pushed those thoughts away as he ran, assessing every turn, every stride of the young woman ahead of him. If anyone saw the pursuit, they knew well enough to stay out of the way. Dimitri had spent many long years in this town. He was known and respected by everyone.

Everyone except Lauren Grant.

The blonde chose that moment to make her first mistake—a fatal one, in his mind. She darted off into a side street, a street that clearly didn't lead to the castle. Which meant that she had no intention of heading back to the safety of her bed.

Do not think about that woman and "bed."

Dimitri picked up his own pace, pounding forward now, and he could hear her squeak of alarm. She knew he was back there, could sense the difference in his pace, his urgency, knew somehow she'd screwed up, but she clearly wasn't going to stop, wasn't going to give in—

He ducked into a side alley, blending into the shadows. She'd figure it out soon enough.

She did. The lane she turned down next dead-ended, and the American's frustrated cry made him a little too happy. He schooled his breath and waited. She would have to come back out this way. She would know he wasn't following her anymore. Which meant she knew he was waiting somewhere in the dark. Waiting for her.

He understood now how cats felt when playing with mice. Only this mouse had claws and a seriously bad attitude. He needed to remember that.

Dimitri's cell phone vibrated in his pants pocket, but this time, it wasn't Kristos contacting him—it was ONSF command. He'd returned to the world-renowned security force a few years ago when the princes had entered military service, and had quickly risen to the rank of captain. He'd lost count of how many times he'd served in that role since he'd first entered the military at age 18, but at least nothing surprised him anymore. The technology changed over time, but the urgent summons for him never got any more convenient. Something was up, and he needed to report.

His eyes narrowed as Lauren came back into view. They were close enough to target that he could hand off her escort to one of his men, if she gave him any trouble from here on out. Now he needed to head back to the ONSF home base at the back of the palace, not the front doors.

The American walked by him, and as if she sensed him staring at her, burst into another panicked run. But he could see her steps were less solid now, her footing less sure. He sprang out of the alley and caught her as she sprawled forward, head-long, his hands clamping around soft curves and rounded muscles as she gasped. He pulled her upright, bracing her against him. "Easy does it, princess. That little jog is going to speed up the effects of the *tsipouro*."

"Let go of me—" Her voice was clipped, or would have been

without the alcohol. The booze wasn't masking her fury now. She'd been stupid, and she'd been caught. He wasn't sure which pissed her off more. She turned back toward him, battering her free hand against his chest. "I said, let go!"

Dimitri's pocket rattled a second time, and he shook Lauren hard enough that she stopped. "Look, princess, you're drunk, it's late, and I'm your ride home. This isn't America, and you don't get to vote."

She blanched, shocked at his anger or his nearness, he didn't know. He didn't have a chance to ask either.

She slumped toward the ground, a deadweight.

This time well and truly passed out.

Just as his cell buzzed again.

Three

Lauren's eyes blinked open, and she forced herself to remain completely still, the waves of vertigo doing more to pin her to the bed than...

Wait a minute. Bed?

A familiar voice floated over her, but it did nothing to reassure her. Dimitri Korba was speaking in rapid Oûrois, his words delivered in the same brusque, professional tone that she'd heard him speak when he'd been hauling her and her friends through Oûros's back country this past week, keeping them out of the spotlight of the paparazzi. Them, or more to the point, Emmaline, who'd made a splash with her whirlwind romance with the prince of the realm.

Figures that Em gets the prince and I get the frog. But she honestly wasn't upset about that. Emmaline had been dealing with so much for so long, while Lauren's life was damned near perfect. She didn't have the right to complain about anything. Not when in almost all cases, she had the ability to change her circumstances or walk away without thinking twice. Of course, that "almost" was an issue, but not tonight. Tonight she simply had to get back to the palace. Right after she could see normally again.

Another burst of chatter, this time not Dimitri, refocused her. He was talking to someone on some sort of screen, standing near enough to touch. She shifted the minutest inch, then froze.

Something was around her now-bare foot, tethering her to the bed.

It wasn't thick or clunky—not a manacle. But it wasn't a heavy rope either. Zip tie? Twine? Whatever it was, it was attached to the bed or the post and was silent. So not a chain, not metal. Had to be plastic or cord of some sort.

Fury ripped through her, followed closely by outrage and embarrassment. She was to blame here, dammit. She'd gotten herself into this predicament. The last thing she remembered was running past Dimitri, sprawling forward, then...nothing.

The asshole clearly had hauled her here like a sack of grain.

And where was *here*, anyway? She squinted at her surroundings without moving her head. They were in some kind of office. She wasn't on a bed after all, but a low, flat couch, the kind of thing that could double as a cot if need be. The room was utilitarian, some kind of command outpost. A desk, a chair, this cot thing, and electronics. Dimitri hadn't turned on the light, probably hoping she stayed asleep until he finished whatever he was doing. Then he would cut her loose and get her back to the castle.

At least, that was what she assumed he was going to do.

How dare he tie me up at all?

Another bolt of irritation cut through more of her fog. She tested her wrists, her other foot—only one was attached to the bed. Only one needed to be, of course, to keep her in place. But why a foot? Why not her wrist?

The panic, she realized. Dimitri had realized that for her to wake up with her hands bound would be infinitely scarier, and he apparently hadn't wanted her to be frightened. He'd simply wanted her to stay put.

Gee, how chivalrous.

But what were they doing here, anyway? As she turned her head slowly, Lauren realized that Dimitri was standing far closer to her than she first realized. Shielding himself with the chair, he stood at attention behind his giant desk, his eyes glued to the screen as he spoke. Whether he knew she was awake or not wasn't material. He couldn't look down, not with the focus of his supreme overlord on him, or whoever was on the screen. Cyril Gerou, she assumed, the chief advisor to the king and Dimitri's boss.

So that explained why he wanted to keep her quiet. Probably wouldn't be good form to reveal that he had a drunk, passed-out American in his little captain's office or whatever this place was. And he might not want her to slip away while he was giving his report, but that was too bad. He'd definitely crossed the line by tying her to a freaking couch. She smiled, feeling better by the second. Because you just didn't tie Americans to couches. So Dimitri would have to pay for that.

She reached out and tugged gently on his pants leg.

Right in the middle of his sentence.

To his credit, Dimitri didn't flinch. The only reaction she noticed was him becoming, if possible, even stiffer, his muscles knotting beneath the thin cotton of his trousers. And she could tell those muscles were tense too, since she reached up with both hands to encircle his left thigh—and her fingers didn't touch. His legs were tree trunks, and she imagined them, suddenly, beneath her, her own legs spilling over him, her hands on his chest.

Right. No.

The idea of getting anywhere near this man in an intimate way had every one of her instincts screaming "danger." She'd learned the hard way not to disobey her instincts. She chose her partners with excruciating precision—they had to be discreet, easy to hide, and easy to manage. With those provisions in place, she had plenty of play toys to choose from.

Dimitri Korba was definitely not a play toy.

His breath seemed to catch as another flurry of words poured out from the screen, and Lauren refocused. It *was* the advisor, Cyril, speaking to Dimitri in such harsh tones. Then again, he'd always sounded harsh to her, despite the fact that Oûrois was arguably one of the more beautiful languages in the world.

Dimitri's breath hitched again and she realized that she'd unconsciously moved her hands up his leg as she'd been lying there, trapped in her own thoughts. Now her questing fingers had slipped up dangerously close to the good captain's groin, and she could tell by the strain on the fabric that Dimitri was not unaffected by what she was doing. Power curled inside her, and she smiled with a triumph that reached all the way to her toes.

Then she reached up farther yet, stretching to the extent that her tethered foot would allow.

Dimitri's shaft was full and ready, and she brushed the top of his trousers, reveling in the sensory explosion. Her foot was now taut enough against the zip tie that her toes had fallen asleep, and her heart rate had definitely picked up. The tactile pleasure of the rough cotton twill of Dimitri's khakis stretched tight across his groin and his backside, both of which she was kneading, squeezing, pressing beneath her fingers. Being bound and yet in control at the same time was unlike anything she'd ever experienced before, and she reveled in it, her breath coming harshly between her parted lips before she clamped her mouth shut.

For a second, she imagined Dimitri naked, and white-hot need seared through her.

Back it down, she admonished herself. This could only be a tease. If she kept things in check, no one would know. Because no one could know.

She needed to stay away from Dimitri.

Still, the man had tied *her* down. And he was right here, so hard, so hot, so different from anyone she'd allowed herself to touch...

She skated her fingers up the hard curve of his shaft, fascinated by the way he didn't move, didn't twitch, other than the unmistakable throb beneath the touch of her fingers. Dimitri's voice remained solid and sure, untroubled, as he answered Cyril's questions. He leaned forward, and she felt the powerful flex of his hamstrings beneath her other palm. Once again, her mind returned inexorably to the image of those legs, naked and strong beneath her, on top of her, straddling her, and she almost whimpered.

She wasn't an innocent, and there were plenty of guys out there hotter than this giant. Well, prettier guys, anyway. Dimitri Korba was arguably one of the hotter men she'd encountered in recent memory, at least when he didn't look at her with a snarl marring his lips or disdain in his eyes. She knew better now, though. She knew he found her attractive. Her or at least the idea of her, which was enough for what she needed. From attraction, it was always a very short distance to control, and the idea of controlling Dimitri Korba in secret, for merely a moment or two...

She could totally pull this off. And no one would know. Because, again, no one *could* know.

As she pressed her fingers into him, teasing him with smooth, hard strokes, Lauren thought about all the ways she could tantalize the man in the few short days—maybe a week, maybe two, but no more—that she'd be stuck in Oûros. She'd make sure they were barely in the same room with each other, but she'd give him a glimpse, a taste. She knew from experience that was the way to make a man insane—denying him what he thought he wanted. She'd have fun playing the game until she could get out of Oûros and on with her life. Maybe she'd see him again at the wedding, if the wedding between Kristos and Emmaline actually happened.

She hoped it did. For their sakes, she really did. No one should go through life expecting relationships never to work out. She did enough of that for everyone.

The sudden silence in the room didn't fully penetrate her awareness until it was a hair's breadth too late. Then Dimitri's hand snaked down and wrenched hers away from his body, and he pressed her down into the couch.

"Something you want, princess?"

Four

Dimitri had never been so close to losing control since he'd been a hotheaded teenager roaming Oûros's Royal Beach for the first time. But now, holding Lauren's hand against his chest, his body levered over hers, it was about all he could do not to drown himself in the woman right there. Which probably wouldn't look too good on his next report.

Keeping her hand clasped in his, he used his other to unsheathe the knife at his belt. With a quick flick, her ankle was cut free of its zip tie, the handmade noose falling limp.

He stood in one clean movement as Lauren quickly massaged her foot then scrambled up as well. He didn't miss the way she swayed, then caught herself, ratcheting her body down with every bit of ruthlessness that he was using, though for an entirely different reason.

"How much *tsipouro* do you have in you?" he asked, pitching his voice deliberately rude. A blush marred her cheeks, the bane of her pale coloring. "You gonna vomit before I get you back to the castle, or can you hold it together?"

"I don't need your help," she retorted, though as her gaze raked him, he was glad the evidence of his arousal was all but erased. God love Oûros National Security Force training. As well as parents, who were as keen-eyed as they were not stupid. The number of women he'd nearly been caught with would make the American's toes curl.

Not that she wouldn't be a pleasure to be caught with. He surveyed her as she took another second to get her mad on. Lauren Grant was the most perfect woman he'd ever seen— flawless in the cold sterile way of a classical painting or piece of sculpture, and spellbinding in the way her haughty eyes had grown hazy with need and her lips had parted, her breath coming fitfully as she'd stroked him. She'd had no way of knowing he could see her every movement in the overhead convex mirror above the screen. She'd also had no way of knowing he'd been looking at anything other than Cyril pontificating on the screen.

But when he wasn't making eye contact with Cyril like the exceptional soldier that he was, he'd been watching *her*. And damn if thinking about her face now as she'd touched him wasn't getting him hard again.

"You ready?" he said, the words a slap. "I can carry you if you're sloppy drunk."

"I said, I don't need your help. You tied me to a *couch*. You're lucky I didn't wake up screaming during your little one-on-one with Cyril."

"Couldn't be helped." He shrugged, savoring the emotions playing across her face. She was affected by him, there was no two ways about it. "If I'd gagged you, you could have woken up vomiting and died before I could cut you loose."

That stiffened her spine. "I do not vomit from alcohol."

"You might have with *tsipouro*." He pointed. "Your purse and shoes are next to the water bottle. Probably good to drink something nonalcoholic if you can. Bathroom through that door."

She lifted a brow, but the panicked relief on her face was unmistakable. He barely avoided smirking as she squinted back at him. "How do you know I won't try to escape from there?"

Then he did smirk. "No windows."

She was back out into the main room faster than he would have expected, somehow looking fresher, smoother. As if she'd come out of a spa instead of a utilitarian washroom. Their brief separation had done little to improve her mood, however. "I should have you reported for restraining me. You had no right."

"Your safety is my primary concern this evening, after my duty to my country, and your safety required me to haul you along while I reported in to Cyril. Besides, I figured if you did wake up and realized where you were, you'd have tried to get away without anyone noticing, especially if you thought I was on a command phone call. Which I was. Couldn't take the risk."

"I could have screamed."

"Nope. Not and look like the drunk, spoiled little rich girl that you are. That wouldn't exactly fit with the whole haughty-bitch thing you've got going on, would it?"

Anger flashed between them so hot, he was surprised his eyebrows weren't singed. "How dare you," she seethed.

"There's pretty much nothing I wouldn't dare, princess." He held the door for her, and she stomped out in front of him. They entered the courtyard again, and she looked around, clearly trying to get her bearings.

"This is the military compound attached to the palace."

"Yup." He pointed. "We go that way."

She hesitated for a second, then fell into step with him. "We've been through this area before, and there's a corridor to the main building. Why take me around to the front?"

He flashed her a smile. It was easy to bait her when she stepped so easily into the trap every time. "Cameras line that corridor and feed directly into the royal residence. Who knows if they're being monitored, but they're definitely recording. You really want to be seen sneaking into the main castle with a captain of the ONSF? That's a sure way to get some talk started."

She might have blushed, he couldn't tell. But her words, when they came, were frostbitten. "I assure you, I couldn't care less about what you people think of me."

"Most of us, no," he said, enjoying himself far too much, but he didn't care. A beautiful clear night in Oûros, and he escorted a stunningly gorgeous woman back to her bed. There were worse ways to spend the evening. "But you do seem to admire the queen. It'd be a pity if her opinion of you changed, and for what reason? We're doing nothing wrong."

She opened her mouth to issue a retort, then shut it again. After a few moments of stony silence, they exited a small, automated gate with the help of Dimitri's pass card and stepped out onto the wide paved sidewalk. From here it was a five-minute walk to the front gates of the palace. Not yet midnight, and the American's wits were coming back to her with every deep breath of the sweet night air.

Her wits *and* her sharp tongue. "Who put you up to this?" she asked. "Who assigned you to me?"

This, he would need to dance around. "No one," he lied. "When the evening ended and you weren't with your friends, I got suspicious. They said you'd gone to bed early, but there was no record of that on the cameras."

"You're watching me?"

"We watch everyone, princess." He didn't try to tamp down the amusement in his voice. "What the cameras *did* show was you out in the front terraced gardens, wandering through the flowers—until you weren't." Kristos had fed him this information, and what Lauren didn't know, wouldn't hurt him.

"You have cameras in the gardens too?" She sounded dubious, but he let her stew in those thoughts on her own. There were cameras in the gardens, of course. But he wasn't actually in charge of palace security. He wasn't even usually in charge of the blonde's security. She'd become his pet project at Kristos's behest, and mostly because she was the least predictable of the four girls who were now official guests of the royal house of Oûros. In his work, Dimitri didn't appreciate unpredictable. Unpredictable caused problems. And this time, above all others, should be a period of calm and contentment for the royal family. They'd had enough problems to last a lifetime. Even one as long as his.

"It was Emmaline, wasn't it?"

He blinked at her. "What?"

"Emmaline. That's who asked you to track me. She worries too much about everyone but herself."

They were coming around the final corner now, with the palace walls before them, the gates open, guards stationed every few feet. They nodded easily to Dimitri, their eyes sweeping over Lauren with no judgment. He glanced at her and could see why. She didn't look like she'd been passed-out drunk a bare half hour before. She looked cool, clean, unmussed.

Perfect.

They cleared the gates and followed the lit walkway up to the main palace. He didn't want to ruin the moment with more talk. He already suspected their time was short, circumscribed by their stations and temperaments. But the American had asked a question, and he was bound to respond. "Not Emmaline. Standard procedure only, princess. Sorry to disappoint."

"Hmm." They took the last few steps to reach the front doors of the castle, doors that were opened promptly by smartly dressed staff who ushered them into the grand foyer. Lauren didn't get more than ten feet inside when she turned to Dimitri.

"I can find the rest of the way myself. Thank you so much for your escort. It was a lovely walk."

He gave her a short bow, but he could feel the moment when her gaze left his body, like a blanket slipping away so that he must face the morning chill. As he straightened, however, he could also immediately identify the stiffness in her body, the way she held herself completely statue-like, as if she was about to break. Only this time, she wasn't looking at him.

"What," she asked very quietly, "is that?"

Her eyes were fixed on the antechamber beyond him, a shallow, cream-colored room with a long table and ornate shelving, used as a staging area for the endless flow of petitions, gifts, and written correspondence that flooded through the palace gates.

Dimitri turned instinctively, his gaze sweeping the space. There were packages, stacks of flyers, letters. "What?"

"That." She lifted a hand that had only now begun to tremble, pointing an elegant finger to single out a small, richly wrapped package in black and white. Her face looked stricken, her eyes filled with both a panic and desperation that Dimitri would never have thought possible in someone with as much power and influence as he knew she had back in her glittering ivory towers. "Get it out of here."

"But what—"

"Please!" She grabbed his arm and stared into his face for a panicked moment. Then her control crashed down again, her expression lightening, her mouth curving gently into a smile.

But there was no denying the haunted look in her eyes. "Please, if it's what I think it is, it should be removed from the palace." Her fingers tightened. "Immediately."

Five

Lauren tilted her head exactly eighteen degrees, moving her body into a three-point stance that she knew showed her figure off to best advantage. Not that anyone was looking at her, but in her experience, someone was always looking at someone, and she wanted to be prepared.

It was the only armor she had.

Dimitri moved forward rapidly, barking to the guard in terse Oûrois, relaying another order on its heels. King Jasen and Prince Kristos, both to be summoned immediately, once the danger was assessed.

The first blank wash of fear ebbed away as quickly as it had overtaken her. The king and the prince? Over a box? Lauren opened her mouth to take it all back, to play down her reaction, to smooth everything over—but words wouldn't come right away.

Dimitri stood, scowling down at the package, and she blinked, trying to refocus. "You're sure?" he growled.

"Yes, sir," said the young woman in a palace uniform at his side. "Absolutely, sir. Nothing inside."

Another wave of panic seized her. *Relax!* she ordered herself, but unlike Dimitri, she wasn't as good at masking her emotions when she wasn't the center of attention. It was as if she could only dance on the marionette's strings when the curtain was up. Something she needed to work on, but—

Then eyes were upon her once again, and her training kicked in. She lifted her chin, willing her expression to clear as Dimitri scowled in her direction. "You know who sent this?"

"I thought I did." She nodded, unsure how to play this. *Go with something he can understand, something simple, easy. Something not insane.* "That—that packaging is a signature look of someone I know, someone who plays with electronics, tracking devices, that sort of thing."

Dimitri's brows went up. "Tracking. Who is this person?"

She blinked at him. "Oh, um." *Stupid!* She should have known he'd ask that question first, and Henry Smithson was no more a tech-head than she was. But he was dangerous, at least to her, and he or one of his stooges could quite easily enter the castle grounds if he wanted to. His little present proved that clearly enough. What if he was here, in the city? What if she truly had something to worry about?

"Who is it?" Dimitri asked again, and she shook herself back to the present.

"Henry Smithson—he's not a criminal." *Not exactly.* "He's just—a friend. Of the family's. Who sometimes likes to play games." *And oh, the games he played.*

"Henry Smithson." Dimitri flicked a glance to a man standing at the side of the room, then back to her. "American?"

"Expat. Lives part time in England, part time in…I don't know. Wherever it suits him, I guess. I thought he was in Brazil. But again, he's not going to be in any criminal database. He's simply a very rich man who…"

"Likes to play games." Without saying anything further, Dimitri appeared to dismiss the woman at his side, who turned and left silently. Dimitri waved the box toward Lauren. "What else has he sent?"

She managed a shrug. "What do you mean?"

"He's sent you other things, in boxes like this. You or perhaps your family, but I'm thinking it's you. What? And when did it start?"

Smile, dammit. Tell him something that makes sense. "Well, the reason why I was alarmed…He'd send digital recorders with conversations of my voice that I couldn't imagine how he'd captured. But it wasn't all bad." Smile. *Smile.* Wave your hand. "He'd also send chocolate and jewelry, clothing sometimes." And also dead things. Scorpions. Locks of hair from her own head or her sister's. Newspaper clippings of injured friends. "It became a little unnerving because I didn't know what it might be, or why he might be sending them."

"And always in this type of box?" He gestured with the package again, and Lauren fought not to get queasy.

"Yes, I'm so sorry. Looking at it now, it's an ordinary box, I know. Black paper and white ribbon isn't that distinctive. But, well, it's what he always uses. And that's why I didn't want it in the palace. I thought—well, I thought it was some sort of recorder, but…" She shook her head. "If you say the box was empty, then I'm so sorry. I must be completely turned around." She lifted a hand to her mouth, feigning mortification. She didn't need to act all that convincingly. "Or maybe a bit tipsy."

Dimitri didn't waver. "Does this Smithson know you're here?"

Her stomach knotted. "I didn't think so, but…"

He spoke her next thought aloud. "The paparazzi." His scowl deepened. "In the wake of Emmaline and Kristos's announcement, and all the coverage that followed. If you weren't on his radar screen before, you are now. You say he's a friend of your family's? Or of yours?"

"My father's, most directly." *Straighten your spine. Smile.* "He certainly paid a lot of attention to me, but I was a little girl when we first met, and a bit excitable. I was an easy target." She waved toward the box. "Still am, I guess."

"Do not apologize for your fear. It's there for a reason." Dimitri's gruff absolution hit Lauren exactly the wrong way. The panic she always endured when it came to Henry Smithson clawed at the back of her throat, urging her to tell him the truth, but her ingrained sense of self-preservation smacked it back. Now, she needed to get out of there. To do that, she merely had to play to Dimitri's expectations.

"Thank you." She smiled and deliberately made it quavery, moving her hand to her hair as if to swat away some imaginary wisp. "I—oh, should I stay for the king? I feel so silly."

"Not at all." Dimitri gestured to one of the staff members, another female, who stepped quickly to Lauren's side.

"Come with me, Miss Grant. I'll take you to your rooms."

"Thank you—I..." Too much? Too little? *Get out of here,* urged a voice in her head. She didn't know how well Dimitri had studied her over the past few days, but the captain wasn't a complete idiot. Surely he could read people's emotions and know the ones that resonated the strongest. And surely her fear was pinging off the radar.

She turned to the staff member, smiling broadly. "That would be lovely," she said, forcing herself to slow down, to modulate her voice despite the impact of the alcohol and her own fear making her want to shout. She couldn't look again at Dimitri, though. Instead, she left the foyer without a backward glance.

Her heart pounded all the way back to the guest chambers, where she, Emmaline, Nicki, and Fran all shared an extended guest suite. When she approached, she heard their voices, and she steadied herself further. Usually the sound of her friends' laughter would have been soothing to her, presaging a carefree respite. Not today, though. Not when her mind was reeling. They'd know too much, pepper her with questions. She didn't want to face them.

Impulsively, she put out a hand and stopped the attendant. "Thank you, but—is there someplace I could go to be alone for a little while? I don't want to worry my friends, but I...I'm not feeling too well."

The training of the palace attendant was evident as she nodded, completely unperturbed by Lauren's request or by her trembling hand. "Of course, Miss Grant. We have a lovely sitting room down the corridor. When you are feeling more yourself, you may retire to your suite at your leisure. Would that be acceptable?"

"Of course—yes. Thank you." Lauren closed her hands into fists to keep from crying, a reaction completely out of step with the attendant's words. She was still a little drunk, was all. She was overreacting. She needed to pull it together.

The room was as advertised. Small, cozy, and quiet, it seemed a lovely oasis as the attendant stepped quickly across the room and turned on two low-light lamps. There was a long couch and two chairs in front of a gas fireplace, which the attendant helpfully turned on despite the fact that it was early summer. A cheery flame leapt up in the grate, and Lauren's knees wobbled a little. One of the chairs had a cotton throw folded over it, and she angled for it now. Vertigo struck her hard, but she steadied herself enough to turn and thank the attendant.

"No problem at all, Miss Grant." The woman bowed and left the room as quietly as she'd entered it, and Lauren practically dove for the chair, pulling the soft blanket around her with shaking hands.

For a long minute, she stared at the fire climbing in the grate. Then she pawed at her purse, snapping it open long enough to pull out the phone. She didn't need to dial anyone, though.

The text was waiting for her.

How I've missed you.

Six

Dimitri strode through the halls of the palace, fury arrowing through him. Fury at *what*, he wasn't sure, but he had a whole lot of mad going on.

The American sure knew how to pick her freaks.

Henry Smithson wasn't merely a friend of her family's. He was a friend of just about every royal and moneyed family in the civilized world. Hell, King Jasen knew him, though he'd also confirmed that neither he nor the queen had ever received packages from the man. Certainly nothing in such a distinctive box.

That wasn't even the worst of it, though. The ONSF had a dossier on Smithson an inch thick, same as it did on any moneyed mortal who dedicated themselves in service to a Greek god. In Smithson's case, the billionaire financier had chosen a particularly nasty deity to don the toga for: Typhon, god of monsters. Yeah, him. Even though Zeus had long ago beat Typhon's snake-dripping ass well into the ground, the tempest-loving creeper god still had his groupies, and Smithson was apparently a big fan.

Funny how it was the second time in a single day that

Dimitri had been forced to think about Typhon and his minions. He wasn't a fan of coincidences like that.

To the king's recollection, Henry Smithson was in his late thirties, fit and athletic, and an avowed bachelor. He'd apparently been part of the Grants' inner circle since he was a young man, but now was richer than Croesus all on his own. There'd been some speculation in the media that he was finally considering marriage and family life, but by all accounts, he was currently sailing around the world on his yacht called, because of course it was: Typhon I.

Smooth.

Dimitri chewed on the logistics required to deliver the package to the palace. Even if Smithson had seen the media blitz on Kristos, Emmaline, and the rest of the girls, he would've had to scramble to get a package here the same day that Lauren had returned to the castle. And the package was empty, so how could he have known that Lauren would see it?

There'd been no note, only the crisp handwriting on the card that had accompanied the package addressed to King Jasen. There'd also been nothing to suggest that the box had come from Smithson. It had arrived by special courier, unwrapped, like a birthday present carried in by a family friend. The only notation from the concierge was to follow up with the courier service the next day on what the intended contents had been. Theft was suspected, but as it had arrived at the palace already empty, it wasn't as high a priority. It could wait until the following day.

Dimitri couldn't wait, though. Not if the gods were involved.

Typhon may have been an outcast of Olympus, banished beneath Mt. Etna for eternity, but he still stirred up the seas with the best of them. Known for gifting his minions with fabulous wealth, power and the toys, he cast a long and dangerous shadow. Ordinarily, humans were smart enough to accept such gifts and enjoy them circumspectly, taking care not to attract the interest of the deity who'd so casually transformed their families with generational wealth. But occasionally, humans sought more attention from the gods.

They usually got it.

And that invariably meant trouble.

Dimitri stalked into the guest-apartment wing of the palace, his scowl deepening as he caught the flickering light from the sitting room east of the girls' suites. He wasn't in the mood to interrupt a late-night fireside girls' chat, he just needed to talk to the blonde. Something wasn't adding up.

Fortunately, a quick sweep of the sitting room reassured him that the room was empty.

Or...not quite empty.

He stepped inside, moving silently to where the very top of Lauren Grant's head peeked out of a summer weight blanket. She'd wrapped herself in a cocoon, her purse tucked beside her, her face angled toward the warmth of the fire. He stood there for a moment, weighing his options.

The American wasn't telling him everything. She wasn't telling him much of anything.

But what did it matter,? She wasn't his real concern. The royal family was, especially until plans got settled for how Kristos's engagement would move forward. Then the remaining girls would be ushered along to enjoy the rest of their fancy European vacation. Once he'd confirmed that this Henry Smithson wasn't tangled up in the affairs of the gods but was simply a fanboy freak, he would happily wave them all goodbye.

He had already missed the window of his leave to go see his family on Miranos, but that couldn't be helped. The ONSF reports from the Turkish border were increasingly dire. The military needed to increase its presence to the north, and there were precious few fighters to spread out through the mountainous region. He'd assigned one of Kristos's royal cousins to the job, along with his contingent of hotheads. That might have been a mistake, but sooner or later, the young fools would have to be trusted with real work.

Either way, he had too much to do to play nursemaid.

That didn't change the fact that Kristos had asked him to take care of this woman. Worse, Dimitri wasn't simply honor bound to do what his prince commanded, he needed it. Needed the assignment, needed the mission, just as he'd needed every mission over the past year. Especially those missions that required him to save people from themselves.

He'd failed at that the day Ari had disappeared. Failed miserably.

He wouldn't fail this time, regardless if his focus wasn't the heir to the throne, but some spoiled, insufferable woman whose touch he craved so much, it made his bones ache.

He wanted nothing more than to get away from Lauren Grant. He needed to put her on some plane back to America and never see her again. Because if she didn't get out of his sight soon, he knew she'd drive him to do something he regretted.

Nothing permanent. Nothing stupid. But...still something more than he should.

Even now, he wanted to lean down and take her into his arms, holding her so tightly that he might never forget the warmth of her body against his, the touch of her lips, the feel of her long, lean legs—

Stop it.

He stomped another step forward with perhaps a bit more force than necessary, and Lauren stirred. The blanket fell away from her face, and her hand reached out reflexively to keep it tight around her body, as if that flimsy bit of comfort was sufficient shield against the hornets' nest she stirred up around herself simply by existing.

Well, he was more than in the mood to kick that nest a few more times right now.

Stopping short of the couch, he dragged an ottoman closer and sat on its edge. He leaned forward, resting his elbows on his knees as he stared at her.

He could tell the moment she returned to awareness. It wasn't so much a change in her coloring or a flutter of her lids, but an electric energy that seemed to course through her, warning her that once again, she was being watched. Once again, she was the focus of someone's attention.

What would it be like for this woman to wake up outside the spotlight? He smirked. She'd probably be lost.

"Were you planning to stare at me all night?" Lauren's eyes drifted open with a cold challenge, her face controlled, her tone even. There was nothing to indicate that she'd been sleeping, other than the fact that he'd observed her not thirty seconds earlier, dead to the world.

"Where is this Henry Smithson now?" he asked too gruffly, but the sharpness of his words seemed to ground her. She straightened on the couch, pulling the blanket tight around her.

"I told you, I don't know."

"Has he ever threatened you?"

"Of course not." Her outrage flickered between laughter and anger with such precision that every one of his nerves prickled. She was bluffing. Had to be. Still, Lauren continued. "He's a friend of my father's. I've known him since I was a little girl."

"How little?" He didn't know why he asked it, but the spasm of emotion that arrested her face might have been the confusion of waking up on any other woman.

But not this woman.

Either way, she recovered quickly enough, and rolled her

eyes. "As if I could possibly remember. I was young, and he and my father did business together. I was paraded in front of all of Dad's business clients at one point or another, it couldn't be helped." She tilted her head. "Why? Did you find something in that package after all?"

"We're tracking it down. Officially, we expect to determine that it was emptied on the way to us, since Mr. Smithson cared more about the style of his presentation than its contents. He sent the thing to the palace unwrapped. Is he frequently careless?"

"I wouldn't call him careless, no." As if she realized she was saying too much, she lifted a slim shoulder. "He's too good at business to be truly careless. He might have been conducting a test, to see how the good citizens of Oûros would react to such easy pickings. Or"—she waved off his bristled indignation—"he may merely have been playing a game. He likes games. Perhaps another package will arrive tomorrow, identical in every way, except this time, it will have something in it. That would play to his sensibilities."

Dimitri scowled. He hadn't considered that. Rich people often had too much time on their hands. "Has he recently come into a lot of money, a lot of power? Things suddenly seeming to go his way? Or has his family been wealthy for awhile?"

"Henry? No." Lauren's absolute certainty didn't seem manufactured. "He's scraped and scrabbled to get to where he is —he's known my family since I was a kid, and my dad in partic- ular. The money he's got, he's made himself."

Well, none of that tracked. Ordinarily, any minion of Typhon would be a pampered piece of shit. It's how the god kept his acolytes close to him. Maybe Henry wasn't as tight with the monster god as Dimitri had feared. It certainly would make his life easier.

He narrowed his gaze on Lauren, knowing it was time to ease back on the interrogation. "How are you feeling?"

"Remarkably well, actually." She smiled, and Dimitri nearly lost his breath at the sight. Lauren Grant was pretty all the time, but she was heartbreaking when she smiled the way she was now, without art or intent. She reached up to tuck an errant strand of hair behind her ear, then laid the back of her hand against her mouth, stifling a yawn. In that moment, she could have been any young woman, from any background, wrapped up in a blanket at a college sleepover.

Then, of course, she had to keep talking.

Her brow arched in a smug curve. "Are you seriously stuck being my babysitter tonight? Out of all the jobs in Oûros, that's what they assigned you to?"

"You would be so lucky." The words were out before he could stop them, and his movement seemed unstoppable as well. He leaned closer with a smooth, almost predatory shift, and the American's hand froze mid-drop, her eyes fixed on him. "Tonight I was out and heard the commotion, and I thought to myself: who would be stupid enough to rouse up the locals at this bar that is usually so quiet, making them spend their hard-earned cash when ordinarily they are careful souls?"

As if remembering that her hand hung between them, she shifted it once more to her hair, then lowered it as she tried to back away from him, retreating more deeply into the plush cushions. "You must have been hearing something different than I did, then. The patrons of that establishment were already half-drunk when I got there. I never did catch up."

"And may the gods help you if you did." The anger was back, and he welcomed it. Anger he could understand, manage. Anger had purpose and form. And this woman definitely made him angry, he decided. That was the emotion coursing through him, he was certain of it.

She seemed to welcome it as well and leaned forward now, her lips inches from his. "You truly dislike me," she said, her words a low purr. "What did I ever do to upset you so much?"

He held himself locked in place. "Don't flatter yourself. I don't waste my time being upset by people like you."

"Mmm." Like some sprite of the gods, she wouldn't leave it alone. She moved forward another inch, and now her lips were brushing his, the warm, vital scent of her filling his senses. His entire body demanded that he take her, and Dimitri's reality was narrowed down, focused on the tiny point where their mouths connected. "I wish you liked me more, though. I really do."

She would have pressed forward, but Dimitri reacted to the sound almost before he could process what it was, who it was. He jerked straight and turned, rising to his feet and taking three strides across the floor before the petite dynamo of Nicole Clark burst into the room, her eyes bright and wide, her body practically quivering the way it always did, as if she was constantly high on caffeine.

"Lauren!" She burst out, hurrying forward. "My God, girl, what are you doing here? We've been worried about you. Did you go out—she went out, didn't she? I knew she did." Midsentence, Nicki transferred her gaze to Dimitri. "You had to fetch her."

"No one had to 'fetch' me." Dimitri turned back to the blonde, unsurprised that she'd also risen to her feet, the blanket thrust aside like garbage, her purse clutched to her side. "Dimitri was out and about, and was kind enough to walk me home."

She nodded to him, but her eyes glittered with something he had seen before. Something that set every nerve ending alive with anticipation. She was using his attraction for her to distract him, but in doing so she'd betrayed her own interest all too clearly...

Lauren Grant was desperately trying to hide something. He intended to find out what.

48

Seven

"We can't stay cooped up in the palace forever, right?" Nicki sat forward with her elbows on her knees, swiveling her gaze between the ocean and Lauren. "I mean, seriously. This isn't some sort of weird time warp that we'll never get out of?"

The following morning had the three of them—Lauren, Nicki, and Fran—sitting out on the veranda, a wide covered porch allowing full view of the glorious Aegean Sea without any aerial vantage point for dive-bombing media drones to take their picture. In this moment, Lauren could almost believe they weren't once again trapped at the home of one of the most photographed royal families in all Europe, but simply enjoying the gracious back patio of a family friend. A family friend who wasn't a psychopath, anyway.

"We'll be leaving for good in a few days, I expect," she said, with a confidence she didn't feel. "Now that she's spent two weeks alone with him, Emmaline is almost sure that Kristos isn't a dream, but I think she'll need to return to America and then come back before she totally believes this all isn't a mirage."

"It's so not a mirage." Fran smiled as she set down her glass of orange juice. "Never mind that she's out with the queen this morning visiting on some sort of morning rounds, like we're back in Regency England or something. Every time Kristos looks at her, his entire soul is in his eyes. He must know how skeptical she is deep inside. How much she assumes this is a story that simply must come to an end."

"If he does, then he's very perceptive." Lauren peered skeptically at Fran. "You haven't been shrinking him, have you? Without his knowledge?"

"I don't shrink people." Fran's eye roll didn't quite mask the edge in her voice. "Right now, I'm not licensed to do anything but sit around and read about the work I *should* be doing instead of being on permanent vacation. Just because I have a conversation with a guy doesn't mean I'm trying to crawl into his brain."

"Right." Nicki's derisive voice echoed Lauren's, and Lauren looked at her, startled, as they both broke into laughter. They all hadn't seen each other in nearly a year, only a few times since they graduated college, and yet they'd so quickly fallen back into their old patterns from school that it was almost eerie. Emmaline the caretaker, Nicki the adventurer, Fran the voice of reason, and Lauren...

She didn't know what she brought to the table, honestly. Her money, certainly, but that had never seemed to be a big deal to the others. And it wasn't *her* money anyway—it was her family's, and it had strings. So sure, she was going to spend it when the opportunity arose. But what else bound her so closely to these women? What bound anyone?

This was veering into Fran territory. Fran, who now was regarding her with that sense of "knowingness" that was so unnerving. "So, what's bothering you anyway?" Fran asked. "I mean, beyond your general ennui at all the opulence surrounding us." She grinned and waved, clearly trying to ease

Lauren's tension while she continued her delicate inquisition. "Did your parents call again? Your sister?"

"No, thank God." Lauren warred with herself briefly over what to say to them about Henry's unexpected "gift." They needed to know—something. If only to protect themselves. She'd learned the hard way that withholding information left people vulnerable to attack from the most unexpected of quarters. Attack they weren't always able to withstand. But she didn't want to make too much of Henry Smithson. He had enough people making too much of him.

At that moment Nicki sharpened the conversation, as Nicki often did. "You know, I think your mom and dad should back the hell off you," she said, forking up an egregiously healthy egg frittata. "First they wanted you to get a degree, now they don't want you to work, but instead get married off like some sort of cow to increase the family fortunes? That's seriously sick."

"Well, maybe not a cow..." Fran put in, her wince clear in her tone.

"You know what I mean." Nicki waved her fork, then pointed its tines at Lauren. "You could get a job doing anything in the world, and they know it. This marriage thing is weird. And so fifteenth century."

"They're pressuring you more, aren't they?" Fran had settled back in her chair, watching Lauren with her dark eyes. She'd been the quietest of them all, save Emmaline in college, but her mind made enough noise on its own. She was the only woman Lauren had met who thought too loud. "That's part of the reason for this trip, isn't it? Only you couldn't have imagined how our very first stop would end up taking over the entire experience."

Lauren held herself still so that she didn't slump back in her seat, though she wanted to. She was so tired, and probably a little hungover, regardless of what she'd told Dimitri last night.

Dimitri. Don't go there.

Flustered, she dove into a conversation that was every bit as treacherous. But with these girls, in this place, she could at least be a little honest. Because, once again, forewarned was forearmed. If only someone had treated her with the same kindness when she'd been too young to know she needed to be armed at all.

"It's—weird. They aren't pushing me to get married, exactly, but they clearly want me to get engaged. They actually want a lengthy engagement, to drag it out as long as possible." She focused on her breakfast plate, glad she'd managed to eat enough to keep her stomach settled. "The dual undergrad/MBA was charming to them, but I kind of think they want the pomp and pageantry of a wedding, and all the social media blitz that will surround it. They think it'll be good for business."

Nicki stared at her. "Tell me you're joking."

"Not even remotely."

"Is there someone they have in mind?" Fran pressed. "Or is it anyone with a particular net worth?"

Lauren grimaced. *So not going there.* "I've sort of made it my policy of late not to slow down enough so we can have that conversation. It's been working so far."

Nicki scowled. "But now you're trapped here again."

"Now I'm trapped. I mean, they wouldn't cause a scene or anything in public, but I'm sort of surprised they haven't shown up yet, if you want to know the truth." And with Henry and his unexpected delivery she knew her time was running out. Because where Henry was, her parents were sure to follow, and vice versa. She needed to leave Oûros sooner rather than later.

"Well, this isn't the freaking Middle Ages," Nicki insisted again. "They can't marry you off without your consent."

Sure they can. If they can catch me. "I think they'll move on eventually. I really do. I keep waiting for some big stock market boom or bust. That usually takes over Dad's attention for at least a few months. And as long as I appear to be productive, that helps too."

"Hence the MBA." Fran tapped her lips. "Grad school?"

"I was safe until I turned twenty-one. No one gets married before twenty-one anymore. It's unseemly. But since then..." Lauren trailed off, then sighed. "Honestly, I didn't expect it would be this hard. I toyed with the idea of a fake boyfriend, but there's no one I wanted to subject to that kind of attention. And again, I didn't need a *different* husband from whoever my parents picked out. I needed no one at all."

"But your family is rich," protested Nicki. "I seriously don't understand why they care."

Lauren knew her smile was too brittle, but she couldn't help that. "Money is a form of currency, but so is prestige, so is chatter. The more chatter, the more interest people will take in our family. That interest can translate to awareness of my father's businesses, which could lead to new businesses. I've kept a pretty low profile up to now, but there's money in my profile. Money he'd like to tap."

"Gross." Nicki shook her head. "You don't care about money that much."

Lauren shrugged. "I've always had it. That makes a huge difference—no, it does." She waved off Nicki's automatic objection. "I don't take it for granted. I'm incredibly blessed. But it's sort of similar to you with your physical fitness stuff. Being active is second nature to you. It's who you are and what you know. It's how people define you before they even meet you."

Nicki held her gaze for a long moment, her cheeks faintly coloring. There was a reason behind Nicki's commitment to extreme sports, a reason that Lauren hadn't realized before they'd gone zip-lining their first full day in Oûros, before all the chaos had struck with Emmaline and Kristos falling in love.

Now she knew something about Nicki, something big, and she wasn't going to betray the secret.

"Someone's been reading my psychology journals," Fran said wryly, apparently oblivious to the undercurrents coursing among them all. Lauren took the interruption for what it was, a respite.

"Well, you can't deny they're more interesting than my high-finance reading." Her words were light, easy, but she modulated her tone anyway, turning away so Fran's shrewd eyes couldn't catch her expression. She could feel the anxiety surging up in her as she'd tried to explain this to Nicki, who treated everyone with the same wide-eyed and open-armed honesty. But Lauren's life was different. She hadn't been wide-eyed for a long time.

"Anyway," she continued. "I've been looking at a new itinerary. I think we're probably going to—"

A commotion at the door betrayed that they were no longer alone, and they all turned as the queen and Emmaline entered, both of them looking fresh and happy and full of sunshine.

Then two men entered behind them, and Lauren's mood instantly soured.

Great. She'd thought she was done with him.

Eight

"I thought I was done with this," growled Dimitri as he and Kristos stepped onto the veranda.

When the new crown prince had summoned him from his training rounds this morning, he'd responded with military efficiency, wondering if he'd finally get his orders to go to the border, where his help could do some good. He should have known that those kinds of orders would only come from Cyril. Kristos was so ensnared in his accession duties, he didn't have time to take a breath, let alone focus on the work he so loved.

"Another party?" he continued. "For what?"

"It'll get worse before it gets better." Kristos didn't look amused either, hanging back as his mother and his fiancée swept forward, clearly bursting with news. "Emmaline's so relieved that my mother seems happy, she'll agree to do anything for the few short days she's here. And Mother is so happy to be planning a royal wedding, she's impossible to be around."

"And you?" Dimitri didn't ask the question lightly. It'd been only a few weeks since Kristos had proposed to Emmaline on open network TV...or pseudo proposed, anyway. He'd given her one of his military pins, not a ring, but the effect was the same: mass media hysteria.

"The wedding, I couldn't care less about," Kristos said, shaking his head. "That's going to be a state event so tortured with tradition that Emmaline will probably fall asleep in the middle of it. But as for her?" He shifted his glance forward and focused on Emmaline.

Despite himself, Dimitri felt a rush of emotion at the change in Kristos's face. Though Kristos was only a few years younger than his older brother, Ari, Dimitri had spent most of his time with the original crown prince. Still, the boy had matured dramatically since Dimitri had first returned to the palace and taken on the role of captain of the guard again.

Over these past eight years, he'd seen Kristos bored out of his mind with school, excited with his physical training when he'd first joined the military, drunk and celebratory, devastated with the loss of his men in combat...and completely destroyed when his brother had crashed his stupid, fucking plane into the Aegean. Dimitri had even seen Kristos distracted by, and half in love with, whatever woman had crossed his path on any given day.

But he'd never seen him like this.

Kristos grinned broadly, his entire face transformed as he stared at Emmaline like a boy of sixteen and not the future king of Oûros. "Emmaline is everything I wanted, and a lot I didn't know I wanted. She's beautiful, giving, sweet—"

"Pull it together, Pyramus," Dimitri reached out, punching Kristos in the arm to refocus his attention. "The queen."

He and Kristos moved forward to watch the announcement, but he'd heard the important part already. As King Jasen's closest relatives in Oûros, the Raptis family insisted on hosting an engagement party that very night for Kristos and Emmaline, and of course her friends must also attend now that they were back, blah, blah, blah. Emmaline's gaze swept toward them, and Kristos took another step to enter into the explosion of female planning, while Dimitri stayed back. He didn't care about another ridiculous party. He didn't care about these women.

Well, not all of them, anyway.

Lauren Grant stood between her two friends, the fitness freak and the shrink, holding on to her chair with a little too much grace. He frowned, shifting forward slightly. As if she caught his movement, her gaze drifted to his, then held it for a second. Every ounce of withering contempt that she could infuse into that gaze, she did, then she glanced away.

If the eyes were the window to the soul, this woman offered him nothing but hoarfrost.

Only he knew better than that. It was all he could do to keep from grinning.

"Of course, Dimitri will be on hand to provide security for the event." He blinked at the sound of his name, lashing down his irritation at getting pulled into the conversation.

"Security?" Emmaline asked, her slender body going instantly tense. "Why security? Is anything wrong?"

"Standard procedure," Dimitri said, overriding the queen's voice. The queen looked at him, surprised at his intervention, and he nodded with deference. "Ma'am."

Queen Catherine smoothed her expression. "Exactly so," she said. She didn't look at Lauren, who didn't look at him, and Dimitri kept his gaze on the room in general. Nicki's and Francesca's faces were blank, but genuinely so, not in the calm-façade way of Lauren's. That façade masked about a million untold truths, he suspected. Not the least of which was last night's little scare. Interesting.

Predictably, Lauren recovered first. "I'm sure there's no need for more security than whatever you would normally have." Her gaze swiveled to his, and he was struck again with its cool dismissal. "It's an engagement party, right? It should be safe enough without involving Dimitri. He's done quite enough." Her lips curled with disdain around his name, and he found that he wanted to hear it from her again—and again. Not in her haughty, refined accent, either.

He held her stare, glaring back at her, matching her ice with fire until finally she faltered, her eyes going wide as he put the full force of what he wanted to do to and with her in his gaze. *That's right, princess. Chew on that.*

"Oh, but of course he'll be there," the queen said firmly, though Dimitri didn't miss her glance between them. He quickly shuttered his expression, but he couldn't do the same to his body. In the blink of an eye, even thinking about holding Lauren Grant in his arms, both of them naked and slick with sweat and heat, was enough to make his body completely forget its hard-core training. The woman was a drug, and he suspected his next hit would be deadly. He needed to get out, get away, get some air. And some control.

"Yes, that should do nicely." Catherine continued, oblivious to his internal struggle. "We're not expecting any excitement, but it's always good to have trained experts on hand. There are any number of details to manage when it comes to public appearances."

"I'll get working on that right now," Dimitri said, grabbing for the opportunity to leave. Almost before the queen nodded, he'd turned on his heel and strode out.

He hit the corridor and kept moving, aiming for the closest location for him to take a moment and ratchet down his reactions. He knew the palace like the back of his hand. He'd been here countless times in his long life, most recently becoming a fixture again when Ari, the crown prince, had reached the age of eighteen and joined the military. Dimitri had been assigned to watch over him—if only from a distance—as part of his role as captain of the guard. Instead, they'd become friends, never mind that Ari was the prince of the realm. That was always Ari's way. Everything was easy, unforced. Everything was meant for its proper place. And Dimitri's place had been at his side—in battles large and small. Ari had grown into his position quickly, and Dimitri, as Ari was fond of saying, never changed.

It had taken the crown prince awhile to figure out how true his statement was.

Then came that last, fateful day, when Dimitri hadn't been there to protect the prince.

Now the palace held no more secrets for him, no more mysteries. And it also didn't hold Ari. Without the man who'd unexpectedly become his best friend, the place seemed little more than a pretty, painted shell.

One short hallway and a turn later, and he stepped inside the quiet portrait gallery. The room was, as usual, shrouded in soft shadows. The family didn't come here much. They hadn't before Ari's death, and now, when the portraits of generations past seemed only to remind them of the future that they'd lost, he doubted they'd darkened its doors in months.

Excellent. He needed the time alone.

As usual, he avoided Ari's portrait, preferring instead to focus on the much older generations of the royal family. The quiet, staid paintings had the desired effect. His temper cooled, his body unknotted. He could manage the American, if he kept his distance from her. He could manage her even better if she never spoke. His lips twisted. Like that would ever happen.

He'd made it halfway down the long, narrow room when a flurry of movement at the doorway had him turning around.

"Ungh!" Lauren's momentum took her halfway into the room before she stopped, her graceful arms flexing as she lifted her fists to her eyes. She hissed out a long breath, clearly trying to get control of herself. "This is impossible!"

Dimitri shifted toward her almost unconsciously, picking up every detail, cataloging it, assessing. The blonde thought she was alone, safe. Unwatched. She pressed her hands to her temples, then turned toward the picture at the head of the room and exhaled a long, tortured breath. The image she was looking at was a large portrait of the royal family made after Ari's death. Without Ari in the frame, the royal family seemed impossibly wrong, but Dimitri could tell Lauren wasn't actually seeing the painting. She wasn't seeing anything except the images shuddering through her mind.

He moved closer to her on soft feet, unreasonably pleased that she didn't notice him. The room was mostly dark, the only light where she was, highlighting the royal family. No windows lined the walls either. Ideal for a portrait gallery, and for hide-and-seek as well. But he was close enough now to see Lauren's distress, and his words were harsher than he intended. "You lost?"

"Oh!" Lauren whirled, taking a defensive step back, and the play of emotions across her face would have been comical in any other situation. Shock, fear, panic, anger, all in succession, but the only one he wanted there was the anger. It was clean and fierce and didn't twist up his guts, didn't make him want to punch through walls he couldn't see.

"No, I'm not lost," she snapped. "The queen and Kristos left, and Emmaline was practically bursting with the desire to talk to us, but then an entire *host* of staff members descended for fittings, she got called away to deal with some need with her family, and I—I just couldn't deal with it. I split."

"Uh-huh. Or maybe you just decided to follow me?" He grinned at her, hooking his thumbs into the waistband of his trousers. As he planned, her gaze dropped to track the movement, then shot back up to meet his, her outrage ratcheting up.

"Don't flatter yourself," she snapped, her chin firming.

"You're the last person in the world I'd want to follow." The fire he wanted to see—needed to see—was back in her eyes, and he couldn't deny the relief that spread through him.

He also couldn't deny the way his body reacted, being this close to her. *Dammit.* She might be a stuck-up, spoiled pain in the ass, but she had his number. She radiated with energy no matter where she was in a room, or who she talked with. This close, that energy reached out toward him like a hungry sun, and it was all he could do to stand his ground and not grab it up, gathering in its warmth.

Instead, he went on the offensive, leaning toward her close enough that she stiffened, on guard. She wouldn't back down, of course. That wasn't her way.

He liked that about her.

About as much as he liked the soft curve of her lips, parted slightly below his mouth. As he'd thought before, she was a drug. And he was well on his way to getting addicted.

"And yet you're still standing here," he murmured. "Something you still want from me, princess?"

Nine

Lauren's focus had narrowed to a pinprick, emphasis on *prick*. What was it about Dimitri Korba that so completely turned her brain to mush?

Even now, he stood there, oozing sex appeal like it was his job, and she knew he was screwing with her, knew he could see how much he affected her. Saw it and liked it, which was galling on an entirely different level.

She found the trailing edge of her mad and grabbed for it, wrenching her gaze away from his lips to focus again on his maddeningly dark eyes. "Why are you really on security at this stupid party tomorrow? What else happened with that box that you're not telling me?"

If he was surprised about her change in direction, he didn't betray it. "Nothing." He shrugged. "There's still a lot of chatter about the Americans in our midst, and Emmaline remains news fodder. Additional security is standard procedure."

"Oh, bullshit. You're lying."

Irritation flickered in his gaze, and she poked him in the chest with her index finger. She might as well have been poking a brick wall. "What happened? Did you get another package? You have to tell me."

"I don't *have* to do anything. You're not my assignment, beyond keeping your pretty ass safe at a fancy party." He gave her another half-smile. "Now, you want to talk about the things I *want* to do, with and to you, that's different."

Once again, she found herself staring at his mouth. How long had it been since she'd been kissed by someone as vital and alive as Dimitri Korba? She couldn't remember. Not that she lacked for suitors. But none of them, by careful design, were anything special.

And none of them were anything like Dimitri.

Then she recovered herself. This man was playing her, and here she was, begging to be played. She drew herself up haughtily. Even on her worst days, haughty was always a reaction she could depend on. Good thing, because this was quickly becoming one of her worst days. "I thought you didn't like me," she said, arching one eyebrow. "You've made that clear enough."

"I *don't* like you. I don't like anything about you." Before she could let those words register, before the hurt shot fully through her, stinging her to the quick, Dimitri closed the final gap between them and leaned down to brush her lips with his. "Doesn't mean I don't want to bury myself inside you. Princess."

The raw intensity of his words stung her, and Dimitri's wolfish smile as he pulled back only made it worse. "And you know what? I think you want that too," he said. Somehow, he remained far too close, so when he spoke, his breath fanned against her mouth, causing a response deep in her core that teetered dangerously close to complete meltdown. "You gonna tell me I'm wrong?"

"No." She breathed out the word before she could stop herself, before she could fully think.

"Good." And he reached for her.

Dimitri didn't merely bend down into his kiss, he attacked, his right hand snaking around Lauren's neck as his left pulled her body into his. As if she needed more of a reminder of his interest, his hard shaft pressed against her, but she no sooner registered that sensation than she felt his fingers cup her backside and lift her against him, focusing the hard ridge between her legs where she most needed him. Meanwhile, his mouth plundered hers, not so much kissing her as devouring, his tongue thrusting into her mouth, then withdrawing quickly, his teeth catching her lower lip, then sucking it into his mouth as if he secretly wanted to eat her alive.

Her own hands were on the move as well, grasping at his hair, his shirt, digging into his shoulders and the nape of his neck as she struggled to pull him closer, then closer still. She wanted to laugh, cry, scream, and pass out all at the same time, but her most immediate need was the pulse of him at her core, hot enough to detonate.

What are you thinking? Finally, her sense of safety prevailed, and she shuddered against Dimitri, using every last bit of strength to infuse her words with disdain. "Let go of me," she managed, her words far too breathless, so she tried again. "I said *let go.*"

Dimitri obligingly leaned back, though his chuckle was pure seduction. "Your wish is my command, princess."

"I wonder..." Desperate to look at something—anything but him, she glanced to the side, at yet another gorgeously rendered portrait of the royal family, this one featuring a king and queen she didn't recognize...standing next to someone she did.

"Wait a minute," she said, stepping toward the wall. "Is that—?"

Dimitri's hiss of warning drew her focus back to him.

"We've got company," he snapped, his voice low and hard as he peered at the far-off doorway to the gallery, his hands tucking his shirt into his trousers with rough urgency. "Queen in twenty seconds."

"How do you know that?" Lauren stared at him for another precious second before realization hit her square in the eyes. The queen! And she'd been mauling the security guard! With speed born of long practice, she pulled out her destroyed bun and reknotted it, then quickly smoothed down her dress. She'd worn only the barest makeup, and her gaze snapped to Dimitri. "Face?"

"Eh." He shrugged. "It's dark."

"Oh, great."

"What can I say? I have an effect."

"Yeah, well." She let her gaze drop to rest on the evidence he couldn't quite hide yet. "You're not the only one. You owe me."

She turned around smartly and positioned herself slightly in front Dimitri, so that when Queen Catherine entered the room and flipped on the flood of lights, Lauren was effectively shielding him from view. The queen wasn't alone either. Kristos filed in behind her, looking weary.

"Oh, good. I was hoping to find you together." The look she sent Dimitri wasn't challenging, Lauren realized. It was grateful. Wariness shot through her, stiffening her spine. Why was the queen grateful to Dimitri? What was going on here?

She didn't have to wait long to figure it out. "Jasen finally filled me in completely on Lauren's concerns with the package we received yesterday. I suspect you haven't told her yet about your latest findings. No? Then you can tell us both now."

Lauren couldn't see Dimitri's face, but she could almost sense his grimace. "There's nothing to—"

"Don't patronize us," the queen said breezily. "I know full well that you've been using every piece of our electronics and surveillance systems to find information about Henry Smithson, if he's truly behind this." She shook her head. "I hope he isn't. I've met the man on more than one occasion, and he didn't strike me as a game player. But I admit I'm not always a good judge of villainy. So, what have you found?"

"Not much, Your Majesty, as I suspect Kristos has informed you." Lauren saw Kristos nod almost apologetically and stifled her own smile. She knew that Dimitri had been the better friend of the older brother, Aristotle, but these two clearly knew each other well. "There's nothing to indicate conclusively that the package was from Smithson, and our inquiries have led us only to Rome, where the package apparently originated: a custom jewelry vendor of some sort.

Raphael's, Lauren thought. That settled it. It was one of Henry's favorite boutiques, if only because they had no issue pushing conflict diamonds.

She kept her expression smooth, and Dimitri went on, blessedly oblivious to her sudden awareness. "This jeweler, Raphael's, said the order was placed by a woman, not a man, and that it was to be an anonymous gift of a jeweled butterfly for your majesty. To honor your work with the World Land Trust?"

"Hmm. It's reasonable. And yet the butterfly was sent in an unsealed package? Seems strange."

"The rep would agree with you," Dimitri said. "They had the package sent with all the usual protections. Somewhere along the line, only the box remained."

She felt his gaze shift to her. "Black-and-white is their standard configuration. So it could be a coincidence that it matches Smithson's preferences."

Lauren nodded firmly. "Yes. Yes, it could be, absolutely."

Dimitri went on as if she hadn't spoken. "Smithson himself has proven a bit more difficult to locate. His yacht was last docked in Portugal earlier this month, but there was no indication of where he was slated to travel next."

"He's in Portugal?" Lauren turned to Dimitri, fear surging up faster than she could shove it down. Smithson was that close? "Which yacht? The Typhon I or II?"

The queen gave a soft gasp as Dimitri glared at her. What had she said to upset them so? She was the one who should be upset. "Like, just tell me the size, the color—is it white or black? He only has two. One he keeps solely for European travel. The other is bigger, more capable of going long distances."

"Black," Dimitri said, and Lauren managed to breathe again.

"Okay. That's the Typhon II. That's the bigger one—I don't know how big." A lie, but Dimitri didn't need to know that. She'd studied Henry Smithson the way a cop studied a serial killer. He was that dangerous to her. "He could go anywhere, especially from Portugal. He could be heading back across the Atlantic."

As she spoke the words, she knew she'd said too much. Dimitri practically turned to stone in front of her, and the queen took a step forward, her hand lifting in a gesture of reassurance. "You must know you're safe with us, Lauren. We'll put every resource at your disposal."

"Oh! No, no." Lauren lifted her own hands, tilted her head, shook it ever so slightly. The way she'd been doing since she was little, though with far less occasion to practice recently, since normally she didn't slip and betray her fear so obviously. *What is wrong with me?* "I do apologize. I only mean to say that, assuming that package was sent from Smithson, which is a big assumption, if he's on his larger yacht, he's likely not going to be landing on our doorstep. I'm terribly sorry that I did anything to worry you. I must seem completely silly."

"Pay no mind at all, dear." This time the queen did step forward, and she reached for Lauren's hand with a warm smile. Turning, she tugged her forward toward Kristos. "Sweetheart, could you escort Lauren back to her friends? I'll want to chat with Dimitri a moment more here."

Once again, Lauren sensed the danger, but she could do nothing as Kristos bowed first to his mother, then to her. He held out his hand, and she took it, feeling Dimitri's gaze scorch through her thin dress as she exited.

But what was he thinking, exactly?

Whatever it was, she needed to get back in control of it, fast.

Ten

"How much of a problem is this going to be? Smithson, I mean. And what is Typhon's role in any of this?"

"We don't know that he has a role." Dimitri looked evenly back at the queen, who was scowling at him. It made her look, if possible, more majestic, but it was still not an expression he enjoyed having leveled at him.

"To quote Kristos, 'bullshit.' What aren't you telling me?" She shook her head to stave off his denial, then checked her watch. "Walk with me. Stefan is getting the guest list from Raptis. If I'd been briefed of this disturbing package in a timely manner and the possibility that anyone under the influence of Typhon was looking to infiltrate the royal court, I could have ensured this party didn't happen. Now it would seem awkward to cancel it."

He winced as he followed her out into the hallway, then fell into step alongside her. "King Jasen didn't want you to be alarmed. There's been nothing to prove that the box was intended malevolently in any way, or even that it's attached to Smithson."

"Nothing except that poor girl's face. My God, Dimitri, are

we actually debating this? I've barely met Lauren Grant, but I know the girl maintains her public profile with the severity of a drill sergeant. Yet here she looked like she was about to faint. What has that man done to scare her so deeply?"

Dimitri blew out a long breath. "We don't know. According to preliminary data, Henry Smithson is a long-time friend of the Grants. He was mentored by Lauren's father for the first several years of his professional life, and he has been a mainstay at their public events for the past fifteen years. Nothing more."

"Lauren would have been a child when that started?" She sniffed. "And now he's romantically attached to her? That's obscene."

"We don't know that either," Dimitri countered. "From all indications—"

"Well, she reacted in the manner of someone being stalked, so it's a pretty good supposition. No." She shook her head. "Even if his intentions are honorable, even if his affiliation with Typhon is just the whimsy of a billionaire idiot with more money than sense, Smithson is far too old for her. I don't care how rich he is. And there's something about this that feels...exceptionally wrong to me. I don't like it."

Dimitri didn't miss the shift in his monarch's expression, and he kept his face carefully neutral. Queen Catherine was notorious for her matchmaking wiles, but he wasn't engaged in this assignment to keep the American away from an eager pursuer. And he certainly wasn't trying to cock-block some idiot future husband for a bored blonde. His dedication was to the royal family, but he had his limits. "Again, so far, we've had no proof to link the empty box to Smithson. And it is, in the end, just an empty box."

"Fair enough." Queen Catherine huffed in irritation. "It makes me nervous, though. Raptis has attended many state dinners where Smithson was our guest. If Smithson's on the list for the event tonight, I can't very well ask Raptis to uninvite the man."

"And you think he is?" Dimitri felt his blood quicken. If he could see the man in person, he could look for clearer evidence that Smithson was a true Typhon acolyte, beyond just slapping the god's name on his boats. The sapphires and diamonds. The ink. The brands. Typhon's followers had grown more discreet over time, but they all had their tells.

"It's all too likely. Raptis is always interested in currying money. And Smithson has money." She worried the beaded necklace triple draped around her neck. "Smithson has also been nothing but proper in all his dealings with us. When did he name his yachts—and do they have those names painted on them in any sort of obvious way? If so, that has to be recent. He was here at the New Year celebration, and none of my briefings included that. Typhon himself hasn't left Olympus, but there are so many monster gods...could one of them have slipped through without us knowing, then breached the borders of Oûros long enough to connect with Smithson?" She waved an agitated hand. "We've been distracted since Ari's disappearance. It could have happened."

Dimitri grimaced. "I'll find out." He hadn't been here at the New Year's celebration. He'd been buried in the military with Kristos. At the time, he'd been happy to be away from the royal family, but had that been a mistake? Had he left them vulnerable when they needed him most? "There's something else, too. I found one of Typon's monsters in the grotto last night, harassing a nymph."

"You intervened?" Catherine stopped short, turning to drill him with a glare that brooked no bullshit. "Tell me the nymph was unharmed."

"I did, and she was. I threw them both in to a pool."

"Excellent." She smiled. "But...you're sure he was a monster god?"

"Very low level, but yes." Dimitri shrugged. "If it'd been a servant of any of the other gods, I wouldn't bring it to your attention. But I don't like the trend here."

"Agreed. It could be nothing, but it could be something we need to watch." Catherine started walking again. "You're going to have to protect Lauren personally, Dimitri. I mean that. Don't let her out of your sight."

"What?" Dimitri scowled at her profile. "Your Maj—"

"Oh, dispense with the Majesty nonsense, I beg you. Jasen isn't here, and I don't have time for the formality. I'm worried about the girl, and I don't do well with worry. It's my least favorite occupation."

"But I won't be here long enough to protect her, at least not beyond the event Wednesday. Cyril has me slotted—"

"And I'm saying that the most important need of this family, at this exact moment, is to avoid a scandal of any sort. Especially since we've been catapulted onto the public stage with Kristos and Emmaline's engagement. All eyes are on us, and on the king. It's an unexpected boon, but it doesn't come without its headaches."

Dimitri shook his head, disbelieving his own ears. "Your Maj—Catherine, I'm a captain of the ONSF, not some kind of hired-out bodyguard."

"You've protected every member of the royal family when the need dictated—and for quite some time."

"Yes, I have," he countered. "But Lauren Grant isn't part of the royal family. She's a guest in a highly public location. We have people for that." They turned sharply down another corridor, this one flanked by two attendants who bowed to the queen. She nodded back graciously, then swept forward, picking up her pace.

"We do have people for that," she said, her words decisive. "And one of those people is you, who, if I am not mistaken, took an oath to be bound to serve whatever your monarch commands. Or did I miss a clause in that arrangement? You did agree to it quite some time ago."

Dimitri gritted his teeth. Queen Catherine had a way of making the most high-handed request seem like it was your sworn duty, and here she was doing it again. "I will, of course, do whatever the Crown requests," he said curtly as they turned into the conference room.

Stefan Mihal, Oûros's top diplomat and half-cousin to the royal princes, stood at the head of the table, staring at a file folder, but he wasn't alone. It was the first time in a while that Dimitri was actually glad to see the royal family's chief advisor, Cyril Gerou. Maybe he could talk some reason into the queen.

Cyril's face was neutral. Stefan's was as well, but then again, Stefan defaulted to neutral. The royal ambassador glanced up when the queen entered the room, bowed perfunctorily, then held up the file. "You're correct in your assumption, Your Majesty."

"You could go with Aunt Catherine, you know. Keeping up appearances, and all that," the queen said, turning to accept a similar file folder from an attendant who'd appeared at their side. She scanned the document. "Oh my."

"Yes." Dimitri frowned at them both as Stefan kept talking. "Smithson has been invited to the event."

A black bolt of anger and anticipation surged up inside Dimitri, unexpected but brief. "Then, fair enough," he said. "Lauren doesn't go to the party. Problem solved."

"Not solved so neatly as that, regrettably," Stefan replied, apparently unperturbed by the queen's grimace. "In addition to inviting Smithson, the ambitious Raptis has invited his good friends, Lauren's parents. By happy coincidence, all three of them are traveling on the Smithson yacht at this time, though there was no indication Raptis knew this when he extended the invitation. The lot of them are expected in port Wednesday morning."

Dimitri's scowled. "Your information is better than mine."

"Not better," Stefan corrected. "Merely more current. While you were on duty today, the inquiries we made into the whereabouts of the Grants yielded far more fruit than our initial research on Smithson. The Grants apparently are not nearly as diligent about their personal security as their host, or simply prefer to keep a more public presence."

"So Lauren has to attend," the queen said, tossing the file on the table. "Her parents will be there. We can't very well keep her from her parents."

"She could leave the country," Dimitri put in, which earned him a thin smile from Stefan, and scowls from Cyril and the queen. "Look, I shouldn't be in the middle of this. And I'm not equipped to play babysitter at a fancy dress party. That's his job." He poked his finger toward Stefan.

To his credit, Stefan didn't deny it. "We could dress him up, but enough people know Dimitri as a captain of the ONSF. It would arouse suspicion to have him so close to Lauren."

"You're going," the queen snapped before Dimitri could jump in. Cyril blinked, clearly startled at her royal vehemence, but she didn't back down. "She trusts him," she said to Cyril.

"She what?" Dimitri stared at her. "You can't be serious." He sent a longing look to Cyril, but the advisor looked as shocked as he felt. "I'm due—"

"We can make arrangements for that," Cyril said, lifting his hand to quell words that Dimitri wouldn't easily be able to take back. Catherine was his monarch, even when she was being ridiculous. The only one who could override her command was Jasen, and he wasn't here to lend his voice. "Stefan will take the first line of defense for Ms. Grant, should she need any, and with any luck, she will not. Dimitri will be on hand to monitor the girl from a distance, but more importantly, to monitor Smithson."

He stared at Dimitri. "Somehow, that box got into the palace without going through any normal channels. It wasn't on the scheduled delivery manifest from the local couriers, and there was no record of it entering the country, let alone the palace. We were lucky, you could say, that it didn't contain more than air."

"No record? But the video feed showed a truck—"

"Unscheduled. The regular driver wasn't anywhere near the palace when that truck entered the drive. And the man who was driving it isn't showing up on any of our databases."

"Hired help," said Stefan dismissively. "A one-time hire at that. The box would have tripped our sensors, except there was nothing to trip, since it was empty. It exposes a low-tech weakness in our security if nothing else. Something we'll need to address."

"And the names of Smithson's yachts?" the queen demanded, squaring her shoulders at Cyril's and Stefan's surprise. "He calls them the Typhon I and II now. Lauren shared that."

Cyril spoke first. "Typhon hasn't been anywhere near the gates."

"But he rules over everything that slithers!" Catherine snapped right back, with unusual sharpness. "And don't even get me started on the shapeshifters he commands. It wouldn't be so hard for one of them to escape, especially if we weren't looking for it. Plus—Dimitri, tell them."

Dimitri grimaced as Stefan and Cyril turned to him. "There was a disturbance in the gardens last night. A low-level monster god harassing a nymph. I separated them, chased the dickhead back into Olympus, but he was one of Typhon's, and he mouthed off."

He hadn't told Catherine about this part, but Cyril needed to know, and the advisor nodded subtly for him to continue.

"Nothing specific, just the usual rhetoric of one day the gods would rise, and we'd be sorry for thinking we could control them."

Stefan snorted. "They've been saying that for a thousand years."

"Agreed. But given this Smithson guy..."

"We have to treat it seriously," Cyril finished for him. "Even if Typhon is merely attempting a show of strength, it's one we need to match. I agree with the queen, captain. You'll need to be on hand for the party to watch over Ms. Grant."

"Of course, sir." Dimitri's head had started to pound. He'd have to pull it together around the blonde. Keep his focus on the mission and only the mission. "So, Wednesday night, then. How long will she be at the event?"

"Three hours, max," Cyril said. "We won't be alerting Raptis of our concerns. You'll be there as part of the detail for Kristos, in the background. The party will have dining, dancing, a speech, then all guests will depart."

"I'll tell Lauren. She'll want to be prepared—" The queen turned to him unexpectedly. "Unless you'd rather speak with her, Dimitri?"

No chance in hell would *that* be a good idea. "Be my guest."

He had his own battles to wage to make this assignment work. And none of them involved getting anywhere near Lauren Grant.

Eleven

"What do I need to know?" Stefan asked quietly.

Lauren looked across the limo to Oûros's answer to James Bond, who was also her date for the evening. The other girls were following in a separate set of limos, but she'd been sent on ahead to be at the Raptis house before her parents arrived.

Her parents. God.

Stefan didn't press her with another question and instead let her root through her response to the first one on her own. She hadn't even been surprised when they'd come to her with the news of Smithson's attendance at the ball. She'd known from the moment she'd seen that damned black-and-white box that he'd be making an appearance in Oûros sometime soon.

Coming in with her parents, though—that was a master stroke. One she should have anticipated.

"My parents won't cause a scene, if that's what you're wondering," she finally said. "Nor will Smithson. We're on good terms, as far as anyone knows. My father is eager to see me married off, and it would seem that Smithson has been designated the boy most likely."

77

"Though he's hardly a boy."

She grimaced. "And he's nowhere near likely."

Stefan's lips twisted in amusement, and Lauren flapped a hand at him. "My personal feelings about him aside, he's cunning, and he's got the Midas touch. He's made an extraordinary amount of money in a comparatively short time, and he's a fast friend of my parents."

Stefan glanced at her, one elegant brow lifting. "He didn't come from money?"

She shook her head. "He met my father when he was a college intern, and he was an orphan, didn't know his parents, the whole up-from-nothing story. He worked his way through school on his own, learned society manners and negotiating skills as he needed them. He's my father's proudest achievement." She grimaced. "Fortunately, he's never officially offered to date me, so I've never officially turned him down." She caught herself nervously spinning her bracelet. "I really don't think my parents have any idea how dangerous Smithson is."

"And how dangerous is he?"

Lauren colored. "This all sounds completely over-the-top. I'm sorry."

"You're genuinely worried. Explain why."

"I—I've started to believe some of the things I've been told about him. That he's a man who operates outside the law. That he's done things you can't find in dossiers or police reports. Things that get covered up." She knew it wasn't enough, and she swallowed, saying the words for the first time to anyone who wasn't a trusted member of her staff. "That he's made deals with crime syndicates all over the world. And that he's successfully made those deals work, or he's successfully screwed the people who he's realized don't have the strength to screw him back. He's laundered money, trafficked contraband. He's got the

Russian mob on speed dial. And the Chinese. And the Korean mafia as well."

"You said you've been told this? And you have proof to back it up?"

"Not even remotely. He's the one who told me." Stefan's gaze sharpened on her, and she shook her head. "This is what he's murmured to me in dinner conversation at my parents' house over the past few years. The way you might tell someone about the new sport you've taken up or the latest diet you've tried. I've never heard a whisper of any of this outside those conversations, and I've been completely unable to verify any of it via a third party." She glanced out the window, unseeing. "Believe me, I've tried."

"So if he's ever questioned…"

"He'll know I'm the leak." She shook her head. She couldn't tell Stefan her real fears, her concern for what Henry would do to her family—her sister. He wouldn't understand. "I can't discount what he's said, though. Henry has never lied to me. He hasn't had to lie. But I can't involve the authorities until I have proof. And I have. No. Proof. The few whispers I do catch in the wind turn to smoke by the time I get to the source. I can't risk moving until I have something real."

"Understood." Stefan studied her from his side of the limo. "Explain his attention to you personally."

She sighed. "I wish I could. He has enough money to attract any woman, and yet he's been fixated—in my mind alone, perhaps, but it's my mind that's in sway here—on me. Since I was barely more than a kid. At first, it was the whole doting-uncle thing, then it got weirder."

"Sexual."

"Ugh, no. Not that. Not exactly." She wasn't looking directly at Stefan, but she knew his face wouldn't register any emotion at her words. Not relief, not revulsion, not curiosity.

For all his suave good looks and powerfully built body, the royal cousin was the master of the non-expression. "He called me a little snake, once, and then the next time he showed up, he gave me a pin with a snake on it. A terrible thing to give a little girl, right?"

Stefan's gaze had grown more intent. "A monstrous thing," he agreed. "I assume you gave the pin back?"

She laughed a little grimly. "I'd been trained better than that. I accepted it as if it was a great honor, and that pleased him. His next gift was a diamond bracelet for my sixteenth birthday, and that of course was lovely. So for him, I think the snake pin was more sort of a power thing. He liked keeping me guessing."

"Hence the gifts in the black-and-white boxes. Some good, some bad."

"Hence that, yeah."

They rounded the corner and entered a large stone gate to a drive that snaked up the side of the mountain. The Raptis estate was outside the capital city, but the countryside had already devolved into the forested paradise she'd only recently begun discovering. "Is this the only way out of the estate?" she asked.

"The only way for public transit. The grounds have other access roads, of course. Those are being watched covertly. We expect no trouble there."

"Good." Another wave of shame drifted over her. "Look, this all comes down to me trying to avoid a guy I don't want to date. I'm sorry for putting you through this."

"As I told you during your debrief with the queen, there are no apologies necessary for ensuring one's safety." He was right, he *had* said that, while the queen had been searching Lauren's face for any sign of weakness, any crack in her armor. Lauren knew she'd shown none. From the time she'd been a young child, it had never been the actual bad news that rattled her, it was always the *expectation* that bad news was about to come around the corner. That was what made her nervous. Once the trouble started, she could handle it.

She hoped.

"In addition, your presence here presents a liability to the Crown, should anything happen to you while you're a guest in our country. We take that very seriously, no one more so than Queen Catherine." Stefan waited for her to nod. "Finally, the fact remains that this Smithson made a suspicious delivery that got all the way inside the palace without being flagged, and that's not acceptable. If you hadn't noticed it, what would he have done, assuming he's the one who sent the package?"

"He'd have sent another. Something more noticeable."

Stefan's lips twisted. "You speak as if from experience. He's done that before."

"A time or two."

"How far did he go to get noticed?"

She swallowed, remembering the college boy Adam. Sweet and clueless and heartbreakingly obvious in his adoration as she'd tried to push him away after Smithson had reared his nasty head again. Sweet and clueless and in traction in a hospital bed not three days later, with never a suspicion as to how he'd gotten there, other than some hit-and-run asshole who'd clipped his bike. She'd known, of course. The large bouquet of black-and-white roses had been a bit of a tip-off. "Pretty far. As soon as I acknowledge him, though, he goes away. Sometimes he wants to see me, sometimes he merely wants to know I'm aware of him, but he goes away after that. Or at least he has up to now."

"And now?"

"I don't know." She sighed. "I haven't heard from him in maybe five months. Every time a few months go by, I want to believe he's forgotten me."

"It would seem you are not all that forgettable. When did he rename his yachts?"

"I..." Lauren blinked at the sudden change of subject, but she rallied quickly. "Not long ago—maybe a year? He said he liked the sound of the word. I thought it sounded too much like typhoon, but then I looked it up and saw it was a seriously creepy Greek god..."

She broke off, then grimaced as her words caught up to her. "Ah, no offense. I know your ties to Greece are pretty strong here in Oûros."

Stefan smiled. "None taken. We don't care much for him either."

For some reason, that made her feel better, and she exhaled a shaky laugh. "I mean, right? Of all the gods he could have chosen...anyway, I honestly didn't care. He was always looking to show off, and if this made him happy, then yay."

"Yay, indeed. Here we are." Stefan leaned forward and adjusted Lauren's collar, where the tiny microphone lay embedded among the spray of crystals. "Raptis has woeful security, so he's accepted ours with open arms. You won't be scanned. Everyone else will be."

They exited the car, and Lauren scanned the walkway, shocked at the wave of relief that washed over her as she recognized a familiar face. Her voice shook a little as she spoke. "I thought you were my date tonight, not him."

Stefan glanced forward, then slid his gaze back to her. He gave her an uncharacteristic smile. "Dimitri is not your enemy, Ms. Grant, at least not tonight. And he's almost as good in a fight as I am."

"A fight?" Lauren blinked at him. "I can't imagine you two getting in a fistfight."

"Oûros is a small country, but we have big egos. Dimitri

Korba possesses one of the biggest." He winked at her. "Try not to stir up his pride."

"I—" But Stefan turned from her to greet the owners of the home, Mr. and Mrs. Gaspar Raptis, whose house towered over them in multiple tiers of opulence. When Raptis realized that Lauren was the daughter of his "dear friends," the Grants, his eyes practically lit up with avarice.

"Welcome!" he beamed, waving enthusiastically at the driveway. "Your parents, they are already here."

"What?"

Stefan remained at her side, loose and easy, but Lauren felt as if she'd been turned to stone. She pivoted in a careful three-pointed step, smiled an exact three-quarter smile, and tilted her head precisely eleven degrees as she registered the three people striding across the wide white drive, as if they'd emerged from a stroll through some garden idyll.

Three, not two.

She forced herself to focus. Her parents looked as they ever did, her mother blonde and exact, her father equally blond but far more expansive, his formerly excruciatingly fit body only now going to seed as the years, fine food, and expensive alcohol caught up with him. They both smiled at her with reasonable cheer, but then they would. She'd done a good job being the model daughter. They could have no complaints on that score.

Smithson's, however, was the harder gaze to meet. He was the smartest man she'd ever known, and she'd realized eventually that he had a sort of sixth sense about her. He knew her weaknesses, her vulnerabilities. He could, at the beginning, actually seem to read her thoughts.

She'd gotten very good at helping to convince him of what she was thinking since then, helping him believe what she needed him to believe. And so at this moment, she knew better than to act too coy. He wanted to be coddled and appreciated, yes. But he didn't want to be discounted. He'd meant to scare her with his little box trick. He had. He'd want to know that.

She stepped forward and hugged her parents—her mother delicately, her father more robustly, ever the doting daughter and proud progeny. Then she turned to Henry Smithson and swiftly raised her hand to strike him.

As she expected, he caught her hand before she could complete the blow.

Twelve

"**L**auren!"

As the older blonde's sharp cry echoed through the courtyard, Dimitri didn't know what surprised him more. The flourishing smack the American had communicated that she had every chance of landing, or that she'd let the man opposite her catch her in time. As Dimitri discreetly radioed the arrival of Smithson to his men in the field, he watched the man neatly fold Lauren's hand over his and kiss her knuckles, smiling broadly as he lifted his head.

"You must forgive me, but I couldn't resist." Smithson's voice was smug and self-satisfied. Apparently, the attempted smack pleased him far more than anything else Lauren could have done. Had she known it would?

Dimitri suspected she did.

"You scared me to death!" Lauren seemed to relent, then leaned in for a brief hug as her mother kept spluttering. "I made an absolute fool of myself looking for whatever you'd sent in the box, only to realize you'd never intended to send anything at all."

"My sincere apologies." Henry Smithson spoke with sharp,

squared-off edges to his words, much like the man himself. Smithson was tall and pale, as blond as the Grants. He was built well—slender, but hard. Someone who took care of himself with diligence. Though he didn't appear to be tatted with Typhon's signature ink—and wore no obvious jewelry that would tie him to the god, Dimitri didn't like his energy. His eyes were dark and intense, and he swept the space every few moments, as if he expected trouble. When none came, he turned to continue his introductions. He shook Stefan's hand as if it was a competition, and Stefan, being Stefan, showed no expression at the firm hold. "Stefan Andris, yes? Royal cousin, diplomat, general man about town. Your reputation precedes you."

"Hopefully not in its entirety," Stefan said smoothly, to another round of polite laughter. When he turned to escort Lauren up the stairs, Henry moved in swiftly, taking her by the arm. Lauren betrayed none of the fear—the terror—that she had the day before while talking about Smithson. She was laughing, happy, actually appearing a little charmed by Smithson's high-handedness in taking her away from Stefan. Dimitri and the security team had planned for this, but not so soon in the evening, not when the remainder of the entourage had yet to arrive.

The small contingent moved up the stairs toward them, Mrs. Raptis leading the way as—thank God—the next vehicle turned into the gate at the bottom of the hill. Not an official limo, but the plant they'd had idling nearby. "Oh," Lauren said, turning. "Is that Emmaline and Kristos?"

"We shall all greet them!" Raptis neatly solved the awkward moment by keeping the limelight on himself, and Lauren played her hand by disengaging from Henry's hold to turn back toward the parking plaza. As her gaze found Dimitri's, he tensed.

She was still scared to death.

The glance lasted only a breath, and then she was trotting

down to the car, which, of course, didn't contain Emmaline but another friend of the family's. Then the royal caravan *did* show up, and all was set to rights.

In the soft light of the setting sun, however, Henry Smithson's gaze remained on Lauren as she greeted her friends. Hungry. Self-assured. Resolute.

True minion of Typhon or not, it'd be Dimitri's pleasure to permanently kick this asshole to the curb.

With the arrival of the royal family, the rest of the party followed in short order, and soon the house was full to bursting. Dimitri skirted the perimeter of the main reception room, with its miniature stage for pontificating, and its wide dance floor. The Americans seemed too subdued to his eyes, but anyone who didn't know them well wouldn't necessarily guess. And Lauren, for her part, kept up appearances the best she could. She'd already danced with Smithson twice, laughing and blushing as if she were bowled over by the attention. She'd danced once with her father, another time with Stefan, and once with Kristos.

Now, finally, the evening was drawing to a close, and Dimitri could practically feel the air crackle with tension. With a celebutante's unerring sense of timing, Lauren astutely guessed the musicians were embarking on their last dance of the evening, a traditional Greek celebratory number. Smithson was engaged in a lively conversation with King Jasen, so she slipped out of the room without anyone noticing her. Whether she legitimately needed air or she was merely bored, her absence likely wouldn't be noticed as anything other than a capricious escape. She wouldn't be back until well into the speechmaking, he was certain, while the rest of the party would be trapped by their own politeness, listening to Raptis ramble on about the future of Oûros.

Dimitri's gaze swept the floor, alighting first on Stefan, who was also scanning the room, and then on Lauren's parents, cheerfully drunk and looking...far too happy with themselves.

He double-checked Smithson's position.

Gone. *Dammit.*

King Jasen was making his way to his seat of honor, but Smithson had vanished.

Stationed by the door as he was, it was easy for Dimitri to blend back into the shadows toward the corridor, but before he could turn away, he felt a small, strong hand on his arm.

He looked down into the fierce face of Nicki Clark. "Where's Lauren?" she hissed. Dimitri looked up and saw Stefan bearing down on him as well, his normally impassive face now bent into a scowl. "I saw that creep leave right before I realized she wasn't in the room anymore. That's no good. He's seriously the worst. I want to find her."

"Miss Clark." Stefan reached them and laid a hand on Nicki's shoulder, staying her as Dimitri shrugged off her hold. "Creating a scene is not to our advantage. Not here."

"Well, it sure as hell—"

Their argument dissipated into a fierce whisper as Dimitri exited the reception room. The Raptis manor house featured expansive rooms and narrow corridors, but Lauren, he suspected, would behave the way most stalking victims would. She would head outside, someplace that wasn't closed in, so she couldn't be trapped. Somewhere there would be some people, but not too many, so she could be alone without being isolated.

Front or back veranda?

The front afforded the parking crew, but the back would have the staff setting up for the fireworks display Raptis had announced so proudly earlier in the evening. That was where she would be, he thought. Easier to explain away.

As he walked, he checked in with his men, each new report causing him to lengthen his stride. *No, no, no.*

Smithson, it seemed, remained one step ahead of them. Time to change that.

Dimitri had been to the Raptis home enough times on detail with Ari that he knew the layout. Moving quickly, he signaled a few of the house staff, men and women he'd seen before and so knew were hired by Raptis and not planted, to accompany him. His orders were precise, easy to understand. These people were not fools and knew the value of accommodating the royal family's security team. They hustled out ahead of him toward the back of the house, their momentum giving him easy cover.

By the time he stepped out onto the veranda, however, he could see he was already too late.

Smithson had found Lauren.

The older man leaned into the cool, slender blonde as she stood facing the large house, her body plainly in sight. As she'd no doubt suspected, the veranda wasn't at all abandoned, with quiet staff members moving chairs into place and lighting sparking torches at the perimeter of the space. Between the spitting crackle of the flames and the flickering lights, the torches gave him a greater opportunity to approach the couple, but he went slowly, easily. Smithson wouldn't do more than talk, not here. He wouldn't harm Lauren, not with this many witnesses.

But sometimes words could wound far more effectively than a blade. Not often, but it happened. And it was happening now.

"—fascinated with you since the moment I saw you, dangerously, emphatically so. You know that, my sweet—"

Dimitri's eyes sharpened as the last word was garbled. It couldn't have been what he thought it was, he clearly had misheard. But still, what was Smithson doing? Was this a *marriage* proposal? Here?

"Mr.—" Lauren faltered, tilting her head artfully. "Henry, I'm flattered, you know that I am. But with your wealth and position, you could have any woman in the world. You don't truly want me."

"You're wrong." The words were spoken quietly, but there was such steel behind them that Dimitri paused, shifting his weight to the balls of his feet. Lauren also seemed to realize her mistake.

"Then—if you do, which again, I am desperately flattered by, give us time to work through a relationship like two normal people. With my studies, I haven't had a chance to breathe."

"Your degrees were completed a year ago, and you've not remained long enough in one place since then until now. Don't think I'm not aware as to why. You knew of my interest, Lauren. You didn't reach out, when you easily could have."

"I'm only twenty-three—"

"And I have loved you for easily half your life. First, yes, as an uncle, a friend. But you have grown into the woman I always knew you could be. And I can't bear to be apart from you any longer. I *won't* bear it."

"But—"

"I know your hesitation, Lauren. I do." The sudden admission appeared to take Lauren by surprise, and Dimitri stiffened as well, alert. He had circled to the right of the pair so he could see them both clearly. Lauren's flustered nerves and fear, some of which he suspected was artifice, some of which he knew wasn't. Smithson's hard triumph at having cornered his prey. "Your parents have explained how much freedom they've given you—too much freedom. No, no," he lifted a hand to stay whatever protest or agreement Lauren was about to share.

At that moment, Dimitri's earpiece crackled, and he instinctively looked toward the door, as if he could picture the wide front veranda atop the circular drive, and the third new vehicle that was now idling there, low and sleek and belonging to Smithson. The bastard was going to move tonight.

"But freedom is not for everyone, Lauren. What have you done with yours? Dashing around the world, playing at running a business, playing at having a life. It is time you live your life in earnest. I can show you how."

"Then perhaps we should wait until I know I can be the mature wife you need?" Lauren sounded a little desperate now, and Smithson seemed to react to it, a wolf leaning in for the kill. "I'd be better able to handle the duties and responsibilities of your social calendar—and know for certain what business I would want to pursue—in a few more years. I can get focused, make decisions."

"I will not wait another year, certainly not three. I've everything already prepared to leave tonight." He reached out, cupping her chin to lift it. "I get what I want, Lauren. I've always gotten what I wanted. You know that perhaps more than anyone. And now what I want is you."

"Oh my *Gawd*!" The strident voice of Nicki Clark, sounding like she was cheering on the game-winning goal in the World Cup, caterwauled over the space, causing both Smithson and Lauren to jump. "Stefan, will you *look* at all the sparklers!"

Thirteen

Lauren wheeled around, shocked to see Nicki stumbling forward as if she'd downed an entire bottle of *tsipouro*. Which would have been a trick, because the girl barely drank enough to give herself a buzz. But you'd never know it given the way she plowed forward, knocking into a small collection of chairs before Stefan reached her.

As usual, the unflappable diplomat was fast and efficient, but Nicki seemed to be overmatching him with her sheer physicality. She flailed her fist, cracking him in the jaw, and even Stefan seemed surprised at the force of the blow. He bent to gather her up, and she sprawled forward, halfway down the stairs, barely keeping her feet.

"Ms. Clark!" Stefan gasped, reaching for her, and his sharp gaze swept to them. "A hand, if you would, Smithson," he called to Henry. "She'll hurt herself if she keeps it up."

"Of course." Henry didn't hesitate, but Lauren was so grateful for the reprieve from his touch that she shamefully didn't move forward to help recover Nicki, who'd begun singing at the top of her lungs—Nicki, who was the worst singer she'd ever met. By the time Henry reached her, Lauren finally recovered her wits. She surged forward as Nicki took her first remarkably well-aimed swing toward Henry, but someone grabbed Lauren's hand and stopped her cold.

Then Dimitri was right up in her face, the shock of his nearness and the surge of his touch overbalanced only by the intensity of his gaze as he squeezed her arm hard enough to bruise. "Come with me, now. Don't argue."

She didn't so much agree as breathe in his general direction, but that was apparently enough for Dimitri. He yanked her off the veranda and through the torches so quickly, she barely got her skirts up in time to run, and then they were off through the darkness, his hand locked on her wrist and his legs pumping so hard, she was pretty sure he would have dragged her bodily down the lush lawn if she tripped and fell. Luckily, she didn't.

"Where—where!" was all she could manage as they crested another rise and then were into the trees, the thick knot of forest she'd so admired around Raptis's mountain home. Dimitri didn't answer, but he didn't have to. In another hundred feet, the trees cleared enough that she could see the bright moonlight pick out a strip of dirt tracks, the four-wheeler perched atop those tracks barely more than a golf cart.

"Get in," he said, thrusting her forward, and she moved automatically, responding to the command in his voice. But as she settled into the vehicle and he turned the key—it *was* a golf cart of sorts, no sound whatsoever emanating from its engine— her brain switched on again.

"I'll be missed—Nicki!"

"Nicki knew you were in trouble. She created a distraction." Dimitri's voice was a harsh growl. It didn't sound like him at all.

"Stefan...?"

"He wouldn't have let her do it if he'd known. He was surprised." He flashed a grin, the first emotion she'd seen on him other than furious intent. "He doesn't do well with surprises."

"But they'll look for me."

"Most reasonable place you could have gone was back inside to get help. We've got maybe twenty minutes. That's more than enough time to get you off the mountain."

Lauren flopped back in her seat. "No, this is all too much, Dimitri. You'll just piss Henry off, and he's not a man who likes to be pissed off. Better for me simply to face him."

"Not going to happen." The golf cart intersected with a larger road, closer to the main highway that had brought them here, and another vehicle stood there, a hulking heavy-duty truck. "Into the truck."

"No! I have to— "

"Into the truck or I'll put you there, princess. I do not have time to fuck around here." He lunged for her, and she jumped back, but her options were pretty limited. It was the truck or the forest, and Dimitri was her assigned bodyguard. She had to trust him, though he was making things so much worse. By the time she'd hauled herself up into his monster truck and buckled in, he'd already gunned the engine to life and they were off again, bouncing onto the road and shooting forward at high speed.

Dimitri started talking again. "Smithson had additional vehicles here tonight. They showed up as the party went on. All three of them alike. There is no doubt he would have left with you and possibly your parents in one of those vehicles, or, more likely, you and him together and your parents in a second limo, under some pretext of a drink back at the hotel or a tour of his yacht or some other bullshit that would sound both polite and reasonable. We would have lost track of you, and then you'd be in the wind."

"But you're overreacting. You're doing this all wrong!" Desperation rocketed through her. "You can't simply stick me in some sort of mountain château the way you did with Emmaline. These are my parents! They'll be looking for me. Henry will be looking for me. If he suspects the royal family had anything to do with my disappearance, he'll create the biggest media crapstorm you could possibly imagine until I'm released."

"He won't suspect the royal family. They didn't order me to follow you outside. They didn't order Nicki and Stefan to create a distraction. As far as anyone will know, you ran away and hid, and someone is either harboring you or you're using your own considerable connections to escape an unpleasant situation. Your parents will not make a public stink about it until they understand the fallout back to them."

"But I can't truly hide, Dimitri. That's not reasonable. Which means sooner or later, this is going to end very badly for me."

"Maybe. But it beats the alternative." Dimitri yanked his phone out of his pocket and tossed it into her lap. "Scroll through the pictures."

She picked up the device. There was no pass code, and a simple swipe showed her he'd already been in the text app. The first pic was a snapshot of a document, and she frowned, brushing the screen with her fingertips to stretch it wide.

She flinched. "Oh."

"Yeah, oh. Marriage certificate, prenup, all your asset-transfer paperwork. Everything that's yours, now and in the future, will be his. Neatly done. We found that in your parents' suite aboard the Smithson yacht. There's another copy in Henry's."

"Do I want to know how you got past Smithson's security?"

"You do not." Dimitri angled onto another road, and she got the sense they were heading away from the capital city and down, toward the sea. "So far, no one has seen these documents except me. Cyril and the king will receive copies if and when it's appropriate."

"Plausible deniability." Lauren shook her head. "I didn't think you'd need that in a monarchy."

"It's never a bad policy. Brace yourself."

Without more warning, Dimitri braked hard and cut the wheel, and they slid off the main road and down a path that was little more than a goat track. Trying not to squeal like a six-year-old girl, Lauren grabbed on to the door, the ceiling bar, anything she could get her hands on as they bounced and roared over skittering rocks and precipitous drops. Eventually the road evened out again, but she was swimming with vertigo by the time the trees opened up onto a narrow strip of sand. Ahead, she could see a legitimate road feeding onto the beach, a few picnic tables scattered around. Off into the water was a boat, its prow lit up with a single light.

"What was wrong with the road?" she asked, unsurprised that her voice was shaking.

Dimitri shrugged. "Shortcut. We get out here."

He didn't wait for her to answer but got out of the truck. For a moment, however, Lauren froze. She had no phone. She had no money. She had nothing to wear but the clothes on her back, and no one to trust but this brute of a bodyguard who listened to absolutely nothing she said, despite the fact that she was the one speaking reason and he was the one hustling her into a boat to go God only knew where.

"This is the most ridiculous thing I've ever done," she muttered as Dimitri jerked the door open and reached up a brawny hand for hers.

"Let's get moving, princess," he growled.

Fourteen

Dimitri checked the controls over the captain's shoulder, nodding with satisfaction. Lauren was standing on the deck, rigid and in control, but at least she'd accepted a large, heavy blanket to ward against the shock he knew was going to hit her sometime very soon. The fact that she remained upright was in her favor. The fact that she was breathing steadily, her eyes clear, her chin high, was too.

Then again, maybe nothing fazed the woman. He didn't know her, not really. He didn't want to know her.

Not really.

Dimitri refocused on the electronics in front of him. As expected, there'd been no communications from the party. With any luck, everyone was still in turmoil, searching the grounds. He'd covered a good three miles in the fifteen minutes they'd spent in the golf cart, and his truck had eaten up the terrain since then.

Both would have been cleared away by his team already, so there was nothing there to find. Lauren would have been declared an on-foot escapee, and the search would extend to neighboring homes. The royal family would be in an outrage, her parents panicked, that slimy bastard Smithson furious.

The boat was looking better and better all the time.

He thanked the captain, asked a few questions. This was a good plan, a solid plan. It would give him the time he needed to ensure the safety of the woman while maintaining deniability for the family. Excellent.

Satisfied, he moved back out on the deck with Lauren. The mini yacht was owned by Theodopolis Papalia, but he was in New Zealand right now, and he'd long since lent the craft out to the ONSF to help with the recovery of plane fragments from Ari's fatal crash.

Ari. As usual in the months since the crash, Dimitri cast his glance to the sky, thinking of his friend. He hadn't forgiven the prince for flying off so foolishly into a storm. He still couldn't quite accept that Ari was dead. If he was, though, then when Dimitri finally tracked Ari down amid the mists of Olympus, he fully planned to beat the shit out of him.

Lauren half turned as he approached. "Where are we going?"

"Island a few miles out to sea. It's called Miranos. I suspect you haven't heard of it."

She frowned. "Fishing ports, right? Villages. Town. Whatever. Not a tourist destination."

Dimitri settled in beside her, trying not to smile. "Everywhere in the Aegean is a tourist destination these days. Miranos has long made its money by fishing, but it's become a popular location for divers. It's rustic, but it's clean. Good people, good food. You'll be safe until we figure out how to proceed."

"This is such a mess," she sighed. "I don't know whether to thank you or scream at you."

"Be a shame to scare the fish."

"I guess." She seemed fragile suddenly, wrapped up in her

blanket, and he edged toward her. He'd dealt with his share of frightened people going into shock. That was part of the work they did along the border, ensuring the safety of the villagers from marauding bands that snuck into their country. Usually, they reached those villages in time. Sometimes they didn't.

Fear was something he knew, understood. And it wafted off the blonde now in little fits and gasps, as if she was trying to control even this.

Still, she didn't move away from him. And that was progress. Without asking, he put his arms around her, pulling her back to his chest, squeezing her close through the thick woven blanket. She let him do it, which was more a testament to her frame of mind than anything.

Nevertheless, something about her actions seemed wrong to him, off-putting. He couldn't quite figure it out. It was as if she was acting the role of the exhausted celebutante, knowing she should submit and so submitting in exactly the right way, when he knew damned well that she legitimately was exhausted, wrung out. What was he missing?

Her soft sigh recalled him. "I get the feeling this isn't exactly how Emmaline and Kristos spent their time out of the media spotlight, huh?"

He laughed. "Not exactly. But you'll be safe."

"I was safe before." But she said the words automatically, as if she'd been telling them to herself for so long, she wasn't sure what else to say.

He decided to push for more. "What exactly was in the boxes this man sent to you when you were younger?"

"Gifts, mostly." She leaned against him a bit more heavily, and he welcomed the warmth of her, the light scent of her shampoo and perfume mixing with the salty air. "Jewelry, books, electronics sometimes. And about every third or fourth time, sometimes less, sometimes more, there'd be something that wasn't a gift. The empty box trick he definitely pulled a few times. But then there were...dead things, too."

"Dead things."

"Yeah. Dead scorpions, a couple of times. And spiders, once. Beetles. All of them dead, thank God." She shuddered, and Dimitri tightened his hold on her. "Ashes too. I didn't understand that one until a week later. I was at a prep school camping trip, something stupid like that. I'd thought he was sending me a care package of some sort. It took a week for my mom to tell me that the family dog had gone missing."

Dimitri was glad she couldn't see his face. "He killed your dog?"

"I don't know. I didn't ask him. But the timing was a little eerie, you have to admit."

"And you *spoke* to him after that?"

She laughed, the sound bitter and jarring in the breeze. "Well, I wasn't exactly going to ignore him. Not after that. I hadn't told him I was leaving for camp. My mother had. It never occurred to me. After that, I told him more, or made sure he knew in advance. He claimed that he worried about me, but it was a control thing. It's always a control thing with him." She shook her head. "I don't know why I ever thought I could escape him. But maybe..." She broke off. "Those contracts. Maybe he was simply being thorough. Maybe they were fake, a bluff. A negotiating trick. That's something he'd do...something my dad probably taught him."

"Maybe," Dimitri allowed. *Do you understand what you're saying?* He didn't speak the words out loud. He didn't trust himself. This was a woman with more money than she knew what to do with, and she was honestly contemplating a life that none of her friends would have considered remotely acceptable: to marry a man she didn't want, didn't love, didn't trust, and was afraid of. A man who'd—maybe—called her a name that sounded familiar to Dimitri, the barest snatch of a word but...something he recognized. Echo? Ekti? Something.

Either way, and regardless of his potential affiliation with Typhon—which was looking more likely all the time—Henry Smithson had definitely proven himself to be a mentally unbalanced stalker. Not even Kristos's sweet Emmaline, who'd pretty much spent her life doing things for other people, would have found the situation tolerable.

And how was it possible that Lauren's parents had allowed this to go on? How could they not have defended their child against this man? Perhaps at first, they might have discounted Lauren's complaints, her fears, her panic. But surely it had continued long enough, often enough that they would have turned the bastard into the authorities at some point...Right?

Assuming she'd ever told them. But she had to have told them, surely. She couldn't have kept such harrowing secrets to herself.

Then again, Lauren and her family were rich. Unreasonably, unfathomably rich. Maybe they did things differently.

And it all still seemed somewhat false to him, a role she was playing. As if she'd given him enough information to string him along, but not the crucial piece, the piece he needed to know. What was she truly afraid of?

Dimitri didn't fully realize when he dropped his head toward the crown of Lauren's hair, his lips brushing the soft strands in time with the boat as it moved out into the open sea. The trip to Miranos wasn't long, maybe two hours, but they would be safe there. Lauren relaxed further in his arms, and he held her tightly, his skin prickling when she reached through the blankets to clasp her fingers around his.

His heart did an odd shimmy in his chest, but he knew this wasn't the way this was supposed to go. He didn't want this woman to get under his skin. He didn't want this woman to be anything but safely stowed cargo. And if he didn't watch it, she was going to be more than that.

Then again...

Remember who this is, here.

Dimitri went very still as Lauren's hand continued to stroke his. She'd moved her head precisely to the side, enough to allow him access to her ear, her neck. She'd stopped talking, but her body was tense, too tense, too straight, for all that she leaned against him, allowing him to take her weight. He had thought her mind lost to the rhythm of the open sea, but that wasn't it at all, was it? She wasn't wondering what the adventure ahead lay in store for her. She was trying to figure out how to manage him. To control him, the same way she thought she could control Henry Smithson, in the end.

He should give her more credit than that, he knew, and yet...

Lauren took the decision out of his hands.

She chose that moment to turn in his arms, letting the blanket fall away. Snaking up her hand to his head, she pulled him toward her, and he let her do it too. Let her bring her mouth up to his, taste his lips, steal her other hand down the hard planes of his chest to rest on his rib cage, and all the while he could tell that she wasn't truly in the moment, wasn't taken away with the desire. She was *faking* it.

Or faking some of it, anyway. She couldn't mask the shortness of her breath, or the way it passed fitfully over her lips. She couldn't fake the tremor in her fingers, or the racing of her heart. She was using her own body to help hone her diversion. And doing a damned fine job of it.

Except no one—ever—had faked it with him. Not at the level of sheer desire.

Especially not someone as into him as Lauren Grant clearly and most definitely was.

How did she think she could get away with it?

The answer came to him in a flash. Because she always had. She'd always needed to, wanted to. She'd always been in control of every situation, which could only mean that no one had ever made her feel out of control. No one had gotten her out of her own pretty, calculating head for long enough that all she could do was focus on her body, her senses, her pleasure.

Had no one ever truly seduced her? Had set aside her money and her power, and gone after her for the sole pursuit of savoring every inch of her skin, every shattering breath? If so, that was certainly a shame.

Someone should do something about that.

Dimitri lifted his mouth away from her lips. He could sense Lauren's confusion, but she was too smart to say anything but sigh and snuggle against him, the very image of the broken, trembling flower.

Oh, she was trembling, all right. Because of him. And he'd only hit her with the barest fraction of the full demigod package.

Dimitri smiled into the darkness, over the blonde's head.

Maybe this visit to Miranos wasn't going to be completely useless after all.

B athed in a wash of brilliant sunshine, Lauren lay awake the next morning, glaring at the whitewashed wall of the bedroom, the dark tile gleaming at the edge of a thick white rug. It wasn't opulent, and it definitely wasn't the palace of the crown family of Oûros. That was where she should have woken up.

She hadn't. Instead, she was in a world of wrong.

She had to get out of here.

Sitting up in bed, she swiped for her phone, which was always no more than five feet away from her—and came up with nothing. She bit out a tight curse, remembering the most infuriating part of her predicament. No phone. No money. And she knew virtually *nothing* about this rock where they'd landed. Hadn't Dimitri said this island was a dive spot? There had to be some sort of Internet café here then, right?

The smell of something obscenely good finally permeated her foul temper, and she turned her head. Bacon? The scent of grilled meat and spices filled the air, and she swiped again for her phone to check the time.

Nope.

No clocks either anywhere in the room, though light poured in from two sides, giving her a stunning view of the pristine white sand beach and shockingly blue waters of the Aegean far beyond. Still, none of that could compare to knowing what was actually going on in the world.

"Neanderthals," she muttered, throwing off the covers. She was wearing her clothes from last night, and as she padded out of her room, she realized the room opposite hers was a tiny bathroom, and there was...nothing else. Just these two rooms tucked up at the top of a narrow staircase. So, a villa, then, not some kind of bed-and-breakfast or inn, which was what she'd assumed the night before. Whose house was it, Dimitri's? A friend's? The questions crowded into her mind, but she had no way of answering them. After washing her face and hands in the sink—without a mirror, she noticed, so she also had no way of knowing what she looked like—her stomach insisted she head downstairs to explore the smells of breakfast.

Seconds later, she wheeled into the kitchen, and stopped cold.

Dimitri stood in profile at the stove, his body clad only in loose sweatpants that hung low on his waist. It was the first time she'd seen him anywhere close to partially undressed since that first day on the beach, when he'd been wearing a sweat-soaked T-shirt and shorts. That had been amazing enough, but this...

She stared at the tattoo that covered his shoulder and spread onto his back. A roiling mass of clouds, detailed and inked in a dozen different shades of gray, with the jagged streak of lightning slashing through it—

"You sleep well?" he asked without turning, and Lauren blinked, trying to get her bearings.

"I—yes. Can I borrow your phone?"

"No service out here." He waved the spatula. "We'll head into town later today, and you can make contact."

"No service?" she turned and looked out the windows that lined the wall. "How is that possible?"

He chuckled, apparently unconcerned. As if a lack of cell coverage weren't grounds for immediate meltdown. "The island has always been pretty sketchy with phones and Wi-Fi, but tourists don't seem to mind. We have sat phones for safety, should we need them."

"Oh—well, give me that, then."

"That'll have to wait for town as well, I'm afraid. Phone's dead, and I don't have a charging unit here. We left too quickly for me to round up supplies. It's only us this morning." He brought the pan over to the table, which she saw had been set for two. "You hungry?"

"No. Yes. Sure."

His warm laugh rolled through her, setting off whorls of panic within her that she couldn't quite process. Dimitri wasn't the threat here. Sure, he was half-naked, but that wasn't a threat. Really.

She sat at the table, and he served the meal, meat and roasted vegetables and hummus and bread and olives. As he padded back to the sink, she couldn't help but stare at his back. The tattoo covered only the very top of his shoulder and ended mid-back, and the slashing thing was a trident, cleaving the swirling water as if it'd been thrown from a great distance. Muscles rippled on top of other muscles, and his powerful shoulders tapered down to narrow hips before flaring out again to thighs the size of Thor's. There was a strange mix of scars as well—nothing terrible, nothing horrifying, but she got the impression that Dimitri's body had been used, and used well.

He'd used it last night to help protect her.

An unexpected wave of emotion swept through Lauren, startling in its intensity. Dimitri had moved quickly and decisively at the Raptis mansion, pulling her out of danger without any concern for Henry and his money or power. He'd whisked her away to safety, and when they'd stood together on the boat, he'd held her. Simply held her, surrounding her with his strength and solidity, as if trying to show her that nothing and no one could harm her, not while he was on the job.

She'd let him hold her, too. She'd done it to stoke his attraction, to try to control him, but...but if she was honest, a part of her had simply wanted to be held. A part of her had simply wanted someone strong to stand in the breach with her, to offer a united front against a terror she'd carried around so long that it was like a second skin.

But she couldn't afford to be weak and needy. Not now. Not ever.

No one else could get hurt because of her.

Lauren managed to return her gaze to her food again before Dimitri turned around and caught her staring, but it was a near thing. And then he sat next to her again, all skin and heat and strength. She opened her mouth to protest, but he was already focusing on the enormous platter in front of him, digging in as if he hadn't eaten in days.

She picked up a fork and eyed the food, spearing a few vegetables that looked at least reasonably familiar. Since Dimitri was wolfing down his food, she occupied her time with eating as well.

It was...heavenly. Apparently, Dimitri could cook too.

What else is he good at?

Lauren gripped her fork a little more tightly, determined to stab herself if she didn't straighten up. "So, what are we going to do today?" she asked. She could have kicked herself for not demanding more details from Emmaline about her own idyll, but her escape with Dimitri already seemed vitally different. Kristos was far less...dangerous than the rough, uncivilized captain of the ONSF.

"Eat. You'll need your strength." He grinned at her and nodded at the plate. "Unless it tastes bad?"

"Oh—oh, of course not. It's delicious." Sudden awkwardness engulfed her, and she glanced at her plate. Food, at least, she could manage. "Thank you."

He snorted. "Delicious, it is not. But it is local fare, and it'll fill you up, I promise you."

He continued with an animated description of the island's cuisine, clearly trying to put her at ease. Unfortunately, she found herself focusing less on the food and more on his face, his mouth, his eyes...anything to stop looking at his naked chest. She flushed as she realized what she was doing, and she reconsidered her idea of stabbing herself with a fork. It was as if she'd never seen a man before.

Dimitri, fortunately, didn't seem to notice. At least he didn't until she realized he'd stopped talking, while she sat there with her fork poised over her plate, her focus on his pecs. Gently, he reached over and took the fork out of her hand, laying it on the table. The touch of his hand galvanized her, her entire body quivering with anticipation, but he didn't do anything further. Merely sort of patted her fingers, then stood.

It wasn't until he turned away that she got it. She narrowed her eyes, pushing out from the table.

"You're doing this on purpose, aren't you?" she snapped.

He looked at her innocently. "Doing what?"

"This! That!" She pointed at his naked chest. "Something has happened, and you're shielding it from me, distracting me with the whole He-Man routine. What is it? Is it my family? Henry? Have they made calls? Are they on their way here?"

His eyes widened in what appeared to be genuine alarm. "Not at all. I told you I've had no contact—"

"Oh, bullshit. You're a captain of your country's security force. Of course you have a real phone on you." She threw her napkin down and strode toward him. He backed up until his hips met the sink, and she still kept coming. Standing this close to Dimitri was dangerous, but she could control it. She could control her reactions too. She knew that, but that didn't stop her from standing a little too close, leaning in a little too far. Dimitri smelled of spices and heat and—*Focus!* "What is it you're not telling me?"

He didn't answer right away, and she flapped her right hand in front of his face. "Hello? I asked you—"

"Enough." He moved so quickly that she didn't see it coming, but he grabbed her hand and there was that jolt again, the vital leap of energy between them, that at once grounded her and made her blood feel too fizzy in her veins. "You keep coming after me, princess, and sooner or later, you're going to catch me. Do you have any idea what you're going to do when that happens?"

"You're disgusting." She tried to pull away from him, but he held firm. He stared down at her, laughter in his eyes.

"Disgusting? That's really what you think of me?"

"I—" Lauren blinked as he pulled her hand toward his lips, brushing the fingertips as all the blood drained out of her head. "I don't—stop that."

"Stop this?" He pressed her hand more firmly to his mouth, his warm lips drifting down to the hollow of her palm until his mouth slipped over the edge of her hand, and she felt the pressure of his teeth bite down.

Need shot straight through her and exploded in a burst of panicked lust. *What the hell was happening here?* They'd kissed and she'd enjoyed it, sure, but this—this—was off the charts. This didn't make sense. The ocean outside suddenly sounded like it was roaring. The sunlight seemed to beam like lasers, filling up the room with its radiance. Her insides spontaneously melted with a speed she'd never experienced before, and she gasped, her right hand trapped, her left hand pressed against Dimitri's chest, his eyes riveted on hers, tempting her, taunting her...

A crackling voice rang out with abrupt authority. "Dimitri! You're—oh!"

The spell shattered. Lauren turned, her right hand captured in Dimitri's, as an old woman pushed into the kitchen from the front room of the villa, her arms laden with food. Though stunned for exactly half a second, as soon as the woman saw Dimitri and Lauren together, she burst into an excited, shocked, or certainly startled flood of Oûrois, her accent so thick that Lauren couldn't follow her words. She asked practically fifty-seven questions all at once, one on top of the other as she dropped the loaves of bread on the table along with dark purple fruit.

Dimitri startled Lauren by kissing her hand once more, firmly. Then he squeezed her fingers and pushed her away.

"Hello, *Grandmother*," he announced with an almost odd emphasis on the word, striding across the room. The old lady's eyes widened as she took in his lack of a shirt, then she batted at him ineffectually while he picked her up and swung her back and forth like a plump doll. The two devolved into another conversation while Lauren braced herself against the sink, willing her brain to come back online. The woman was laughing and crying at the same time, back to speaking a million miles a minute, and as Lauren watched, a new realization struck her.

No one was paying attention to her. At all. She might as well not be in the room, a situation that hadn't happened to her in—forever. Far from being offensive, it was wonderful. Freeing. And made Lauren suddenly feel safer than she had in longer than she could remember.

She turned toward the sunshine, and walked out.

Sixteen

Dimitri shook his head slightly as Calista stumbled in her nonstop patter. With a gesture, he urged her to keep it up as they both watched Lauren drift down the porch. His sister's eyes rounded as she babbled on, but the moment Lauren stepped down the short staircase and onto the sand, she sucked in a deep breath—and punched him in the arm. The strike was remarkable strong for an eighty-year-old woman.

"Your *grandmother?*" she protested, glaring at him. "Has it come to that?"

Dimitri grinned. "Well, what else could I say? Lauren Grant is a guest of the royal family, a xénos. And she's leaving on the first boat we can put her on. It's not like I'm going to spill my entire life history to her."

"She wasn't looking at you like any outsider," his sister sniffed. She turned her gaze out the window again, watching Lauren as she disappeared around the corner of the house. "She looked like she wanted to eat you for breakfast. Which makes me sad for her. The disappointment will be crushing."

"I suspect she'll survive."

"Yes, but the nightmares."

As they bantered, Dimitri studied Calista's profile. Long, thick white hair curled around his sister's lined face, and her skin was a little looser at her jaw than the last time he'd seen her, but her dark eyes remained sharp, her laughter bright and full. No matter how much else had changed between them, some things never would.

His sister had been like him in almost every way when they'd been children, a year younger but every bit as fiery-tempered, always up for an adventure. When they'd learned that Dimitri had enough of the throwback demigod gene to allow him the choice of Hemitheos, she'd at first been irritated that he'd gotten the nod from the gods and not her.

But that hadn't lasted. Calista had encouraged him to embrace the gatekeeper's gift at twenty, to make the choice to serve the crown and live as a demigod, not a man. And even though she hadn't fully understood the sacrifices it would entail back then—neither of them had—she'd never stopped treating him like a slightly older brother. Even as he'd only aged one year for every ten of hers, even as they'd buried their parents, then their aunts, uncles and cousins—and eventually her first two husbands. Even as he'd seen her beautiful children grow, thrive, and have children of their own, she'd always been there for him.

"Now you're the one looking at me like a xénos," she grumbled good-naturedly, sending him a sidelong look. "You've never seen an old woman before? Show some respect."

"I've never seen an old woman as cranky as you," he said. "And you're too thin. You need to eat, Callista."

"And you need to tell me more about this American." She pointed a long, knobby finger in the general direction of where they last saw Lauren. "I heard about Kristos's engagement, even all the way out here. It's about time he stepped up to his responsibilities. Ari's been dead a year."

"Not dead," Dimitri said sharply.

She flapped her hands at him. "Gone then, gone. You can give me that. And Kristos is here, the royal family is here. The country must go on. But back to your girlfriend."

"Not my girlfriend."

"Okay, she's smarter than I thought. She's with the new princess? A friend?"

"She is."

"Is she in trouble—or is *she* the trouble?" She eyed him. "I mean, why's she with you?"

Dimitri flashed her a smile. "Besides the obvious?"

Calista snorted. "So maybe not so smart after all. Still..."

The sound of an engine starting had them both turning toward the door.

"*Shit*," Dimitri snapped. He was out the door in ten seconds, but it didn't matter. He'd left the keys in his four-wheeler. Of course he'd left the keys in his four-wheeler. Of course he'd left the keys, and of course Lauren had taken it. The same way she'd probably taken for granted that everything she saw was hers the moment she laid eyes on it.

He shook his head, his anger dissolving into a rueful chuckle as Calista strode out behind him, laughing her fool ass off. Together, they watched as Lauren roared down the beach in the beach rover, completely in the opposite direction of town. She'd figure it out soon enough.

"Seriously, she's the trouble or she's *in* trouble, which is it?" Calista asked.

Dimitri sighed. "Both."

It took him an hour to track Lauren down. Not very difficult, given the size of the only town on Miranos, and the fact that she was the only blonde on the island. He saw the vehicle first, parked in front of the main pub. There would be a TV there, and a phone, he knew she assumed. She wasn't wrong. Because she also wasn't stupid.

He entered the bar and waved to the bartender, Anker, whose grin broadened as he looked up from Lauren, who sat hunched over Anker's ancient phone. "She said you would pay for her coffee, my friend. I said to myself, a beautiful woman I have never seen before comes to my bar, of course she is friends with Dimitri Korba. Unfortunately, she has been having no luck with my phone. I told her the connection on the island, it is not so good. It is the price we must pay to live in paradise. But oh! Good, you can help her."

Lauren turned to him then, her eyes narrowing as she saw what he held in his hand. "Your phone was charged all along!"

"You Americans are all too connected." He handed the sat phone to her. "Call the number I last dialed. Nicki Clark will pick up. Stefan tells me she's been hounding him by the hour for information, that she wouldn't go to sleep until she knew that you were safe. And even then, she slept in the communications room."

"She—worries." He could tell she was thinking something else, and her words sounded false to him, anyway. From what little he'd seen of Nicole Clark, she didn't worry. She acted, reacted, attacked, confronted. He didn't envy Stefan having her underfoot, literally. She was probably coming out of her skin. If there was one thing Oûros's most polished diplomat didn't like, it was any lack of control. And Nicki Clark had that in spades.

Lauren's voice recalled him. "But she's the only one there?" she asked, clearly mapping out her communications strategy. "Not my parents?"

He shook his head. "They continue to search. Cyril took them into the mountains, stopping at every château along the way. He has assured them that you cannot leave the country without our knowledge. Oûros is not that big."

She grimaced. "I have to contact them, Dimitri."

She did, yes. But that idea seemed strangely wrong. At least for the moment, until he understood the full scope of the threat against her. "Remember the pictures we took. We don't know what else he's put in place."

Her face shuttered, enough to let him know that his barb had hit its mark. "Fine. Then I definitely need to make some calls."

As she dialed, Dimitri watched her. Though her makeup had been scrubbed off and her clothes remained far too fine for Miranos, she looked fully at ease in the tiny bar, fully in control. He rested his elbows on the counter as she spoke, and nodded to Anker as he slid him a steaming mug of coffee.

"Your wife?" Anker asked, timed to ensure that Dimitri choked. "Ah, your girlfriend, then. She is pretty. Stubborn too."

"You noticed that."

"I notice everything." Anker winked. "I asked her why she is here, and she said you are worried for her unnecessarily." He eyed Dimitri. "She thinks you are foolish for trying to protect her."

"She'll get used to it." Dimitri took another sip of the dark brew as Lauren scowled. She spoke rapid English, which he could follow, though he found himself getting distracted from her words by the sheer attraction of her anger. She honestly was lovely when she was happy, but she was magnificent when she was mad. Which probably didn't bode well for a relationship.

A what? He shook his head. Demigods didn't have relationships, not if they were smart. Clearly, he needed more caffeine.

"I need you to keep an eye on Fran and Emmaline. Especially Emmaline," Lauren was saying now. "If another one of those packages shows up, do not fool around with it." She waved her hand with irritation. "Whatever you do, Nicki, don't make a scene. That'll make him happier than anything else."

Dimitri scowled, considering her words. Lauren was channeling anger, but there was no missing the undercurrent of fear that laced her words. When he woke that morning on the couch, his first thought had been to contact Cyril, and his second had been to check on Lauren—a thought he'd resisted, knowing that fear had exhausted her.

What must this be like for her? She was the billionaire heiress of one of the world's richest families. She'd doubtlessly had an army of maids and nannies and shopping buddies surrounding her like a pink cloud since she'd been born. This kind of woman wasn't supposed to know fear of any sort.

And yet, Smithson sending her a few nasty presents wasn't enough to account for that fear. Even presents that were creepy as fuck. He'd had to have hurt her personally worse than that, in a way she couldn't prove. In a way, she was clearly unwilling to tell him yet.

Dimitri scowled, forcing himself to keep tabs on Lauren's conversation with Nicki while his mind roved over the rest of the data he'd collected. Surprisingly, Cyril supported Dimitri's decision to remove Lauren from the mainland, a reaction he thought had more to do with Cyril's relief that they couldn't be held accountable for another American if she wasn't in the palace proper. But the reaction of the Grant parents and Smithson himself had been less relieved, Cyril had told him. They were outraged, all three of them.

The current story that Cyril was spinning was that Lauren had used her considerable money and influence to spirit herself out of the country, with the intention of shopping in Milan or Paris to clear her mind. She'd been stopped due to her unfamiliarity with the terrain and the people—and the fact that she'd decided to run away when she was miles away from any actual town. So discreet inquiries were underway, and of course she would be noticed and found. Sooner rather than later.

Which meant that eventually, exactly as she'd told him, she was going to have to face Smithson.

Dimitri took a long pull on his coffee. What would it be like to have everything and still feel threatened by one man, threatened to the point of a deeply personal fear? He couldn't imagine it. He couldn't understand how Lauren had put up with it.

Then again, his life was far simpler, for all that it was unusually long. For the past sixty some years, he'd served his country and his king. He would happily sacrifice his life for either, or for his family, should the need arise. In the meantime, he simply needed to stay focused on his work, and let go of attachments to people who invariably would drift out of his life as easily as they drifted into it.

"You are looking very dark, my friend," Anker observed. "A woman so pretty, she should not make you so sad."

"He should be sad for other reasons." The familiar voice had Dimitri turning around, his heart undeniably lighter with it.

"Alexi!"

"Do not talk to me." His grandniece held up her hand and scowled at him, then peered critically at Lauren. "You have a beautiful American woman, and who sees her first? Grandmother. This is unacceptable. And she's dressed in yesterday's clothes. What sort of monster are you?"

Lauren, as if sensing they were talking about her, swiveled around. She took in Alexi with an interested gaze. His grandniece gave a low whistle. "She's more beautiful than Grandmother said." In true family form, she punched his arm as Lauren slid off the stool and moved several steps away, heading out the door. "You are married, then?"

That stopped Dimitri from going after Lauren. He stared at Alexi. She of all people knew that was impossible. "What? *No.*"

"Good, then she cannot stay with you. She will stay with—"

"Also no." Dimitri shot out a hand, staying Alexi's words as he clasped her arm. Lauren was bent over the phone, talking fast. She couldn't know she was being recorded by tech built into Dimitri's phone. He wouldn't tell her either. "She's in danger, Alexi. I can't have her bring that danger to the family, only to me. She's my responsibility."

She lifted her brows. "So you *are* married, then," she quipped. "Does she know you're a demigod?"

"She doesn't," Dimitri said heavily. "And she can't. Which makes you my sister."

Her eyes gleamed with delight. "Noted. But she still needs something to wear. How long will you be staying?" At his dazed look, she laughed. "Well, she can't stay holed up in your villa, Dimitri. We will celebrate this night, yes? And go shopping this day. She speaks only English?"

"Oûrois as well." Lauren stepped toward them, her face carefully composed as she handed her phone to Dimitri. "Thank you."

"Ah, excellent," Alexi said. "Then we will get you new clothes and supplies to make your stay with my monstrous *brother* acceptable. He will keep you in his little villa so that you may remain safe, but you'll come to our house this evening, yes? You must."

Lauren, who surely had more party experience than most women in the world, seemed nonplussed, whether by the invitation or the word "safe." Her gaze swiveled from Dimitri to Alexi and back, until finally she nodded. "You don't need to do anything for me, truly. I'm fine."

"Nonsense. You are the guest of my brother, and you have brought him back to our shores for longer than a few hours for the first time in a year. This makes you a miracle."

"A year?" Lauren shot him a startled glance. The timing clearly didn't escape her, and he shrugged.

"It's been a very busy year."

"It has been a year of mourning, and not only for the crown

prince. But go—shoo." Alexi pushed Dimitri away. "Let me dress this beautiful woman. We'll see you later. "

For the second time that morning, Dimitri watched Lauren walk away from him without a backward glance. He found he didn't like it. Didn't like it at all.

He swiped open his phone to connect with his tracking service. At least he could keep her safe.

Seventeen

Within twenty minutes, Lauren had not only wheedled Dimitri's sister out of her phone—this one hopefully not tracked within an inch of its life—she'd also gotten her to take her to the one place in town with decent cell service. The local sports bar and bookie shop. It all made a weird sort of sense. Even complete Luddites needed connectivity to place their bets and watch the latest games. With assurances that she wanted only to take care of critical wire transfers, she stepped to the side of the bar as Alexi ordered them both food and drinks. Breakfast already seemed hours ago, and Lauren hadn't really been focusing on her meal. Not with Dimitri in front of her in his half-naked glory.

Dimitri. When he'd kissed her, there in his house, it legit had felt like the earth had moved beneath her. Was she more exhausted than she'd realized? Was the island playing tricks on her?

Her attention was recalled by the crisp voice on the phone. It took only a few tries to get transferred to a real human, one of the perks of her name, she knew. You learned to take the good with the bad.

Lauren put the transaction through quickly, double-checked all the other accounts, and changed all the passwords, leaving strict instructions on what constituted any further "authorized" changes. The process only took a few minutes, which was the whole point of setting everything up in advance. At least now her money was safe. That was the easy part.

But she had another call to make. One she didn't want to make on Alexi's phone, if she could help it. The bank call was safe enough, even if Dimitri had a bead on his sister's device. This one, Nicki had insisted needed to be more private. Plus, she had a second reason to find an untracked phone.

She made a show of wandering back into the little pub, wide-eyed and eager. Since it was afternoon, the pub was hopping—or as hopping as she expected it ever got on this tiny dot of an island. The clientele was mostly male, which was in her favor. She needed to single one of the guys out and...

Shit. She didn't have any money. She wasn't going to be able to call anyone if she couldn't buy a phone from some hapless tourist. That wasn't going to happen without cash. She'd have to find another way.

Trying not to let her irritation show, she rejoined Alexi and prepared herself for a long meal and a longer day trying to find clothes. It wasn't that she didn't appreciate Dimitri's sister. The woman was sweet, practical, and strikingly pretty—her dark eyes big and flashing, her riot of curly black hair a perfect match to her buoyant personality. But Lauren didn't have time for her. She didn't have time for anyone. "Here you go," she said, handing back the phone. "I only made the one call, and it shouldn't charge you—"

"Keep it." Alexi grinned at her, and Lauren blinked at her, startled.

"I can't keep your phone. I'll run up charges."

"Then Dimitri will pay them." Alexi pointed to the phone.

"It's what he calls a 'burner.' Charming name, don't you think? You burn it up and throw it out. Only mine stays good for much longer than he seems to think."

"He gave you a burner phone?" Lauren frowned at her. So maybe the phone wasn't tracked after all? "But why?"

"Because he's a big, overprotective ox. And I say that with love and affection. But I have six of those phones in their boxes at home, minutes already charged to them, and I don't know when I'm going to get to them." Alexi smiled at Lauren's confusion. "With Dimitri, you don't always get reasons. He simply does things."

"When did he start, though? Sending you phones?"

Alexi cast her gaze skyward. "It was a year ago, of course. After Prince Ari died." She smiled grimly. "That's why he said he gave them to us—so we could call him with any information about the prince's plane. Such a tragedy, truly. We lost Dimitri that day as much as Aristotle. He said we might find—he didn't know. Something. Wreckage of the plane washed up on the island. Information from the fishermen or divers. Something. He spared no expense—and not only for the family, but friends and neighbors as well. The local fishermen. Everyone."

She shook her head. "We suspected he mostly wanted us to be safer. He took it very hard when Ari died. Went dark for days, wouldn't eat. Came here, you know, but we didn't see him. He combed the beaches and coves for debris. Very sad." She sighed. "He blamed himself."

Despite herself, Lauren found herself leaning closer. She didn't need to pry into Dimitri's life; it was none of her business. And yet the idea of the rough-and-tumble captain scavenging the rocky shoreline of this tiny island for wreckage that he had to know wasn't forthcoming made her unaccountably sad.

"Why did he think Ari's plane would wash this far south?" she asked. "I thought he took off from the mainland and crashed..." She frowned, trying to remember the details. "Wasn't it near Thassos?"

"You know the story! But of course you do. I forget that the whole world was watching our little country for a while. Yes, Thassos is where they found the wreckage, after that storm blew up and the seas finally calmed enough for the search. But Dimitri, he was convinced Ari wasn't heading to Thassos but to Samothrace, east of us. There is a small landing strip there, and the royal family has a house, as they do on many of the Greek islands. Dimitri became convinced everyone was looking in the wrong place." She sighed. "He couldn't let it go."

"And did you? Find any wreckage?"

Alexi shook her head. "We didn't. There was no wreckage to be had. And everyone looked. When he started giving out his phones to the fishermen, men you'd think would simply sell the things off to tourists and make some fast cash, they didn't. We all felt for Dimitri and for his quest. The only things that have ever turned up, however, are parts and debris from Turkish planes. Which makes sense—we are one of the easternmost islands in the Aegean, and if the seas wish to offer up her finds, it's often those that have washed over from Turkey. But that's it. Dimitri looked over the Turkish debris for a while, then he, eventually, trusted us to know what it was we were looking for." Her expression turned rueful. "He's never stopped sending the phones, though. When he does, then we'll know he's finally on the path to healing, yes?"

They passed the rest of the meal on lighter topics, but Lauren couldn't let the search for Ari's plane go. She puzzled over it while they shopped—a euphemism, as when someone else is buying you clothes, you accept whatever largesse they see fit to give. As they moved through the tourist section of Miranos, a surprisingly thriving minimarket that catered to divers and sun worshippers alike, her attention drifted again and again to the open waters of the Aegean.

"It's beautiful, I know." Alexi stopped beside her, shielding her eyes as the sun glared down on them. "You will see, this is only the beginning. The sunset celebration is truly breathtaking."

"This is the western coast," Lauren said. "This is where he thought the plane would have washed up?"

"Yes." Alexi pointed to a spot where the island stretched into the sea, like the defiant prow of a ship. "The water is relatively shallow there, and there are reefs that are treacherous to navigate. It's a natural holding spot for anything the sea might wish to share with us. Dimitri used to camp out there when...ah, when he was little. A long time ago. Ironic that now that he's a grown man, it's become such a mix of despair and hope for him. Every tide brought new possibilities and ultimately new disappointment."

Lauren scanned the open water. From this height, she couldn't see the beach below them, where Dimitri had his villa. She knew without asking, though, that the beach was connected to the distant promontory. How many times had he taken his beach rover out to that lonely spot, casting out for an answer that wouldn't come? Her heart shifted uncomfortably in her chest. Dimitri wasn't her problem.

She closed her fingers around Alexi's phone. Right now, she had plenty of her own problems to solve, and now was as good of a time as any to get started.

"Give me a minute?" she asked Alexi, waving the phone as the other woman nodded, apparently happy to settle onto a boardwalk bench to wait.

Lauren wheeled away, walking fast. Angling herself toward the center of town and the lone cell tower, she looked in either direction, though what she expected to see she didn't know. No one knew she was here. No one could reasonably guess that she was here.

She hoped that that would stay the case, despite the calls she was making now.

She dialed the number and turned back to face the ocean. Her heart was in her throat as it rang—and rang.

No one picked up. Lauren closed her eyes, knowing she shouldn't be so grateful. Her sister Maddie could have missed the phone call entirely, or been at one of her interminable practices. The only way to know that she was actually following Lauren's instructions was to finish out the protocol. She swiped the text icon for the same number, keyed in the three letters. Her phone jumped in her hand less than a minute later.

"Lauren! Where are you? Mom and Dad are so pissed!"

Lauren closed her eyes against the sudden rush of affection. Maddie hadn't been a planned child, to hear her mother speak. Her father, however, had doted on her from the beginning, in a way he'd never quite seen his way clear to doing for her. Lauren didn't mind, because Maddie was so much younger than she was—eight years. A lifetime, it seemed, sometimes. Maddie had been a true gift to their family—she was sweet, special. And Lauren would make sure she would always be protected.

"Hey, sweetheart," she said now, past the lump in her throat. "I'm fine, but I'm going to be out of touch for a few days, okay? I didn't want you to worry."

"Where are you? Are you in *hiding*? Mom said you totally ran away from a party." The excitement in her sister's voice made her heart ache. "You're a renegade. This is so cool."

"Yeah, it's real cool," laughed Lauren. "But keep my secret, okay?"

"Are you kidding? Of course. You better bring me back some awesome stories, though."

Lauren sighed, looking out over the sparkling Aegean. "I'm working on it."

They clicked off, and Lauren stared down at her phone, but only gave herself one long breath before she started dialing again.

When they'd talked a few hours earlier, Nicki had been absolutely insistent that Emmaline had to talk with Lauren personally whenever she was not around Dimitri—and she wouldn't breathe a word of the reason why. That kind of restraint was definitely not like Nicki.

She pushed the call through and heard the connection click, then smiled wide as Emmaline picked up. "Lauren?" her friend asked, a little breathlessly.

"Em!" Lauren stepped beneath the cool shade of a brace of trees, instantly feeling better. Em just had that effect on people. "What's up? Nicki was acting like you needed to share a state secret with me."

"I...oh," Emmaline said, and even with an ocean between them, Lauren could feel her friend's tension ratchet up. "Crap, I didn't think about that. Do you think this line is safe?"

Safe for what? Lauren glanced at the phone. "It's a burner that no one is tracking." She hoped. "I think we're fine."

"Okay, well—I mean, I have to tell you this, Lauren. You need to know. You're on that island with Dimitri, and—I mean, you need to know." Emmaline was talking at a speed of an auctioneer, and Lauren had handled enough delicate conversations in her life to know when to just be quiet and let the other person speak. Even as her eyes widened at Emmaline's next words.

"Oûros isn't the country we thought it was," she blurted. "I mean, it is, but it's so much more than just a cute little kingdom on the sunny side of Greece. It was founded by one of the descendants of Hercules and eventually became border control for the gods, keeping them corralled in Olympus and barely ever letting them pass through to earth."

Lauren blinked. "Border control."

As if she thought Lauren might tell her to stop, Emmaline rushed on. "There's a gate, okay? And the royal family—Kristos's family—are the gatekeepers, and they've been keeping the gods on their side of the wall for something like twelve hundred years and it's a seriously big secret. Seriously, no one knows. But they told me, because..."

As she faltered, Lauren supplied the obvious reason. "Because you're getting married, and that was something you should know up front." Her words sounded normal, even sane. Even if there was nothing sane about what Emmaline was saying.

Even as she thought that, though, Lauren found herself turning this new information over in her mind. She knew the fabled history of Oûros, of course. She'd learned the basics of the country when she'd learned the language—the founding by a member of the Heracleidae, the literal hundreds of temples and statues still very much intact. But an actual connection with the real gods of Olympus? Wherein the intrepid royal family was set up as gatekeeper to Earth? Was that possible?

I mean...maybe? It certainly would explain the country's strength over the centuries—its wealth and safety, and its undeniable beauty. The Oûrois people were some of the healthiest in all of Europe, and the country had never suffered plague, nor war, nor blight...

But Emmaline was talking again, and Lauren refocused sharply when she heard Dimitri's name. "Wait, say that again?" she demanded.

Emmaline exhaled a shaky breath. "I said, that's why they were so freaked out about Henry Smithson going after you so aggressively. They think he may, you know, have a connection with the god Typhon. Not the actual god, I don't think, but one of his minions. They don't like him."

"Yeah," Lauren managed. She immediately recalled her conversation with Stefan in the limo, how she'd outlined Henry's use of the name Typhon on his boat. When he'd said that the royal family wasn't a fan of the god, she'd thought he was making a joke to put her at ease. But now...

She cleared her throat. "Are you okay?" she asked Emmaline, because in the end, that was all that mattered.

"Me? You know, I am. It's not even a question of me believing them—I do. I totally do. And I told them I'd be telling you guys and Kristos didn't officially forbid me, so...here I am. I knew I had to tell you as soon as possible. Like, right now. Especially now."

"Okay, but why?" Lauren asked, genuinely confused. "Because of Henry? They really think he's, ah...joined some sort of Typhon cult?" Once again, it sounded preposterous, but with as skeevy as Henry was, she somehow could see him falling in with the god of monsters. And if the gatekeepers of the gods thought that Typhon was amassing supporters or something, she could see how that would be a problem. But Dimitri was handling that problem, right? That's why she was here. Alone with him. On a gorgeous island in the middle of the Aegean.

She grinned. If this was what she had to do to keep the world safe from the gods, she supposed she could handle it.

Emmaline sighed on the other end of their cell connection, still sounding unreasonably upset. "I mean, yes, but, um Lauren —there's more."

Lauren's brows climbed. "More."

"Yes. It's... well, it's about Dimitri."

Eighteen

Day had begun to edge toward evening, and Alexi had dutifully checked in three times over the past few hours. That did little to assuage Dimitri's concern about Lauren's safety, but it was important that she not feel trapped here. It was important that she trusted him enough to allow him to keep her on the island for her own safety. The last thing he needed was a headstrong socialite calling in favors from the Greek embassy and causing an international incident that would look like, to anyone on the outside peering in, a lover's quarrel.

He shifted in the deck chair, his eyes fixing on deceptively calm sea that gleamed beneath the swiftly setting sun. He knew the issue between Lauren and Smithson was a hell of a lot more than that, of course, but this wasn't a conversation anyone in the Oûros royal family wanted to have with outsiders. Least of all the king and queen. No. He needed to keep things as quiet and close as possible. Which meant he needed to keep Lauren as quiet and close as possible.

Dimitri's phone buzzed, and he plucked it out of his pocket, recognizing the number immediately. Cyril's voice was cool, crisp. And the man was clearly on speaker phone. "Report."

"She's safe," he said gruffly. "Meeting a town's worth of witnesses. Shopping. Eating. Everything in the open, exactly as if she's a tourist on holiday. No sign of Smithson or anyone unusual on the island." He paused. "I can get her to mainland Greece tonight if you'd like. It will take some doing to keep it quiet, but it could be arranged."

"No." This was from Stefan, who paused, clearly waiting for the go-ahead to continue. Then he spoke again. "Our intel on Henry Smithson is proving increasingly problematic. It appears Ms. Grant's suspicions about his business practices are well-founded. There is reason to believe that he has begun financing insurgency forces in Turkey and Armenia, with outliers who might be rallied to his cause with sufficient motivation. That he hasn't acted yet to find Ms. Grant is simply a matter of him not knowing where to look, we expect. Any attempt to move her to another country could potentially prove dangerous to her, requiring official action, which we don't want to initiate if we can avoid it."

Dimitri nodded, though they couldn't see him. "Any information on your end from her call to Nicki?"

"Ms. Clark offered assurances and confirmed that nothing new has been received in the palace." He paused. "She knows something more, but we can't interrogate her without causing suspicions to rise. And I'm not convinced her information would be worthwhile."

Dimitri stifled a snort. Stefan wasn't convinced that anything Nicki Clark had to offer was worthwhile. Her brash behavior might be blinding him, but in this case, he was probably right. Nicki knew only what Lauren had told her about Smithson, both today and throughout their relationship. Based on what he'd learned about Lauren, so far, he suspected she hadn't shared much.

"What has Smithson done to Lauren?" he asked instead.

"Beyond these stupid gifts he's sent her. There's something more."

"That intelligence is being accumulated now," Stefan said. "But his affection for Ms. Grant is, at a minimum, suspect. By her own admission, the attention began when she was a child and increased every year, becoming romantic in nature only when she turned eighteen. Within the letter of any law in any territory." Stefan's words seemed to disgust him, but he was right. Smithson had not assaulted Lauren by any account, neither before nor after she'd turned eighteen, and he'd acted at all times within the boundaries permitted by her parents, as evidenced by the fact that they maintained ties to him. There was something distinctly wrong about his attention, but it wasn't criminal. And, perhaps most damning, Lauren herself had not brought charges against him. Even if her reasons were sound in her own mind, there was little she could do without having stated her case to the authorities.

"Smithson's relationship with her father showed signs of strain at approximately the same time, but the two clearly reached an amicable resolution, and now they remain tightly connected," Stefan continued. "We will continue to compile data and cross-reference to all his other known relationships and romantic partnerships."

He hesitated. "There's...something else, too. Something I don't think we can ignore."

Dimitri's nerves prickled. "What is it?"

"The link to Typhon. You mentioned the unsavory gifts that Smithson has given her. She told me about them too. How did she describe them to you?"

"Dead things. Bugs, spiders, beetles. Like that."

"She didn't mention the snake pin?"

Dimitri sat up. "What? No. What snake pin? Did she describe it?"

"Other than say it was a pin with a snake decoration, no. It was apparently the first gift he ever presented to her, and she accepted it politely. She said he hasn't given her anything like it again—no other snakes. But with everything else we're discovering..."

"Echinda," Dimitri blurted. "Son of a bitch."

Before Stefan could prompt him, he rushed on. "Smithson called Lauren by that name during the party—I'm almost sure. His voice was muffled, but I thought he said something familiar, and that tracks."

"He called her that?" Stefan asked, sounding aghast. "That's not good."

"No shit." Dimitri blew out a breath, his gaze returning to the empty sea, half-expecting to see the monstrous god himself surging out of the water. "He's gone off the deep end, if he thinks he's summoned Typhon's beloved into being. And who would be that stupid? Gods aren't generally interested in sharing. If he thought he could summon Typhon's lover into human form and take her for himself, somehow...no. That's insane."

"Well, Smithson is clearly acting irrationally," Stefan countered. "From what you've experienced with Ms. Grant, could she make a man defy a god?"

"I—" Dimitri cut his initial answer short, then laughed a little grimly. "Honestly, when you put it that way, I don't know."

"Well, I'd suggest you find out. Understanding Smithson's motivations are going to be key, if we expect to extricate ourselves cleanly from this situation. In the meantime, keep Ms. Grant secured."

Dimitri grimaced, weighing the words, trying not to let his mind stray to the way Lauren had reacted to him physically since they'd first set foot on the boat to Miranos. Maybe she'd warm up to him enough to confide in him, maybe not. But he would keep her safe. That was nonnegotiable. "Of course," he said smoothly. "How long?"

"Twenty-four—forty-eight hours. Miranos is close, your childhood home. You had a hysterical woman on your hands, the guest of the royal family. You needed to make a quick decision, one that kept her out of harm's way. You have done all these things. Further, you are an esteemed military captain, with lengthy service and proven integrity. It's a reasonable story, as long as Ms. Grant is returned to her family safe and whole within the next forty-eight hours. That's your number one assignment."

"Forty-eight hours?"

"No more. We'll leak awareness of a false location to the parents within the next twelve hours, along with our potential concern that Ms. Grant may be afraid of Smithson."

"I wouldn't do that—"

"It's necessary to maintain the illusion, and to determine the full scope of the danger to Ms. Grant. We cannot know what sort of threat the woman's parents pose otherwise. The information will be reversed within an hour of its release, and Smithson carefully watched. If he makes any move toward the false target, it changes the game. At that point, your plan to head for Greece might make more sense."

"Right." Dimitri nodded. "Forty-eight hours, then."

Cyril took the line again. "What phone activity has she had? Other than the call to Ms. Clark. We tracked an incoming call to Emmaline from Miranos, and we have to assume it's from her."

Dimitri sat up a little straighter. "That's possible, but easily tracked. She's been with my sister all day, and she has no money or devices on her. If she's placed a call, Alexi will know. We're rendezvousing shortly." Dimitri's gaze flicked toward the horizon as he heard the familiar sound of a beach rover. "Now, actually. I'll check in tomorrow. Let me know if there are any developments."

"Well... there's something you should know before you speak with her again. She may know of your, ah, status, with the royal family."

Dimitri's gut tightened. "My status."

"If she spoke to Emmaline, she knows." Once again, Stefan's voice rang through his earpiece, the demigod's voice flat with disgust. "Apparently, Kristos and Queen Catherine saw fit to tell Emmaline about the true nature of Oûros and the royal family as gatekeepers of the gods. Emmaline somehow convinced them to allow her to tell her friends."

Dimitri came to his feet. "She *what?* Nicki confirmed this?"

"No." Stefan said. "Nicki didn't know when we spoke last night—there's no way she's a good enough actress to keep a lid on her reactions to information like that. But we have to assume they all know today. And if Emmaline arranged for Lauren to call you...I just wanted you to be prepared."

"Right." Dimitri groaned, rubbing a hand over his face as he tracked the nearing beach rover. He signed off from

They signed off, and he stowed the phone, but remained on the porch. Alexi waved as Lauren exited the vehicle, and the two of them shouted back and forth before Lauren turned toward the house. As Alexi roared off again, Dimitri noted Lauren's handbag, a new purchase, and her long, loose trousers and top, also new. She carried another shopping bag with her, and from what he could see, she now had enough clothing for a week. At least her clothes looked easy to move in, quick to dry, unrestrictive. Exactly the ensemble you'd need for an island getaway...if you were actually trying to get away from someone.

Right now, he narrowed his gaze on to her purse. He'd need to see what she'd bought, what Alexi had given her. If his guess was on point, he'd bet Alexi had given Lauren a phone. Who else had Lauren called, besides Emmaline? Her accountant? Her lover?

Did she have a lover, given her worry over Smithson? He supposed he should care more about that possibility, but whether she had a man back in the States or not, that man wasn't here. And Lauren was capable of making any decisions she wanted regarding her own pleasure.

His lips twitched as she trotted up the steps, and he wasn't able to wipe his expression fully clean before she saw him. "You're looking satisfied," she said. Her manner was easy, light. While Stefan didn't think much of Nicki's ability to hide her reactions to the truth about Oûros—and about its people— Dimitri wasn't at all sure he could say the same about Lauren.

Still, he could play along for a little while, and see what could be seen. He leaned forward with his elbows on the railing and gestured to the sun. "It's almost sunset. There is much to be satisfied about."

"Hmm." She swiveled to take in the sun as well, her face half-hidden by giant sunglasses. "You do this every day? Just, you know, stand here and watch the sun go down?"

"No. We only do it on the days when we wish to be good to ourselves. The rest of the time, we make do with a lesser life." He held out his hands. "Let me take your things and put them inside. I will get us both a beer so we can celebrate the sunset appropriately."

She willingly handed him her shopping bag, then hesitated with her purse, keeping it close to her body. "I'm good with this. But thank you." He had no choice but to take her bag and retreat. Dropping it inside the door, he fetched the beers quickly enough as his mind clicked through the possibilities. He needed to see her phone before they met up with the others. And that would be right after sunset, so he didn't have a lot of time.

How could he get Lauren worked up enough that she

demanded a shower before she saw anyone else? Especially if she potentially thought he was a demigod?

Dimitri grinned. The solution was, of course, obvious. He'd always been known for his excellent ideas in the field. It was good to know that his instincts didn't fail him while he was on leave.

He pulled the tops off the beers and headed back outside.

Lauren was sitting on one of the sling chairs, angled toward the sun. A thin crawl of clouds had surfaced on the horizon, running purple against the water. It looked more beautiful than any photograph he'd ever seen, and he'd watched tourists try to capture its magnificence a thousand times over. Some things you had to experience in person.

He handed her a beer. "Good, yes?"

"It's pretty, I guess." Her smile softened her sarcastic words, and when he held his beer out to her, she clinked hers against it. "What are we toasting to?"

"To the sunset. It's enough." Instead of taking a seat beside her in the matching swing chair, though, Dimitri folded his body to the porch, his head level with Lauren's knees as he lounged back on one elbow. He was close enough to her body to feel her heat, sense her sudden tension. But it wasn't the tension of a frightened woman, he thought. Simply one who was uniquely, subtly aware of him...and who maybe, just maybe, thought he was the descendent of a Greek god.

He took a long pull on his beer. He could work with that.

Nineteen

Lauren held her beer in a death grip. What was Dimitri doing? Or, more to the point, was he actually doing what she *thought* he was doing, so obviously showing his interest in her? If so, how did she feel about that?

More to the point, how did she feel about that, *given that he was a freaking demigod?*

There was no doubt that Emmaline believed he was. And just as Lauren's conversation with Stefan now made more sense in light of the royal family's entanglement with the Greek gods, the portrait she'd seen in the Andris family gallery now took on greater meaning as well. Dimitri—or someone who looked exactly like him—had been standing next to an entirely different king and queen...a king and queen from decades ago, if their clothing was any indication. It was him. She knew it was him. And if so, how old was this guy?

And did he really want to hook up with her, like he was so seriously acting like he wanted to do?

She was no stranger to the act of sex. While any sort of real relationship might have been off the table due to Henry's particularly vicious brand of jealousy, she had needs and ran in the kind of crowd that appreciated discretion more than most. Everyone had something to lose, and anyone with half a brain in his head understood that sex was one thing, romance was another. But was that what Dimitri wanted? And was that what she wanted him to want?

Especially if he was a freaking *demigod*? What exactly did that *mean*, anyway?

Dimitri lounged at her side, his powerful, suntanned legs stretched out beneath his soft gray sweat shorts. He'd been exercising while she was gone, she thought, or at least walking the beach. Sand and salt crisscrossed his shins and thighs, the muscles beneath the suntanned skin now relaxed, pliant.

Lauren kept her chin up as her gaze raked his body, but there was no way the sunset could compare to the magnificent male specimen beside her. He'd topped the shorts with a loose navy-blue tank top that bore no logo or insignia, and he wore no jewelry other than a thick watch that she suspected could shoot lasers to the moon and back. His ocean wave tattoo gleamed in the dying sunlight, its detailed ink threatening to pull her under. She was more than half willing to let it.

Dimitri was earthy, vital, real...and *safe*, she realized.

He was safe.

And he was a demigod.

Better still, Henry Smithson would never know the truth about this gruff, taciturn supposed captain of the ONSF, other than he'd had his hands full with a runaway American for two days or however long she was on this rock. He'd never have any reason to suspect that Dimitri had done anything with her, or to her, or...

"What are you thinking about?"

"Nothing," she snapped, not liking the sound of her own voice. It was too breathless, too sharp. She took a drink of beer, needing the cool wash of liquid as a distraction from her own thoughts. Beside her, Dimitri lolled in the sunshine, his eyes nearly shut as he gazed out at the water. If he hadn't spoken, she might well have believed he'd fallen asleep. But he wouldn't have fallen asleep, right? He was as aware of her as she was of him, certainly. Men generally were, right?

Did demigods sleep? I mean, surely—

"For nothing, it seems to be making you very upset." Dimitri reached over, touching her calf with the back of his hand, the hand that was holding the beer. She had on long pants, so it wasn't like he was touching her skin, but the simple contact sent all the blood shooting from her brain to pool in her belly, her mouth dropping open involuntarily before she could shut it. Of course, he couldn't see her face, her reaction. Thank God.

Pull it together, she implored herself. But she couldn't pull it together, it seemed. She couldn't think of anything except having Dimitri's arms around her, holding her close. She wanted the feel of his body against hers, the touch of his lips brushing close, the sound of his gruff, throaty words whispered in her ear.

She wanted *him*. Whether he was a demigod or a simple captain or just the man sitting next to her on this porch, sharing an impossibly beautiful sunset, she wanted him, and she didn't know how to turn that desire off. Her control was deserting her exactly when she needed it most, and—

"You want to talk about it?" he asked, his words a low rumble, officious enough to make her think he was interrogating her. Yes. Interrogating her was exactly what he was doing. All he was doing. *Focus.*

"Princess?"

"I—what?" Lauren blinked as Dimitri moved with sudden, almost feline grace. One moment he was lounging carelessly by her chair, loose and easy, the next he was kneeling between her legs, his hands on either side of her chair. His dark gaze held her eyes as she gaped at him, unresisting, as he reached out and pulled her sunglasses from her face.

"What is it, Lauren?" he asked, his words barely a murmur, while behind him the ocean seemed to glow a richer, almost electric blue. He looked impossibly gorgeous, staring at her. Hot and vital and real. Not someone who was weak, not someone she needed to protect. Someone who would laugh at the very idea of needing her protection, no matter how much money she had, how much power. Perhaps he simply did want her, the way she now wanted him, the way she burned for him, if she was honest with herself. "If something is on your mind, you need to share it with me. I can't help you otherwise."

Confusion, need, and want all clanged together in Lauren's brain. What was he saying? How was she supposed to reply? Did he think—

His next words hung it. "What are you afraid of?"

"This," she snapped, and leaned forward too quickly for him to back off. With her free hand, she reached for the back of his head and pulled him toward her, so they could kiss, a real kiss, not the half-pitying smooch she'd experienced with him the night before. Once again, Dimitri let her pull him to her, giving as good as he got but nothing more—nothing.

The earth didn't move, the sea didn't rise up and attack them. The sun didn't shower confetti rays on them. What the hell had she been thinking would happen? How could she seriously have believed—

She broke away from Dimitri in embarrassment and more than a little disgust—at him, at herself, at this entire stupid situation. "That."

His eyes lit up with amusement, and his mouth quirked up. "You were afraid of kissing me?"

Pull it together, she implored herself again. She seemed to be begging herself that a lot these days. Dimitri wasn't a demigod—or, even if he was, demigods probably meant some-thing very, very different in Oûros. That had to be it. Connec-tion to the ancient gods merited a fun dotted line on the Ancestry.com family tree, nothing more. She needed to deal with the man as a *man*...and that was more than enough.

"You kiss me like it's your job, and it's *not* your job, Dimitri," she said, waving her beer at him. "I don't need your pity, and I don't need your duty, though kudos to the Oûros National Secu-rity Force if it trains you to keep lonely women entertained. I thought—I mean, I thought—" She was having a hard time focusing with Dimitri so close.

"Perhaps you think too much, princess," Dimitri murmured, and this time, the ocean did seem to murmur with him, the sound of the shooshing tide carrying along the sand. But surely she was making that up.

He leaned forward as she shifted back into her chair, pursuing her until his lips brushed hers once again. Teasing, tasting. He drew his tongue along her lips and she shivered at the almost electric taste of him. Now this is what she'd expected.

Her mouth opened on a sigh, and Dimitri pressed into her intimately, angling his head as he deepened the kiss. He tasted of salt and beer and lime, and Lauren's mind completely blanked for a moment as he pulled her beer bottle from her unresisting fingers and set it away from them. Her hands seemed to naturally find their way under the loose fall of his tank top, and she shuddered as her fingers connected with the rock-hard planes of his abs. Demigod or not, Dimitri wasn't a lean man, whipped to precision. He was thick and hard, almost bulky, his muscles bulging beneath her fingers as he moved his mouth away from hers to trace a line along her chin, up to the delicate skin by her ear.

"I assure you, kissing you is no duty," he said, the soft tickle of his words sending whorls of intense desire down her neck. She slid her hands to either side of his torso, anchoring him to her, wanting nothing more than for this to continue. He did her one better, reaching out and pulling her closer to him until his groin pressed into the vee of her legs. The evidence of his arousal was as hard and fierce as the rest of him, and Lauren arched her body further, practically whimpering as his hand snaked around her waist to press her more tightly as her head fell back.

Dimitri used the angle to explore her neck, his rough, unshaven skin pressing against the hollow of her neck and shoulder while his lips ranged over her collarbone. His tongue replaced his lips and then his teeth, grazing over the delicate skin as if she were a meal to be consumed bit by careful bit. Explosions of desire had pretty much detonated everything south of her belly button, and she tilted her hips up more, wantonly, mindlessly, needing him closer, needing him inside her. Needing him to fill her with all his raw vitality until she was in his arms, wrapped by his body, nothing and nowhere and no one but his.

Somehow, one of his hands had slid up between their bodies, and it captured her left breast through the thin fabric of her clothing, touching, exploring. She shuddered as his fingers found her nipple, brushing across it as it peaked eagerly beneath his touch, the slow tease so brutal, her eyes practically watered with need. She was almost through a half sigh when he palmed the full weight of her breast, squeezing it hard as she gasped. His head lifted quickly, and he stared at her, his eyes mutinously hot. Had she ever seen eyes glow so fiercely, swirls of melted gold and bronze that trapped her as surely as his body did? Would she ever have the strength to look away?

"I didn't hurt you?" he asked. His hand softened its hold, rolling the round swell in his palm. But he didn't return his fingers to where she needed him most, wanted him, that tight pleasure-pain of her peaked nipples that made her want his hand beneath her shirt and thin bra, not on top of them, touching her skin to skin, heat to heat, need to need.

"No," she managed when she realized he was still staring at her, waiting for an answer. "No." Breathing had become something of a challenge, but she had to make him continue, had to make him understand. "Please, don't stop."

"I have hurt you," Dimitri said, impossibly soft, his words making no sense to her, her body tense and quivering underneath him. He moved his hand away from her, and she almost cried out, until she felt the rough touch of his fingers on her belly, under the hem of her shirt, sliding up toward her breast once more and bunching up the material as he went. "Let me kiss it and make it better."

Twenty

Dimitri took Lauren's groan as all the encouragement he needed. He bent toward her body, reluctantly breaking contact with her so that he could take her breast in his mouth, sucking hard as Lauren gasped and entwined her fingers in his hair. Her body was on fire, and he had done that to her, he had made her forget, made her think of nothing but him. Him and the sunset and beach and his body and hers, wrapped together on this porch, which was now his favorite porch in any country, anywhere.

He didn't need confirmation from her phone that she knew the truth about him, but he was fairly sure she still didn't quite believe what she'd been told. She probably didn't even know what being a demigod meant.

Good thing, he was just the guy to explain it to her.

Not quite yet, though.

"Dimitri," Lauren said brokenly, and he adjusted his hold on her again, pulling her out of the chair in one fluid motion until she sprawled on him as he lay back on the porch. Her hair had fallen loose from her bun and was drifting around her shoulders, her lips full from his kisses, her eyes glazed as she settled against him. She was too far away now, however, and he reached up to her, freezing as she laid a hand on his chest. She couldn't seriously want to stop now. Not now, when he was about to explode from looking at her, when all he wanted was to roll her beneath him and bury himself in the wonder of her body.

Instead, she gazed down at him and smiled, her gaze raking his face, his body. "You're so beautiful," she murmured, drifting a soft hand against his cheek. He stared back at her, willing his body to behave, to do this her way, whatever fucking way she wanted if it kept her touching him, rocking against him, her long legs straddling him and pressing up against his cock with a rhythmic pressure that made his head swim.

"Please tell me you're not simply teasing me," she continued as her gaze fell away. Her hand dropped to his shirt, where her fingers knotted up the material.

He huffed out a short breath, moving his hands to her hips to seat her more firmly over him, knowing his erection was unmistakable through his gym shorts. "Trust me, I'm not teasing here. You—" He broke off as she reached for her own clothes, pulling her top up and over her head, bringing the bra with it. Her body gloriously bared in the setting sunlight was quite possibly the most beautiful thing he'd ever seen, and his control slipped that much more as she lifted her hands to palm her own breasts, her gaze fixed on his face as his mouth went dry. She swayed toward him and he reached for her, his hands sliding up her back to press her close as he kissed her breasts, her collarbone, her neck, and back down to her glorious breasts, full and heavy and *his*.

Lauren shuddered in his grasp, and his need crested again, until before he knew it, he was sitting up, scrambling to his feet with her tight in his arms, swinging her into the house as she laughed and held on. But he wouldn't be fucking this woman on a porch. Not the first time. Maybe the sixth, but not the first.

The relative gloom of the villa's living room was a balm to his senses, helping him to catch his breath. The room upstairs was much too far away for him to consider. The couch was too. Instead, he sank down onto the thick woven rug that covered the tiled floor, laying Lauren down as if she would break. She looked at him, dazed. He could get used to that look.

But for now, he couldn't stand a minute more to be the only one wearing a shirt. He yanked off his tank top, and before Lauren could speak, he rolled back on top of her, stretching her hands high above her as he levered his body over hers. He reveled in the feel of her soft skin beneath him and tightened his abs in an attempt not to crush her.

"Hey—" She wriggled her wrists out of his grasp and brought her hands to his chest, her eyes wide as he braced himself above her. Releasing a purely feminine sigh, she trailed her fingers down his chest, feathering them along the line of hair that arrowed down between his pecs in a line that ended distinctly south of his navel. She followed that line like it was a map, not stopping until her fingers slid beneath the waistband of his shorts. She dragged the shorts low on his hips until the thick ridges of his hip bones were exposed, then slid her palms around his hips beneath his briefs, until her cool fingers cupped his bare ass. Pulling him into the vee of her thighs, she arched beneath him, giving him another heavy-lidded gaze. "I want you," she murmured. "Please tell me I can have you."

"You ask as if you don't already know the answer." He moved to the side and slid off her, his hands going immediately to her loose trousers. Unhooking the clasp, he peeled the soft linen back, marveling at the stretch of smooth skin bared beneath his hands. A thin line of silk lay against her skin, and he slid his fingers beneath it, not with the rough speed Lauren had used, but slowly, marking each sensation, each inch of skin that was revealed to his eyes, to his touch. As he pressed down, the material turned damp, and his own need ratcheted up in turn.

He shifted his gaze to meet Lauren's.

"I, um, hope the answer is yes," she said, and twin flags of color scored her cheeks, making her impossibly more beautiful.

"It's most definitely yes," he murmured, leaning close to brush her lips with his. He tasted the sweetness of her and was suddenly consumed with a need to taste all of her, completely. The incredible smoothness of her skin beneath his rough and calloused palm was at once exhilarating and terrifying. He could hurt her so easily, and yet she moved with a pliant grace that seemed to fit his hand perfectly, her body opening to him eagerly, almost needfully.

He sucked in a tight, controlling breath. Demigods could have sex like any ordinary mortal—and they were better at it, like they were better at most things than ordinary mortals. But unless he wanted to explain a hell of a lot more to Lauren right now than he had any patience for, he needed to go slower, easier. The sea behind him was already restless, eager to match his energy. He was in no mood for a swamping wave to come crashing up the sand.

Not yet, anyway.

He shifted his hand, expecting but not finding silken curls, then realized in a breath that the skin had been shaved smooth. His shaft seemed to swell to six times its normal size, and he schooled himself not to rip the material free right there. It did change his plans, though. It changed them significantly.

"Dimitri—oh," Lauren's word ended on a gasp as he drifted his fingers down the soft folds of her sex, pressing into her, his teeth gritting tight enough to break as he felt her wet heat against his fingers. She was ready for him, but as if there was any question, her hands were suddenly at her own waist, grabbing for her pants to shimmy them down further.

He batted them away easily. "No," he murmured. "Let me."

Twenty-One

Lauren watched almost spellbound as Dimitri wrapped his large hands into the waistband of her linen trousers and pulled them down over her hips. He seemed to wrestle with himself over the scrap of her panties, but in the end hooked them as well, his face rapt with attention as he bared her body to his gaze.

Her heart thumped heavily in her chest, her skin both hot and cold under Dimitri's stare. A curious mix of nerves and confidence surged through her—she knew she had a decent body, she knew she was attractive, she knew these things. And yet this man was different from anyone she'd ever been with before. This was no college guy still figuring out who he was or what he wanted. This was a man—or a demigod?—who looked like he would happily eat her alive.

Oh God, don't think about any part of that.

It was too late, however. As if spurred by her thoughts, Dimitri finished pulling her pants off completely, her panties with them, and tossed them aside in a heap. Then his hands were once more on her hips, and somehow he was kneeling between her legs now, his body bent down, his lips on the inside of her knee. He moved up the interior of her thigh as if he was exploring foreign territory, and she couldn't stop herself from trembling in his grasp as his mouth moved closer—closer—

He stopped, and she almost cried out, but he slid up her body, bracing his arms on the floor to stare at her. His heavy shaft pressed against her belly, and his eyes were dark, searching. "Are you cold? Is this still what you want?"

"You've got to be kidding me." She pushed her fingers beneath his soft shorts. She wrapped her fingers around him, squeezing as his face contorted in a mix of lust and pleasure, then outright need as she ran her fingers over the head of his shaft. "I want you inside me now." Without waiting for him to agree, she latched on to either side of his waistband and pushed down his shorts, over his heavy cock, and along his thighs.

Dimitri swiped with one hand and yanked them off the rest of the way, giving her a glimpse of his rugged body, ridged with muscle, sunbaked to a dark bronze, the narrow strip of hair in the center of his abs arrowing straight down.

"I want all of you," she practically moaned. "Every inch."

"Good," he growled, claiming her mouth with his own. He pulled his body away from her hands again and settled between her legs, the intense pressure of him so close, so nearly perfect that she almost cried out. Then he slid away, skimming her body, leaving her wanting as his mouth traced a fiery path along her neck and over her collarbone. He took one breast in his mouth, his left hand capturing the other, and suckled hard enough to make her arch off the floor. Then he moved away quickly, too quickly, licking a line down her stomach until he paused right over the center of her, his breath hot and moist, but not enough, not nearly enough.

She arched up toward him and he met her with his tongue, the shocking contact turning her inside out as she gasped his name. She twined her hands in his hair and held him there, though whether to brace him or herself she couldn't say. But he didn't seem to notice her. Instead, his attention was solely on exploring, tasting, pressing in, somehow knowing how to tease and excite every one of her nerve endings, kiss by lick by—

"Ohhhh." Lauren froze as a new pressure assaulted her, Dimitri never stopping his sensual exploration with his mouth, but now eased into her with a finger, testing her channel as she trembled beneath him, willing him to go farther and deeper. Pinwheels of light exploded through her brain, and she slipped her hands to his shoulders, her right hand pressing into muscles rippling under the ocean of ink.

"You're so good," he murmured, and the vibration of his words against her clit made her catch her breath. She gripped his shoulders then, her fingers digging in, need spiraling up within her as Dimitri continued the rhythmic thrust of his fingers in time with the teasing lave of his tongue—so right, so good, so exactly where she needed him to be. He pulled back for half a moment, his breath a cool balm against her overheated skin, but she nearly cried out anyway in frustration when he leaned down and flicked his tongue against her one last time.

She shattered against his mouth, panic and need filling her to bursting, then flowing over as she convulsed. He may have cursed, she certainly did, but he didn't leave her, didn't roll away and up, the box checked, the mission accomplished. If anything, he reveled in her climax, his mouth leaving her to kiss her thighs, her hipbone, the curve of her belly, then returning as she was settling to stoke her into a new wave of convulsions, until she didn't know which was ending and which was beginning, and her words had devolved into inarticulate moans.

She was quivering now, practically helpless, and he shifted again, heavily and with purpose, dragging himself up her body until he hovered above her face again. His eyes seemed almost wild, his expression brutally fierce, and his shaft throbbed against her belly, causing her legs to fall open in mute desire. His gaze raked her face, and though he didn't ask the question, she nodded, gripping his arms. "Now," she whispered, and she didn't recognize her own voice. "I want you now."

Dimitri growled and rolled to the side, up on his feet so quickly, she could only marvel at the tight urgency of his body. He strode out of the room and was back before she could reach for the throw blanket, and then he was over her again, warming her body instantly with his, surrounding her with his heat. He kissed her thoroughly, hungrily, and the cycle of desire ratcheted up once more inside her, full and hot, demanding to be sated. But when he would have moved off her again to sheathe himself with the condom he'd brought in from the other room, a new sort of urgency gripped her, impossible to ignore.

She followed him up when he moved to the side, pressing against him until he willingly relaxed and allowed her to push him over onto his back. There was no question that he had "allowed" this too. She wouldn't be able to move this man an inch without his permission, no matter how many cardio kick classes she'd taken or how much iron she'd pumped. But she moved up onto Dimitri's thick body with ease, straddling his hips. He stared at her with a curious mix of intensity and desperation, but he didn't stop her. It was almost as if he couldn't stop her, and the intensity of her power filled her as she took in his face, his eyes, his hands half raised from the floor, the foil packet clenched in one fist, the other clenched around nothing but air.

She slid up the length of his shaft and farther, until her knees were on either side of his torso and her hands were braced on his chest. Slowly, deliberately, she lifted her hands to skim her own belly, drawing them up her body to cup her breasts. She lifted the heavy tips toward him like an offering, then dropped one of her hands to her sex again, involuntarily shuddering as she pressed her fingers against her own swollen skin.

Dimitri looked stricken, and another surge of power curled within her, certain and true.

"You mind if I play for a while?"

Twenty-Two

Dimitri couldn't have spoken if he'd had a gun to his head. And he definitely didn't have a gun. Instead, he had an armful of Lauren Grant, her blue eyes flashing with desire, her golden hair now tumbled over her shoulders, her lithe body writhing on his abs as if she was some sort of goddess of Eros come to life. She swayed down toward him, dropping one hand from her breast and lifting the other from where she'd been teasing him with her slick little clit and braced both of her palms on his chest. She kissed him, hungrily, thoroughly, hard enough to bruise her mouth, and he kept completely still, not wanting to do anything to hurt her. Not wanting to do anything to stop her, either.

Beneath her ass, his cock throbbed, its prize so near that it had to know how close it was to ultimate salvation, but Lauren acted as if the evidence of his arousal wasn't so painfully obvious, that she had to somehow excite him more, tempt him further, drive him fully insane.

"You're so big," she murmured, and he didn't know what she was referencing—his chest, his cock, his head—he didn't care either, because she was shimmying around until she faced away

154

from him, her fantastic ass in front of his face as she bent her head and—

Dimitri's brain almost exploded as Lauren's mouth closed around his shaft. Her body was open, completely vulnerable to his gaze, but his eyes rolled back in his head as she moved her mouth down his length, taking all of him in her mouth before drawing back in one long slide, then plunging down again. His hands fell to either side of his body, limp and unresisting, as he gave himself over to the incredible pleasure of her mouth fully covering him.

She moved, and he could no more stop her than he could talk, but suddenly, the pressure of her body was off his chest and to the side, and he cracked his gaze open to take in her profile—the curve of her ass, the long, sweet line of her thighs, the dips and swells of her belly and breast. She circled his shaft with her fingers and dipped her head yet farther, drawing her tongue along his balls until they bunched up in tight expectation of imminent release. And then, as if knowing exactly how far she could push him, Lauren shifted again, positioning herself between his legs, one hand cupping his balls, the other tight on his shaft, as she watched him with heavy-lidded satisfaction, completely in control of his pleasure.

And damn him, he was happy to let that situation ride.

"You want only this?" she murmured, swaying forward to take the tip of his cock in her mouth, barely enough to give him a hint of the pleasure to come before rocking back again. "Or do you want to be inside me?"

Dimitri groaned. It was an impossible choice. But he'd sworn to himself that he would do whatever she wanted, do this completely her way, and so he forced himself not to grab her but instead stared back at her, trying to gauge her moods, her desire. She leaned over and plucked the condom from the rug and waved it at him. "Because I gotta tell you, I want you to fill me up."

Dimitri's sight went white again, and by the time he recovered, Lauren was ripping open the foil packet, positioning the condom over his shaft. "You've apparently done this before," he managed tightly as she expertly sheathed him in one long, smooth motion, the immediate constriction made infinitely more pleasurable by the fact that her hands were the ones smoothing the latex against him, her fingers were the ones that had slipped beneath once more to cup his balls with a cool, fluttering touch.

"Once or twice," she murmured. She shifted forward, and his mouth went dry as she draped her legs along his thighs, dragging herself up until her knees touched down on the outside of his hips.

"Are you sure this is the way you want to start?" Being on top would give her the most control, he knew, but it also provided him with the most amazing view. His hands finally recovered their ability to move, and he lifted them to skim along her thighs, trying not so much to anchor her to him as brace her.

"You think you'll be too much for me?" She slid her body along his sheathed cock until he was positioned at the vee of her legs, nudging into her as his shaft instinctively swelled to seat itself deep within her. "Because I think that's a risk I'm willing to take."

"Good," he gritted out, as Lauren pushed over him, enough that he fully appreciated how tight she was before she eased back, then moved forward again. The sinuous rocking motion of her body seemed as right and natural as the tides of the ocean, and when she finally allowed him to sink into her, he let out his breath in a long, ragged gasp. He'd not been aware he was holding it.

Lauren also released a soft moan. "My God, you're amazing."

"Mmm…" He sensed her gaze on him and flickered his eyes open, surprised by the raw curiosity in her expression. "Let me guess, I'm the first man who's ever satisfied you?"

She laughed, squeezing him so hard his mouth watered. "The first man from Oûros, anyway. You're a credit to your country."

"We aim to please."

"I'll make sure to put it in my TripAdvisor review."

She smiled with such carefree abandon that he was struck by how different it made her look. Now, focusing only on the pleasure of sensual give and take, with a man she felt safe with, a man who wasn't a threat to either her body or her schedule, she could fully relax and simply be. The pressure within him built as much for how beautiful she was as the sensations she was generating in his body, the fierce, primal desire to make her his rocketing through him. She couldn't be, *wouldn't* be his, not really. But he could bring her pleasure, here and now. That he could and would willingly do.

He slid his hands up her body until they reached the crease of her hips and, when she didn't reach out a hand to stop him, edged his fingers toward her sex. Her gaze challenged him. "I think you've already done your duty there, soldier."

"My work is never done in this regard." To punctuate his words, he brushed against the tight nub of nerves he'd found a few short minutes earlier, gratified when Lauren's amused glance turned into a startled reaction.

"You don't—"

"Let me," he urged, and once again felt a surge of triumph as she capitulated, her body going loose and lax as he massaged her clit, her eyes drifting shut even as she tightened her hold on his shaft and moved with greater urgency. He fell easily into step with her rhythm, his own need surging higher and higher until finally it was cresting too high to ignore.

At that moment, Lauren cried out, a soft gasp of surrender as her body convulsed against his, shattering anew as she gripped his shoulders and called out his name. The sound of his name wrenched from her lips gave him the strength to hold on for a few more precious seconds as he watched and reveled in her carefree abandon, her hair wild around her shoulders, her lips parted, her head thrown back—

Then he was lost as well, and a release as powerful as he'd felt in years surged through him, pounding in his muscles, his brain, his blood vessels as he growled out his own cry of surrender. The world around him exploded with light and sound—just for a second, the barest breath—before he reined his reaction in, mercilessly clamping it down, controlling it.

Lauren didn't seem to notice anything but her own reactions, thank the gods. She collapsed on top of him, totally boneless, and he hugged her to him fiercely, fighting against the possessive force coursing through him. They stayed that way for only a few moments, however, before Lauren shifted against him, sighing with feminine languor.

"Please tell me you have a working shower," she murmured. "We're supposed to be at your family's house thirty minutes from now."

"We do." Dimitri's military mind went instantly to the phone in Lauren's purse, though his body cried out in protest. He shifted away from her, dropping a light kiss on her forehead before he stood. "The shower is basic, but it works," he said, hoping his voice didn't sound too gruff. "Anything you need, though, let me know. I'll bring it to you."

Her laughter followed him into the next room. "I'll keep that in mind."

Twenty-Three

Lauren hugged her purse to her side, almost like a shield. She felt awkward, uneasy, and she never felt that. She and Dimitri had had sex—but that was all it was. People had sex all the time. That was what two consenting, uncommitted adults did when they were attracted to each other. They got naked, and they had sex.

And my God, getting naked with Dimitri had been so much more *everything* than she'd expected it would be. Even now, with him walking beside her so confidently, so casually, she was pretty sure he was drawing all the wrong conclusions about why she was reacting so lamely to his presence. He undoubtedly thought he'd blown her away sexually, and he wasn't completely wrong there. It had taken her a full twenty minutes in the shower before she'd stopped shaking, and his entire house had seemed lighter—brighter—the ocean practically chattering with excitement by the time they'd stepped back out onto the porch. Island sex was undoubtedly the best sex, but that wasn't all that was going on here.

Dimitri presented a danger to her that no guy had in far

longer than she cared to consider. He was strong, stubborn, competent, capable...

And maybe a demigod.

The earth hadn't moved when they'd climaxed, not exactly—no storms had broken loose, and the sea didn't rush up the sand. But it had been the very best sex of her life, bar none. And if that didn't make Dimitri a god, she didn't know what did.

She could almost see him holding his own against Henry. Almost. The possibility of that was heady stuff, filling her with ideas of a life of freedom, of normalcy. A life she knew she couldn't have. Not until she'd solved the Henry puzzle once and for all.

Until then, there would be nothing normal about her life.

But still...

"Lauren! You're here, finally. Dimitri, go help your sister. Lauren and I must *talk*."

Dimitri's grandmother Calista took her by the arm and hustled her around the villa to where a clearing opened out onto a bold promontory. The view was spectacular. Had it been daylight, she would have been able to see for miles out to sea. Now, with the sun fully set, a canopy of stars twinkled in the sky, an awesome counterpoint to the few winking lights of yachts far out in the water. It was breathtaking.

"He's treating you well? He's being good to you?"

"What?" Lauren looked down, surprised, at the old woman who was now poking her in the arm. What had Alexi said her name was? "Oh. Yes, yes, of course. Dimitri is very good to me."

She realized a second later what the woman truly meant and tempered her smile. Did she know about Dimitri? She had to know. But if she didn't, Lauren couldn't let on about Dimitri, right? That would be bad.

"We're not dating, by the way," she finally said, a little lamely. "You should know that."

"Oh, he says the same thing," Calista said. "You both are tiresome with your youth and your words." She waved her hands. "He's a good man, but he needs a strong woman. I get the feeling, that's what you are."

Lauren smiled too widely, not her typical practiced expression at all. She didn't care. *Man*, Calista had said. Not demigod, but *man*. "Well, thank you, but we've only recently met. I'm in Oûros on vacation."

"Then you must come back when you are ready to live here. You see this house? Dimitri built it. With his hands, and his father's hands, and his grandfather's hands. It's a good house, and it will be his one day. He needs something to remember us by when we all are...well." She huffed and flapped her hands at the building. "It's a good house."

The woman's affection for Dimitri was fierce, and Lauren was suddenly at a loss for words. She looked up to the sturdy whitewashed house, lit up with torches and laughter, and tried for a moment to picture herself there, instead of in her apartment in New York City or her flat in London, or her cute little pied-à-terre in Paris.

She couldn't.

Dimitri was a gorgeous hunk of man, but, demigod or not, he wasn't her "forever after." He wasn't even her "for very long." He was a distraction at a time when she needed it, nothing more.

Right?

"Ah, ah, ah! You are thinking about it. Thinking is good." The woman squeezed her arm and grinned at her. "But don't think too much, okay? Too much thinking is useless when action would do."

"Grandma, you're scaring her." Alexi appeared beside them with two familiar drinks in her hand. She gave one to the old woman, the other to Lauren. "I'll be right back," she winked, then steered her grandmother around. "Your friend Mina is here. Don't you want to say hello?"

Their laughter dwindled into the background as Lauren took a sip of her drink, allowing the *tsipouro* to burn down her throat. She glanced at the glass in surprise. She was now becoming somewhat of a connoisseur of the drink, but this seemed—stronger. Smoother too.

"You like it, I can tell. Which means mostly that you have good taste. But then, we already knew that."

Dimitri's rich voice rolled over her, triggering a response she could no more ignore than mask. Luckily, she didn't have to hide it—the deepening night around them did that for her.

"It's my family's recipe," he continued. They should bottle and sell it, but they don't have the time with the work they do fishing." He sighed ruefully. "And I have neither the time nor the head for business it requires."

She narrowed her eyes at him. "Uh-huh. Humility isn't your strong suit."

"It's not a question of humility." He shrugged. "It's more a strategic pursuit. If I know what I am good at, which is many things, I'm happier to let go what I'm *not* good at, so as to spend more time on the things that I enjoy. You see?"

She couldn't gainsay his logic, and instead turned to look at the ocean. The sounds of the party seemed too far away, with him this close. As if he could blot out the world with his presence, creating a tiny circle of calm in the middle of a brewing storm. She could get used to that illusion, she realized. So she went on the offensive again.

"That promontory, with the beacon." She pointed to the west with the hand that held the *tsipouro*. "Your sister was telling me about it today."

As she'd planned, Dimitri's manner immediately sobered. She couldn't help but feel sorry for that, but she barreled on anyway. "She said that wreckage washes up on shore there sometimes."

"My sister, she talks too much," Dimitri said. But he was looking out at the promontory now as well. "She told you, I'm sure, of the wreckage in particular I'm searching for?"

"From Ari's plane." She tried to pick out his expression in the darkness, couldn't. "Have you ever found anything?"

"Not enough to matter. The royal plane had many distinguishing characteristics and many identifying marks against such a tragedy. But when a plane crashes, it doesn't always fall into the ocean in one piece. An explosion could have disintegrated it. The engine could have kept working for a short while even if other systems failed, dropping in a different location from the rest of the plane. There are too many possibilities to fathom."

"Yet you keep looking."

He nodded. "I keep looking."

"What will you do if you find something, though—a scrap of metal that, what—tells you that Ari crashed near here and not near Thassos? How will that help you?"

Dimitri took another long pull of his drink. "It's a good question. Perhaps I'll convince myself that he has died, once and for all. Perhaps I'll have the closure that the few bits and scraps of metal that *have* turned up haven't given me. Perhaps I'll have someone—or something—to blame, finally. When you have no answers, you have too many possibilities. I'd prefer those possibilities to be fewer." He shrugged. "I suppose I won't know until I see it, yeah?"

"Could we go down there?" Sensing immediately that she'd asked the wrong thing, Lauren hastened on. "If we'll be here that long. We may not be, which is fine. Never mind. We don't have to go." *Shut up, shut up!* She blushed hard as she tried to quiet her unruly tongue. Beside her, Dimitri had fallen silent. Not the silence of someone who was angry, either.

The silence of someone who was curious.

A curious Dimitri was not a good thing.

He verified that with his next words. "Why do you want to see the cove? I intrigue you this much, princess?"

She gave him her haughtiest look, pretty sure the effect was lost in the gloom. "I'm stuck on this rock for, what, another day—day and a half? We have to do something."

He didn't hesitate. "It seems that we found a worthwhile distraction already."

"Well, we've done that already, so it's time for something new."

Laughter rumbled deep in his voice. "And you don't think you would be interested in a second opportunity?" he asked quietly. "I could change your mind."

Her scoffing reply sounded impressively derisive, at least. "Doubtful." She turned away from him so he couldn't read anything in her expression. "I'd be far more interested in learning more about this cove that has fascinated you so. You've certainly found a few things, yes? Do you keep them in your house?"

He shifted beside her. "The ones that seemed relevant, sure. The others I left along the shoreline or gave to the local bar owner down there. There's a secondary dock near the promontory, where the boats bring in their weekly hauls—more frequently if they are overloaded, but they are rarely overloaded early. It is not an easy life, fishing. But it's a good one."

"Well, it can't be all that great. You left it for the military."

He shrugged. "Again, I know what I excel at. Or maybe you've forgotten that already."

Twenty-Four

S top baiting the woman.

But Dimitri couldn't help himself. He leaned closer to Lauren as she gave another short laugh, reveling in the heat of her, exactly what he'd sworn he wouldn't do when they'd arrived here this evening. Tonight was supposed to be about rebuilding the emotional distance between them and giving her the illusion of freer rein. He had a completely unreasonable desire to build a cage around her, protect her, but she wasn't his property, she was his assignment.

And then there was the sex. Which had definitely not been a part of the assignment. But damn, it should have been. Nevertheless, he knew without being ordered that he had no right nor place to have any *real* interest in Lauren.

But he did. May the gods help his sorry ass, he did.

The idea of holding her in his arms once more, tasting her skin, reveling in the sheer glory of her body was enough to drive him mad. If he didn't maintain his distance, or at least keep his demigod nature in check, he was going to cripple the woman before he got her safely back to Oûros. And that would serve none of their purposes.

So they'd all be better off if he kept his focus on the mission. Fortunately, she'd made that easy enough.

He'd found her phone, of course—Alexi's phone, more accurately stated. And though his sister believed these phones were burners, they were all linked back to Dimitri. Once he'd had it in hand, he was able to cross-reference the right phone with the right account, and confirm that Lauren had reached out to Emmaline.

So she knew about him, almost certainly. Knew, but likely didn't believe.

He could accept that.

The phones had been Cyril's idea originally. Cyril, who also couldn't quite believe that Ari could die without a trace, that his plane could disappear, with only the barest amount of wreckage to tell the tale of his final hours. There'd been nothing to tie the prince to the debris—not his clothes, not his gear, not the black box. Nothing. It was as if Ari had sunk to the bottom of the ocean.

Cyril had commissioned the phones to encourage chatter about the search for the plane's wreckage, and chatter had definitely happened over the intervening months, but none of it worthwhile. The advisor had called off the distribution of phones months ago, but that hadn't stopped Dimitri. He'd handed them out like candy, asking for a call if anything had been found—a scrap of metal, a twisted bit of electronics, anything.

Now he weighed his options. He needed to deepen Lauren's trust in him. That was paramount if he wanted to ensure her safety. He couldn't ask her outright about the phone calls she'd made—there'd been two, and he hadn't had time to track the second one. He'd sent that information to Stefan to analyze, but he wouldn't get those results tonight.

He also couldn't take the device away from her. At least he

knew about this cell phone, could track it. If she got resourceful and stole someone else's phone he couldn't control, or gods forbid secured a sat phone that she could use anywhere on the island, keeping tabs on her conversations would be that much more difficult.

No, he had to keep Lauren close and engaged and at least reasonably trusting of him. Enough that she didn't decide to run off on her own. She wasn't his prisoner; she was his charge. He had to remember that.

So whatever she wanted to do, he'd do. His body twitched despite himself. *Anything.* "We can go to the promontory tomorrow," he said at length, watching her for her reaction. He had the advantage there. She'd shifted slightly ahead of him now, and was looking back, so he could see her full, lovely face in the lights from the party. "Though I haven't been back to Miranos for a while. There hasn't been much that's turned up. It's been a year, after all. But the boats come in tomorrow with the week's haul as well, and that generally yields something. Not always something useful, but it's a start."

"Enough to keep your hope alive?" Her question was asked without artifice, as if she truly wanted to know. She was as good at playing her role as he was, he realized. But was this a role for her now?

There was no way for him to know, so he contented himself with a shrug. "Hope is not something that dies easily in Oûros. We're a small nation, dwarfed by those around us. We do not have the billions in our coffers that others do to fund our military or our defenses. We are ruled by a royal family who are very much human, who may sicken, weaken, or die. We should have been overrun a dozen times through the centuries, and yet we were not. There is much to hope for."

"I guess. I'm not much good at hope."

His gaze shifted to her face again. This part, at least, was no act. She couldn't know he saw so much. She had to believe she was hidden in shadows. Her expression was starkly forlorn as she looked out over the ocean, and her anxiety arrowed through him, harsh and full.

He decided to press the small advantage.

"Tell me, why don't you report that ass to the authorities? Why don't your parents?"

If she was startled by his change of subject, she didn't betray it. Then again, he got the feeling that Henry Smithson was never far from Lauren's mind. "Henry and my father...you have to understand. Their relationship was almost magical. My father finally had someone he could share all of his time and business acumen with in a way he simply could never see doing with me. And Henry respected him, revered him, and perhaps most importantly, learned from him. By the time he turned his attention to me, he'd been at my father's side for years. I tried to tell my mother what was happening, but she knew how much it would crush my father, and I was a very dramatic child. It was easier to discount my concerns, especially when the very next gift would be something amazingly sweet. It was easy for me to forget too. At least at first."

She shook her head. "Then they had some sort of fight, and after that is when things got more intense."

Dimitri eyed her. Stefan had mentioned this, but didn't have any details, and Lauren's half nod betrayed that she didn't have much either. Her next words confirmed that suspicion. "I never knew what about. It sort of seemed that Dad was angry with Henry, distrustful almost. Which was a shock after so many years when Henry could do no wrong. I almost...I thought about telling him then, everything. The few things I'd told Mom, plus all the stuff I hadn't told anyone. It seemed maybe he would listen."

She trailed off, and Dimitri prompted her. "Why didn't you?"

"Well, I got to thinking that, since Dad was already mad, maybe it would all go away, that I didn't have to say anything." Her smile was rueful. "That somehow, Henry had done the hard work for me, all on his own."

She sighed. "But a few months later, he was suddenly back at dinners, at public events, at golf...it was as if their falling out had never happened. And then he presented me with a stunning set of diamond earrings in front of my father and Dad looked so happy and relieved and it started all over again. The rest is as I've told you. He's untouchable. Half of his business partners are afraid of him, and the other half should be. He has layers upon layers of legal protections, and that's not counting the illegal ones. If I raised my concerns, I would earn his undying enmity, perhaps. But I wouldn't stop him. Nothing will ever stop him, I'm convinced, except his own boredom." Her expression flickered with something close to humor. "I've tried to be as boring as possible up to now."

Dimitri lifted a brow. "I don't see how that would be possible."

Her smile showed that she accepted his compliment and disregarded it as quickly, the polite concession of a woman used to receiving empty admiration. "Unfortunately, I think this little stunt we've pulled may have piqued his interest too far. He's not used to people fighting back." She shook her head. "Maybe that's where I've erred all this time. Instead of evading him without seeming to do so, maybe I should have capitulated, fawned all over him. Maybe if I had, this would all be over already."

Or maybe you'd already be dead. He didn't need to say the words out loud. He could see their truth reflected in Lauren's eyes. Only, she didn't seem upset by the concept. A certain measure of relief clouded her face instead, as if her sacrifice might be worth the greater good in the end.

Rage knotted up inside him in twisted fury. Rage and a surge of protectiveness he had no desire to deny. No. Lauren wouldn't live her life in servitude to another man. She wouldn't live in fear and confusion, wondering if or when Smithson was going to strike. It didn't matter if he was a stooge of Typhon's or just a run-of-the-mill asshole. He wasn't going to be a problem of Lauren's for long.

"We'll go to the promontory," Dimitri said again, more firmly this time. "It's not a far journey—nothing is on this rock—but we'll leave early tomorrow, get there in time to cover every scrap of the place. By sunset, the men will be returning with their nets full of fishes, and we can help them unload." He glanced at her. "I can help them, anyway. There's no need for you to be up to your elbows in dead or dying fish."

She laughed. "And yet you make it sound so appealing."

"It's a gift." He turned her back to the noise of the party, and she seemed relieved to have the bright lights and distraction to create that much separation between them. Yet she didn't stray far from his side, despite the fact that his grandniece, his niece, and again his sister sought to spirit her off. After a few minutes, she always cycled back to him, which kept him from going after her to ensure her safety and protection.

Right. That was why he wanted her close.

Now he watched her across the open space. Her laughter so bright and full, so practiced-sounding to his ears, her face arrested in rapt attention to whatever the young woman was saying, whom Dimitri didn't know. A girlfriend of some cousin, he was sure.

"It is good to see you smile."

He looked down, startled to see his sister at his elbow, her fists on her hips as she peered up at him, but her eyes sharp with approval as her white hair stirred in the breeze.

"Grief makes a man old and bent, no matter how young they appear to the rest of the world. She's good for you."

She turned to gesture to Lauren, and Dimitri's mood soured.

"She's not my girlfriend, Calista. You know that. She can't be. We're here because she's in danger."

"You keep telling yourself that," his sister said, reaching forward to pat his arm. "But you're here because you're meant to be here—and because the gods want you here too. Sooner or later, you'll accept that." Then she poked him, hard. "Hopefully before I grow old and die."

Dimitri winced, closing his eyes. "Calista..."

"I'm just saying!" Her chortling laughter swirled around him and danced out to sea.

Twenty-Five

The exhaustion and adrenaline of the last few days had finally caught up with Lauren by the time she found Dimitri again at the party, and despite her best intentions, she closed her eyes almost before she'd buckled herself into the rover. She came to groggily when the noise shut off again and she realized they'd returned to Dimitri's villa. The night sky was an impossibly thick blanket of stars, and as Dimitri came around to her side, she struggled with the urge to pretend she was still asleep, if only to feel his arms around her once again.

She needn't have worried. "The footing is treacherous," he murmured as he unbuckled her. "Better for me to carry you."

"It's sand." However, she didn't protest as he scooped her into his arms , lifting her easily out of the beach rover and swinging her away.

"It's very deceptive sand. One wrong move and you could slip and fall into it, and that would be very dangerous for you."

"Oh?" She snaked her arms up around his head, turning him toward her. As he bent, she reached up and drifted her lips against his. "And how could all this soft sand be dangerous?"

He clearly didn't need more of an invitation. He pressed his lips against hers gently at first, then with greater urgency, as if the intervening hours since their sunset lovemaking had been more like days or weeks. He braced her without any apparent effort, absorbing all her weight.

Desire stirred in her veins, clearing away the confusion of the *tsipouro* she'd consumed at the party but leaving all its liquid courage behind. "I think if I had a blanket to break my fall, the sand wouldn't be so dangerous," she murmured against his lips.

Dimitri barely shifted, balancing her against his hip as he reached into the back of the rover. A moment later, the thick weight of a blanket bumped against her hip. "I think you're very wrong. But some lessons must be fully experienced to be learned." He sighed as if he was shouldering a great burden. "I will endeavor to go easy on you this one time. But you must be made to understand."

She laughed out loud at the ridiculous words, batting her hands against his body. "Let me go, you big ox."

"Your wish is my command, princess." And he did let her go, but their hands naturally found each other's anyway as she tugged him across the sand. The breeze off the water was deliciously cool as they made their way toward the mysterious Aegean. There were villas high in the cliffs down the beach, but along this idyll, it seemed like they were the only people alive. That it was truly an island paradise shared only by the two of them.

Lauren allowed herself to indulge in the fantasy of being someone—anyone else. Not a well-known face from a tabloid-friendly family, but a girl who found herself alone on the beach with a big, strapping hunk of a man who seemed to want nothing more than to be dragged along behind her to a strip of water that surely was as familiar to him as the back of his own hand. With the warmth of the tsipouro smoothing her edges, she didn't even worry about his is-he-or-isn't-he-a-demigod status. He was just a man...and that was more than enough.

She stopped as they reached the small ridge that marked the tide line, the break between the deep, thick white sand and the damper, hard-packed sand that ran down to the water's edge. "How cold is the water?"

"Too cold for swimming at night, I can tell you," Dimitri rumbled. He dropped the blanket on the sand and kicked off his sandals. "Not too cold for dipping your feet in to feel in touch with its energy."

She looked at him in surprise as she kicked off her own sandals. "That's pretty poetic for a captain of the ONSF."

"We are a surprising military in many ways." He reached for her hand again, and she slipped her fingers into his. She wasn't shy, she wasn't cautious. No one could see them here in this hidden spot. No one needed her —couldn't reach her if they wanted to. Her purse was all the way up in the rover, and she didn't feel strange not being connected to her phone...because it wasn't her phone. Her sister, Maddie, was the only one with access to it, and she also knew it wasn't Lauren's own phone. She wouldn't call it unless something truly important happened. For the first time in longer than Lauren could remember, she was completely cut off. Isolated. It felt deliciously wicked.

Then again, she was cut off, isolated, and unconnected...while walking along the beach with the hottest guy she'd ever seen naked in her entire life. So there was that.

"Do I want to know what you're thinking?" the hottest guy she'd ever seen naked asked beside her.

"You most definitely do not—oh...it's warm." They'd reached the water's edge, and Lauren sighed with rich appreciation as the lapping tide skimmed over her toes. Her sundress barely brushed her knees, so she waded out farther, pulling

Dimitri with her. He paused long enough to remove his pants, and she ogled him. He was wearing boxers, yes but...still.

He laughed at the expression on her face. "There's no one on the beach but us, Lauren. If you would care to walk around in your underwear as well, the fish and birds won't mind. And I definitely won't mind. The sea nymphs, well—they might have an issue. But maybe they won't notice."

"I'm good." Deliberately cataloguing his comment about sea nymphs to think about *later*, she admired his legs as he splashed into the water next to her. They were corded with muscle, yet he moved with the grace and assurance of someone who had been born to the sea. Once again, she thought about how different he was from anyone she'd ever met. Even the guys she knew who were total gym rats, whose musculature rivaled that of Dimitri's, were infinitely different—their bodies too tight and blocky. No way could they move with Dimitri's speed and agility, able to react and redirect at a second's notice.

"You like what you see?" Confidence dripped from Dimitri's words, but not in a self-mocking way. He knew she was staring, though she turned her gaze forward again quickly enough. Knew it and accepted it as his due. How many other women did he have pining after him, she wondered. His grandmother acted as if he was some kind of monk, but that was his grandmother. It wasn't as if Dimitri would share his exploits with an old woman.

She wanted to know those exploits, though. After all, none of this was real. She could discover whatever she wanted, and it wouldn't affect anything. "I suppose I should have asked this already, but do you have any sort of girlfriend or anything?" She tried to sound arch, but knew she came out sounding a little breathless instead. She didn't care. Once again, none of this mattered.

Dimitri's laugh soothed her nerves. "No, princess. No sort

of girlfriend or anything. I would be a pretty poor excuse for a man if I had a girlfriend and yet managed to make love with you on my living room floor this afternoon, and once again beneath the stars tonight."

"You seem very confident of how this evening is going to play out."

He squeezed her hand. "I am well known for my strategic predictive abilities. You watch and see if it happens, and let me know how I do."

"Well, your chivalry is noted. I can give you a list as long as my arm of guys I know who would have sex in a heartbeat—regardless of their relationship status—if they found themselves on a deserted island with someone who practically threw herself at them."

"Miranos is not so deserted as that," Dimitri said lightly. "But tell me about this throwing of yourself at me. It sounds like something I should be prepared for." He stopped their walk and drew her close to him. "Like now, for instance. Show me now."

Lauren couldn't help herself. She allowed a giggle to escape as she pushed Dimitri away. "Well, to throw myself at you, I'll need a running start. Don't you know how this works at all?"

"My training in this maneuver is sadly lacking."

She burst out with another laugh as she launched herself at him, splashing through the water and then jumping up, planning to push him over into the surf. Instead, he caught her easily, swinging her around in the water and locking her to his body, all heat and strength and laughter as he gathered her close. The water swirled and shimmied around them, the breeze kicking up the waves.

"I approve of this American practice of throwing," he said. "We shall have to adopt it here in Oûros."

"Well, you should be careful. You'll never know what Americans might come flying out of the water at you when you least expect it."

"I should enjoy that very much."

Lauren's breath caught as Dimitri leaned into her, nuzzling her mouth until she opened her lips to him. The warm breeze caressed her skin, the salt from the ocean water tasted uniquely perfect, and she sighed as he deepened the kiss, softening her hold on him until he cradled her in his arms.

Twenty-Six

Dimitri's heart thudded almost painfully, but not from the paltry effort it took to hold Lauren above the water. She wasn't a small woman, but perfectly proportioned to his body, as if she'd been carved from the very essence of the earth and sea for him personally. Her laughter thrilled through him, light and free, and it seemed more relaxed with each passing hour. It was as if the farther she strayed from the glittering precision of her life, the happier she was.

He knew why, of course. That it wasn't him, it was the *idea* of him, the idea of being safe, unfettered by consequences, but also unhindered by danger. That the very concept of relaxing in someone's arms without being watched or judged, without being photographed or recorded, was so unusual that she was building it up into some sort of fantasy vacation in her mind, some time out of time.

She shifted in his arms and breathed his name, and he revised his conclusion.

It was probably mostly about him.

He turned her toward the shore again, stepping easily through the water as Lauren leaned against his chest, her hand braced on his shirt, fingers warm against his skin where they slipped into the button-down front. She was lithe and vital and *his*, at least for now. And he'd been on this earth long enough, and seen enough injury and death, to understand the value of living in the moment.

He stopped briefly to swipe up his pants at the shoreline. Lauren giggled as he dipped her, making no move to stand on her own. For his part, he had no interest in letting her. They reached the blanket, and he set Lauren down on her feet, startled when she wobbled, then pitched to the side as if she was in the midst of a faint. He went down on a knee to steady her, and she laughed, pulling him farther down, until they both sprawled on the blanket.

"You're right, this sand is very dangerous," she said. "I don't know how I lost my footing."

"That's only the beginning of your troubles, I'm afraid." Dimitri stretched out alongside Lauren, reveling in the way she relaxed by his side, her face turned up to the stars, her smile easy, unforced. He smoothed out her hair by her face and turned his hand so his palm drifted along her cheek, as lightly as he could manage.

"You touch me sometimes like I'm going to break," she chided him, and he smiled.

"Never that. I touch you like you are made of gold."

She pouted. "That doesn't sound very attractive."

"On the contrary. Gold is hard—hard enough to smash something if you wield it, hard enough to stay pristine over the ages. But apply enough heat, and it melts in your hands, its brilliance undimmed though its form has completely changed. You're gold not because of whatever money you have stashed away somewhere. You're gold because you are strength and liquid fire. And I want to stir that fire in you now, to melt you down into nothing but sensation."

She stared at him. "They *seriously* teach you how to talk that way in the military?"

He smiled as he reached down to his pants, freeing the condom. He wouldn't need it, not at first. But, as he'd already learned from this woman, it paid to be ready whenever she was. "Our training is quite extensive," he said, returning his hand to her waist. "And we learn very quickly that when it's in our best interests to use strategic coercion, we must move ahead with full commitment."

"Mmm." Lauren lifted her hand to caress his cheek. In the starlight, she looked like something out of a painting, a mermaid cast ashore for a precious night, never to return. "And what is it you're trying to strategically coerce me into, Captain Korba? I think you'll find that I'm a soft touch."

"I doubt that quite sincerely." Dimitri lowered his head to brush Lauren's lips with his. He had his opening now, and he knew he should take it. Subtly, easily pump her for information about Henry Smithson, about the threat that he posed to the royal family, if any. About his connection to the god Typhon— real or delusional. About the threat that he posed to her.

And yet, Dimitri found he wanted to do nothing more than stare at this woman, wanted to learn nothing more than what made her happy. He could start there, certainly. No one could fault him for beginning his interrogation with caution.

"Where did you originally plan to go on this European tour you arranged for your friends?" he asked. "Surely you didn't plan to spend the whole of it in Oûros."

Her laugh was wry. "I've learned that your country is bigger than I would have given it credit for," she said with a smile. "And certainly more interesting. But no." Her gaze shifted upward, toward the stars. "We were only supposed to spend a few days here, then all of us would have done the full tour— Cannes for a day or so, then Tuscany, Paris, and London.

Maybe Amsterdam, if we had time. I didn't have it all planned out. Sometimes it's better not to do that. You can get better deals at the last minute—as long as you have enough money to get *something*, no matter what."

"You paid for all of it." It wasn't a question, and Lauren didn't take offense.

"Most of it," she said, her eyes on the night sky. "I wanted to take the vacation as well. I can't travel with a man, and I don't enjoy traveling alone."

Now, they were getting somewhere, but Dimitri resisted the urge to dig deeper. "Yet here you are, traveling with a man to an exotic island. It appears you have broken your own rules, princess."

She looked at him sternly. "It's true. Why couldn't the royal family have assigned a woman to guard me?"

"You're too tall," Dimitri dismissed the idea. "For you to be guarded effectively, it was important for you to be properly swept off your feet."

She lifted a haughty eyebrow. "And that's what you've done?"

He leaned closer to her, so close that when he spoke, his lips moved against hers. "I haven't yet begun that portion of my assignment, princess. Perhaps tomorrow."

"Tomorrow?" Her voice sounded fluttery to his ears. "What about tonight?"

"Tonight, it seems that you are already on your back. So I must make do with what circumstances have brought me." He bent down and pressed his lips to hers, and just that quickly, the desire for her body beneath his surged forth. The waves crashed and thundered, far out to sea, and the breeze stilled around them, holding its breath. Zephyrus always was a romantic.

For her part, Lauren reached up and entangled her fingers in his hair, pulling him toward her, pinning him to her body, shifting him until his knees dropped between hers and she lifted her legs with the strength of a dancer to lock them behind his back, holding him in place. The movement pointed up one of the many advantages of her attire, as their bodies naturally met at the center, his shaft straining against the placket of his boxers as her wet heat beckoned to him.

He stared down at her, and she cracked another smile, at once exasperated and oddly touched. "Dimitri, if you ask me one more time if it's okay for you to make love to me, I'll smack you. I hereby give you ultimate permission to pound the living daylights out of me at any appropriate moment that we're together from now until the end of time. Does that clear things up for you?"

Laughter spilled through him. "Your future husband may object to that. So might the church, were you to become a nun."

"Then I'll have to find a way to make them understand." Lauren reached for him, bringing him close. "Now please, I beg of you. Use that condom by your side and fill me up until I don't have to think about anything at all except you and your body and how good you feel. You think you could do that for me?"

He shuddered as he reached for the foil package. "I think I can do that for you."

This time, they came together not with the curiosity of discovery, but as two people who needed each other at a level beyond words. Not to heal or provide comfort, but simply as a point of connection that transcended the moment. Dimitri sank into Lauren with a sigh. Her breath mingled with his, everything clicking together like puzzle pieces pulled from a hopeless jumble. They kissed, explored, laughed and poured themselves into each other as the ocean danced behind him and the stars dipped a little lower, adding their quicksilver magic to the moment. The song of the sea nymphs came later, drifting across the water as Lauren finally dozed, and Zephyrus stirred the breeze again, murmuring his whispered approval.

It was good, Dimitri thought, it was right. It was more joy than he had ever felt in his long life, and he gave thanks for this moment to every god who'd made it possible as he and Lauren lay beneath the stars, their arms wrapped around each other long into the night.

<h1 style="text-align:center">Twenty-Seven</h1>

The promontory of Miranos was more impressive than Lauren expected it would be. Because the ridge line had obscured the view from Dimitri's villa, she'd prepared herself for a shallow half-moon of water, broken by reefs beneath the shimmering blue-green Aegean, the place almost desolate in its beauty.

Since Dimitri had spoken so much about the ocean trash that he'd seen washed up there, she also expected it to be somewhat littered with driftwood and debris, or maybe a twisted airplane propeller or the shattered bow of some long-ago ship.

Not so.

The promontory looked more like a quaint little port, with boats lined up along one side of the long narrow strip of rock that stretched out into the ocean, and a network of tiny floating ramps connecting the various slips. There were a few small buildings there as well, to process the fish and carry it by truck to the main commercial port of Miranos, and also a seaside bar that she suspected only managed to stay in business because it doubled as the owner's home.

It was the bar where she and Dimitri started, and the

moment she stepped inside, she understood why. The walls were covered with items pulled from the sea—from large strips of metal to exotic scraps of what might have been considered buried treasure anywhere else but the middle of the Aegean Sea, where such finds were commonplace: plateware too degraded to fix a date on, broken cutlery, shattered lamps, bent and broken decking—even an anchor, which Dimitri explained had been raised with much excitement until it'd been verified as less than two hundred years old. When you lived in the waters of the ancients, an anchor two centuries old barely counted as driftwood.

She could see Dimitri's section straight off. A small and unassuming stretch of wall space, its pieces carefully lined the shelves, and a small crown had been carved into the corner shelving, now slightly worn away.

Dimitri touched his hand to that crown now, the action so unconscious that Lauren suspected that he was the one who'd worn the design down over this past year. Could this man truly be a demigod, whatever that meant? He seemed so...human.

"It doesn't look like much," he said, with a grim, self-deprecating smile. "Certainly not enough to justify a year's worth of searching."

"But you launched quite a big campaign when Ari was first lost, didn't you?" Lauren drifted from relic to relic. Most of it was scrap metal with some additional markings that Dimitri had identified as part of the plane, later verified by Crown experts. "I would imagine Queen Catherine moved heaven and earth to find her son."

"She did, but the first pieces were found all the way over in Thassos. This —and these," he said, indicating fairly intact bits of wreckage. The largest piece was an eight-inch section of a door panel, which appeared to have been sheared off from the plane.

She frowned as she examined them. "I can't believe they let you keep these pieces here. They should be in a museum on the mainland, shouldn't they? Or at least under study somewhere."

"They were under study for several months, but the idea of putting them in a museum was rejected by the royal family. Despite accepting the public's need to grieve, they didn't want to create a memorial to Ari's final hours that surpassed what he was as a person in real life. They didn't want him to be remembered only as bits of twisted metal."

"That's fair." Still, she shook her head, looking over the assemblage. "And they never found a body, or anything remotely like a body?"

"No. The storm that blew up the night he left Oûros was fierce. He was testing equipment, and I knew he was excited about seeing what the airplane could do. He had equipment in the cockpit not attached to the controls that he was testing—a watch, specialized phones. All that would've been washed away, and his body wouldn't have survived long in the open water. I never expected to find his body, his clothes...but the electronics should have resurfaced eventually. That was my hope."

"Electronics like the black box or whatever."

"Any sort of recording devices, yes." Dimitri nodded. "Something that could give us some insights into what he was doing, why he was where he was, what went wrong."

Lauren watched him as he spoke, the bleakness of his expression making her heart hurt. All the platitudes that crowded into her mind seemed pointless, ineffectual. She had never loved any of her friends with the deep force of will that Dimitri seemed to have for Ari. She had never been loved so much.

She reached out her hand and touched his arm. "He was lucky to have you as a friend," she murmured.

His lips twisted. "Not lucky enough, in the end. If I'd had

any idea that he would fly that night, I would have broken ranks to stop him—or at least warned Cyril of his plans."

She nodded as she turned back to the bits of sea wreckage, but she didn't believe him. No, she suspected Dimitri wouldn't have stopped Ari. Not that night. Not if his friend had truly wanted to go exploring. He would simply have entered the plane *with* Ari, and then the two of them would have been lost: the crown prince and his faithful friend and bodyguard. Double the tragedy, double the pain. Two families bereft instead of one.

And Dimitri clearly felt everything deeply—his duty to the crown, his love for his friend. Even his intensity in making love to a woman he barely knew. Lauren kept her gaze glued on the scraps of metal as her cheeks heated. Something had been seriously *different* about sex the night before with Dimitri.

Setting aside the fact that he was a wild, virile hunk of man who had muscles for days, every time he touched her, every time either one of them slammed into another climax, it was like the entire world around them reacted. The sea danced, the stars spun, and there—I mean, she would swear that there had been *music*—

"Enough of looking at what we know is of no use," Dimitri said abruptly, cutting off her thoughts as she glanced back at him. "The men will start returning with their nets in a few hours. In the meantime, we should go see what the ocean has brought us.

They didn't go down to the port, however, but along a rocky trail that skirted the wide crescent bay and dove into the forest, heading to where a smaller point jutted out into the ocean. "The reefs aren't so bad leading into the cove," Dimitri explained as at length they left the higher ground, weaving down through a tight jungle of trees and rocks as they made their way to sea level. "More wreckage washes ashore here."

"How did you find this trail to begin with?" Lauren asked. "It's barely visible."

"Those who comb the beaches have always known where it was. They were kind enough to show me when I came to them for help." Dimitri said this as if it were commonplace, the giving up of secrets to help someone in pain. She shook her head at his back, now lined with sweat at the collar as he pushed through branches and tested the rock-strewn pathway.

In her experience, no one gave up an advantage unless they needed to gain greater status or safety. But what status or safety was there to be gained on this desolate island? Only a hundred or so families lived here. There was no status in being the top of a few hundred people, not when you all had to pull together in times of crisis or need.

"Ah, here we are." Dimitri held back a final branch and Lauren saw open sky, heard the crash of water. She moved forward gladly but paused beyond the break in the trees, her jaw dropping open.

"You've got to be kidding me."

"Quite the place, isn't it?"

The grotto was a trash monger's paradise. Metal, tubing, lights, even strings of coins hung from the trees in swaying glory, mute testimony to the rich treasure that lay beyond the water's edge. Lauren half expected to find a crazed old man muttering among the sheets of metal, looking for treasures amid all the junk. "Who put all this up?"

"The scavengers and beachcombers. Anything that was too big or too common to fetch any sort of decent price, they simply started to hang. Over the years and decades, it's become a tradition. You'd think the junk would make the place too crowded, chaotic, but there's a sort of peace that comes from seeing it all together like this. As if the sea will one day give up all her mysteries, if we only wait long enough."

"Any of this from Ari's plane?" she asked, touching one of the relics.

"Not a scrap. Which was Cyril's number-one reason for the wreck to have obviously been near Thassos to the west of us, versus out to the east. But the storm wasn't in Thassos. It was blowing up the coast of Turkey. That's where Ari would have gone."

Lauren frowned. "Turkey? That seems unwise, doesn't it? A small, single-manned plane soaring into a storm over the border of an unfriendly neighbor?"

"As I said, Ari was a master of leaping first, thinking second. He'd never found a situation that he couldn't get himself out of." Dimitri smiled ruefully. "I suspect that's why I've had such a difficult time accepting his death."

He looked so forlorn there, staring out at the sea junk suspended from the trees that Lauren reached out and grasped his hand with both of hers, tugging him forward. "Show me," she said. "Show me where all this stuff washes up."

Twenty-Eight

Dimitri tried to keep his heart from expanding beyond the confines of his chest as he walked with Lauren through the hanging gallery of sea gifts to the open beach. She was dressed simply today, in long, loose pants and tank top, her hair drawn back in a simple ponytail, and only the most basic of makeup on her face beyond sunscreen. Even that he noticed only because she smelled like coconut, instead of whatever expensive designer fragrance she would normally be wearing, if she was in her own world.

A world he couldn't share. Would never share.

He tamped down his mutinous thoughts. Last night with Lauren had been a gift from the gods, and he should honor it as such. As the night had turned to morning, he'd awakened to realize they'd spent hours in each other's arms, their positions as comfortable as breathing and every bit as unconscious. He'd watched her as she slept, memorizing her face, the curve of her lips, the soft brush of eyelashes against her cheeks. He hadn't wanted to wake her, but the birds accomplished that soon enough, their chatter bringing her upright with a rush, dazed and bewildered until she'd seen him. Then the smile she'd offered him, radiant and full of light, had made him feel like he'd slain a thousand dragons for her, all before breakfast.

He was a sap. Ari would be laughing his ass off at him right now.

The thought of his friend brought joy to him, where so often it had brought sadness, and he stepped out onto the bright white sand beach with a lighter spirit. It helped too that Lauren gasped in wonder as she looked out over the beach. "My God, it's beautiful," she breathed.

Dimitri looked around. The beach was similar to any other strip of sand on Miranos, with no signs of civilization now that they'd moved beyond the sculpture garden. Then again, he got the idea that Lauren was probably never truly alone. Even her carefully constructed getaways probably came with a legion of employees and attendants, stylists and planners, cooks and maids and guides. Seeing an open stretch of beach untraveled by any other human most days was probably the equivalent of the Hope Diamond to her.

"What's that?" she asked, pointing out to the reef.

Dimitri squinted into the sunlight and went still. Then he strode forward all the way to the water's edge and beyond, his shoes sinking easily into the shifting sands.

"Dimitri, what is it? Are you okay?"

"Scrap," he said, turning back to her as he pulled off his tank top. "Probably nothing."

She caught his shirt easily, worry and a little excitement plain in her face. "You don't look like it's nothing."

"I haven't seen anything wash up on this shore with my own eyes for six months." He grinned at her, then without thinking reached out and pulled her close for a deep, soul-searching kiss. "See? You're good luck."

"That must be it—hey!" She stepped back, clearly startled, as he bent down and stripped off his pants as well, leaving nothing but his briefs and shoes. He'd ordinarily strip his briefs off too, but he didn't want to frighten Lauren back to the mainland. "Aren't there reefs out there? Won't you get cut?"

He fished out a pair of gloves from his pants and made sure his ankle knife was strapped tightly, then straightened again. "Gloves will protect me against the reefs, but clothes weigh me down in the water. I'm too used to swimming without. Either way, you should stay out of the water," he turned to wink at her. "Sharks."

"*Sharks?*"

He cut off his impulse to laugh by running forward into the sea, diving deep as soon as the sandy bottom fell away. The water felt good against his body as he cut through it, his muscles stretching and straining, the sun beating down on him. As he swam, he allowed the all too familiar hope to fire anew within him, bright and fierce.

If there was a piece of the plane, a new piece, it didn't mean that Ari was alive, necessarily. But it meant that the search could continue anew, would continue anew. It meant that more questions would be asked of more people, more money would be spent on trying to find out what had happened to his beloved friend. His friend who should not have died so early, who should not have died at all.

Dimitri reached the outer reef more quickly than he expected, and gingerly worked his way over to the debris, forcing himself not to examine it too closely. No matter what it was, he was honor-bound to bring it ashore. It might not be what he was searching for, but someone else could be, or someone could use it. Anything rendered completely useless was hung up for its inherent beauty, and this bright blue-silver sheet might possibly be...

He reached the sheet and found the point where it was attached to the reef. Using his knife, he cut away the coral, murmuring his apologies as he freed the large sheet. Getting back to the beach was slow and treacherous, and he finally made it there by using the wreckage as a sort of kickboard. By then, of course, he'd also learned what he needed to know from the bit of debris. And he slogged out of the sea far more tired than when he went in.

Lauren was waiting for him, but her eyes were on his face, not the shiny piece of metal he slung to the sand. Having her here, seeing her expression turn from hopeful trepidation to soft dismay, was enough to undo him. He sank to his knees, not realizing that she'd rushed over to him, was kneeling beside him, until he felt her arms around him, stronger than he would have expected. He sank his head forward and encountered her shoulder, sturdy and certain and true.

The tears that he hadn't allowed to fall for months broke free then, beneath the bright sun, amidst all the beauty and unspoiled splendor of the white sand beach of Miranos. He'd stayed stoic through the funeral and through every military campaign with Ari's younger brother, Kristos. He'd stayed firm in front of his sister and her children and grandchildren, all of them treating him as if he might break. He'd remained resolute in the face of the utterly despairing Queen Catherine, her face ravaged with pain and loss.

But here, in the arms of this woman, he could let go.

And he did.

He wept in silent, shuddering sobs, his breath a sharp bark when he expelled it, the tears that poured forth welling up from places he'd thought he'd never unearth. He shook in Lauren's steady grip, and eventually he held her back, clinging to her as she rocked him on the sand, the stream of his tears like losing his life's blood on the battlefield, blood he would willingly have shed to save Ari from such a stupid, senseless fate. He wept for the friendship that had ended, and the friendship he couldn't let go. His unwavering refusal to let Ari die and get on with his own life remained an open wound that wouldn't heal. It couldn't heal, as long as he resisted the truth. But neither could he accept that truth and give up on Ari. Not yet, anyway.

Not even when Poseidon mocked him with his gifts of twisted steel.

It was a long time before he realized he'd stopped crying, and that Lauren still held him—more loosely now, allowing him space to breathe, to be, while maintaining their connection. He lifted his head and offered her a rueful smile, the tears threatening again when he saw her face was wet as well.

"Sorry," he said gruffly.

"There's no shame in caring for your friend, Dimitri." Her words sounded as if she was a thousand years old, filled with all the ache and pain that she never showed. "Everyone should have a friend like you. The world would be a better place."

Blinking rapidly, as if she'd somehow betrayed too much, she looked at the metal sheet. "Not from the plane, I take it?"

"It's too thin." He shook his head. "It's a piece of some plane, but not the reinforced aircraft Ari had. I should have realized that immediately, but—" He trailed off, and Lauren reached for his hand. He needed her presence more than he wanted to, and certainly more than he wanted to admit. But she didn't push for him to talk about any of that. She didn't push at all. In some ways, maybe she needed the simple connection of a held hand every bit as much as he did. Maybe.

But he couldn't help but think about the reality of their situation. This idyll would last—at best—another day. And then she'd go back to her world, he to his.

How ironic that, though his job was fighting and sometimes death, hers at this moment seemed the grimmer prospect.

Twenty-Nine

Dimitri remained quiet as they exited the sculpture garden to make their way back to the main cove. They'd searched the rest of the reef area again on foot, peering out to sea, but nothing else caught their eye, and gradually, the beauty of the day and the brightness of the sun had served to drive their dark moods away. Now they walked back more slowly than they'd come, and Lauren wondered at that. Was Dimitri focusing on his sorrow over Ari's death? Or was there something else slowing his stride?

Would he miss her?

Grow up. She didn't have the luxury of worrying about that, yet the thought persisted. In a day, maybe more, maybe less, they'd both be back in their own worlds, fighting their own demons—real or imagined. And maybe she *had* overreacted. Henry hadn't done anything intensely crazy in a while. Yes, fine, he'd drawn up marriage documents, but how damning were those, really? The mark of an efficient man, a confident man, maybe. Not a psychopath.

Right?

As they left the shady confines of the jungle, Dimitri angled toward the beach rover. "Need to check in," he said, and she colored with more embarrassment. That was what he'd been thinking about. The messy business of his emotions done, he wanted to connect with something real, tangible. His work in the ONSF fit that bill nicely.

Demigod or not, Dimitri would always be business first.

Lauren grabbed her purse and wandered off a short distance to watch the fishermen's return, while Dimitri recovered his phone. A quick check of her cell indicated no signal, but there were also no texts in the queue from her sister, or from anyone. Apparently, Dimitri's sister wasn't a big texter. Then again, when you'd spent your life on a tiny island where everyone knew everyone, face-to-face communication suddenly seemed a lot more efficient.

As Dimitri had promised, the boats were coming in to the small port, their nets full of fish, or what she assumed was fish, the weight of them dragging the small craft deep in the water. With as much money as the large fishing conglomerates surely made in this area, it surprised her how many men and women were apparently trying their hand at the trade. Trying and succeeding, from what she could tell. Some of the craft were large and sturdy, meant for deep sea fishing, and their boat names were a mixture of Oûrois, Turkish, and Greek.

The dock area exploded into a tightly choreographed burst of activity, and she watched, almost mesmerized, until Dimitri came up beside her.

"So, do you want to become a fisherman?" he asked.

"It looks like way too much work."

He laughed. "Some would say the same of being cooped up in a high-rise all day long, staring at tiny words and numbers on a computer."

"Fair enough." She glanced at him, struck by his smile in the bright sun. He was in his element on this island—probably would be in any place, as long as he could live and work in the sun and surf. "Any news from the mainland? My parents?"

Dimitri sobered. "Apparently, your parents have sided with Smithson in his search for you—not surprising, since, according to Stefan, he is a staunch friend of the family."

At Henry's name, it was as if Lauren's bubble of protection was pricked. She drew herself up, steeling her reserves. "Sided, meaning what?"

Dimitri seemed to be weighing his response, and she rolled her eyes. "I can assure you there is nothing you can tell me about either my parents or Henry that will surprise me. That ship has long since sailed."

He grimaced. "Stefan and Cyril attempted a brief subterfuge, announcing to your parents that they had a solid lead on your whereabouts but that it should be kept in strictest confidence. The chatter we were monitoring from Smithson's boat indicated that such confidence included a call straight to him. He was delivering orders to track you down when the royal family reversed the information, saying their lead proved worthless."

"Does he know you've been tracking him?"

Dimitri shifted. "Potentially. Chatter stopped shortly after that. The bug wasn't discovered, or at least not destroyed, but given the change in conversational flow, it's no longer considered viable as an information tool."

She nodded. It was hard to say if Henry knew he'd been tracked, but his natural caution was enough to keep his men quiet if he suspected it was possible. She'd traveled often enough with her parents aboard his yacht to know his men followed him to the letter, out of a combination of fear and respect more than genuine liking. Then again, Smithson paid for the best, and got the best. Liking the man had nothing to do with it.

"What's the plan, then?" She knew what was coming. They would return her to the fold of her family, with some trumped-up excuse that she'd been hysterical, imperious, demanding, spoiled. Everyone would expect that. She could probably pull that off. In fact, she could *definitely* pull that off.

Dimitri, however, surprised her. He gestured her toward the bar, and they moved down the walkway. "We have several options," he said. "If you would prefer to run, I have the authority to assist you in your escape. If you would prefer to confront Smithson on the mainland, we can arrange for a formal dinner with plenty of people around. If you would prefer to play the spoiled socialite, we can make that work as well. It's whatever approach that you feel you can manage most safely."

She glanced at him as they entered the cool interior of the bar. "You'd let me choose? What's in the best interest for the royal family?"

"That's a movable consideration, as it turns out." Dimitri signaled for drinks, and they settled at a high table. Lauren's gaze moved from fisherman to sailor to dock worker and back as people moved through the bar seeking respite from the heat of the day. "You could show up as the spoiled penitent. That is easiest. The confrontation at the palace is also manageable. Flight is the hardest, because it demonstrates our meddling in the affairs of a non-national, but it can also be arranged."

"Flight would be stupid." Lauren shook her head. As she considered the issue, she distractedly tracked a well-muscled man in dark, shabby clothes, his sun-bronzed skin a striking counterpoint to his expensive, technical watch. The watch seemed overmatched for his outfit, but he looked like the leader of his little band of men. Probably from one of the larger boats. Her gaze lingered on the brightly polished watch as she considered her options. "A confrontation seems dangerous as well, even an exceedingly polite one. Best that I play the brat who came to her senses, a simpering fool. If I can pull it off, maybe that'll be the play that ensures Henry loses interest. It's worth a try."

Dimitri's expletive was succinct. "Stefan suggested you would opt for that approach. Very well. With that plan, it's best to return overnight, after sending messages that you've been located and will return tomorrow. We'll have multiple boats set out from several islands, as well as official vehicles as decoys. With any luck, we'll get to the palace unnoticed."

She smiled, following the dark-skinned man as he moved toward the bar to order more drinks for his team. "You seem to be doing that a lot these days. Shuttling Americans under cloak of night."

"Whatever the job requires."

Dimitri took a slug of his beer, while Lauren's gaze narrowed on the sailor. He wasn't an attractive man, but he looked capable despite his roughness. The watch was the only thing that marked him as acting above his station. It seemed— strange. Not a brand she recognized, but clearly it'd cost serious money.

"Who's caught your eye so effectively?" Dimitri's tone was teasing, but as he turned to follow Lauren's gaze, he stopped.

"That watch..." he murmured.

"Right? Totally too high-end for the guy. I thought so too."

"It's not that." Dimitri set his beer down on the bar, easily, casually. Almost too easily and casually, and Lauren's nerves pricked to high awareness. "I think I recognize it." He reached down to his ankle as if he was adjusting his sandal, then sat up again.

Lauren froze. Dimitri was palming his knife.

"If I'm right, it belongs to Ari."

Thirty

The man ambled back to his table, laughing and unconcerned, looking for all the world like he'd be there awhile. Dimitri racked his memory. He'd seen this man dozens of times over the past few years, and certainly since Ari had died. He wasn't a thug or a pirate, any more than were the rest of the men who made the most of their opportunities on the high seas without directly stealing from their fellow fishermen. He'd never once caused trouble or stood out in any way. Dimitri hadn't noticed the man wearing a watch before, but when he came down to this port, it was to look for found goods among his network, not stolen watches brazenly displayed on a stranger's wrist.

He couldn't be mistaken, though. Ari could afford the finest timepieces in the world, but he'd eschewed the luxury brands for a dive watch that had been custom altered from a Sea Hawk timepiece to incorporate details that made it ideal as either a dive *or* flight watch, since Ari was a fan of both. For this man to be wearing it so openly could only mean he had no idea whose it had been originally.

Nevertheless, the blade in Dimitri's hand itched to cut it off the man.

"Is that the best approach?" Lauren smiled brightly at him, so brightly that it took him by surprise. She kept talking through her teeth. "Do you want to alert this group that you've an issue with this man, and take the watch from him bodily? Cause a scene?"

He scowled at her. "This isn't your business."

"No. Making deals is my business. Which you'd know if you had read up on that dossier Stefan had provided you." She reached out and patted his hand. "How much money do you have on you, and how much money do you think he paid for the watch? He didn't steal it. He doesn't look the type."

That did get his attention, but his scowl only deepened. "The watch cost Ari close to twenty thousand euros. I don't carry that kind of cash."

"Well, neither does he. That's nowhere close to the amount he paid someone for it."

Dimitri snorted. "No. He paid probably five hundred. I have a thousand euros on me." She blinked at him, and he shrugged. "In case we found something today."

She nodded. "Well, it looks like we did. You sure it's Ari's? Lot of watches in the world, and we can only play the ignorant-tourist card once. If he knows you're the one interested and not me, the price will go up."

Irritation ratcheted through him, but he knew Lauren might well be right. She appeared to be a tourist on holiday, one with money to burn but not too much of it. Not anywhere close to the amount she probably normally slung around. He shrugged. "It's worth a try. You make the play, and if you're not successful, I'll cut it from his hand myself."

She leaned over and kissed him as he used his free hand to fish his wallet out of his pocket. "Then for now, hide that meat cleaver you've got there, 'kay?" She palmed his wallet and was gone.

Dimitri held the beer at an angle where he could watch Lauren the whole time, and he didn't sheathe the knife. Despite what she thought, he *had* read Stefan's entire file on her. Multiple times. She was good at what she did—making deals, glad handing, PR shit. He supposed she was good at business, but she never seemed to stick around on any one project long enough to tell for sure. He'd not had any occasion to witness her negotiating skills in person, and he wasn't happy about it now.

Still, he couldn't deny that she looked the part of a wide-eyed tourist as she hesitantly approached the table of men, appearing as out of place as she possibly could with her blonde hair and soft clothes. Thank God his sister had dressed her in local attire, or the price would have gone up a few hundred more euros on general principles.

He turned to the bartender as Lauren began talking in earnest to the laughing man with Ari's watch. The man knew him well, and was also no idiot. "She's safe with him," he said in a low voice. "Put away the knife. I want no trouble here."

"I've seen him before, I know he's no trouble." Dimitri shrugged. "It's not him I want anyway, but his watch."

"His watch!" The bartender's eyes widened. "I thought you wanted wreckage."

Dimitri scowled, causing the man to stand back sharply. "I'd no idea that personal items would be floating around. He's worn it long? A year?"

"No, not so long as that." The bartender scratched his beard. "Six months, maybe. I remember it was New Year's, round about. He had it then. Assumed he'd won it or bought it, but fair and square. He wasn't hiding it."

Dimitri nodded. "Name and craft? Where he's heading next?" He shifted his gaze to the bartender, then away again.

"There is money in it for you." Assuming Lauren left him with any.

The man shrugged. "It's common information, no secret. But I'll give it to you anyway. That outfit, they run the same routes, always." He supplied Dimitri with the fisherman's name, his boat's identification number, and his crew's next location. If Dimitri was right about the watch, members of the ONSF would intercept the fisherman at his next port. He'd be questioned then about the watch, yes, but in a way perhaps more circumspect than Dimitri would have done. Either way...it would be news. Information.

In the mirror, he studied the man as he slipped the watch off his wrist and handed it over to Lauren. The man grinned as she pushed a large pile of euros his way. She threw her arms around the man, thanking him effusively, all while keeping a death grip on her prize. Then, without looking Dimitri's way, she turned for the front door, making a beeline out of the bar and into the open air.

Dimitri glanced back at the bartender, realizing he now had no money to pay for his drink. The man waved him on. "Go. I'm glad for you, Dimitri. Had I known this one watch would help you, I would've alerted you to it long ago."

"You've done me a great service." Leaving the man with the promise of payment, he turned as well. His gaze took in the laughing table of fishermen. They would be met in Samothrace by members of the ONSF and wouldn't be so happy then. Let them enjoy their beer and good fortune while they could.

Lauren was already halfway to the beach rover when he caught up to her, and she was moving fast. "Don't stop, don't stop," she said, though she didn't look at him. He frowned but could sense the anxiety rolling off her in waves, and they didn't speak until he'd started the rover. As they exited the parking lot, she relaxed enough to lose her death grip on the watch, though her hands shook as she handed it over to Dimitri.

He eyed her as he took the watch, then glanced back to the open beach. He quickly slid the watch on his wrist. It hung there with a reassuring weight. "I thought you were a master negotiator. You look like you're about to pass out."

"I wasn't negotiating for *myself*, I was negotiating for you, and for a man who was your best friend. It changes things." She gestured toward the watch. "Is it the right one?"

"It is."

"How can you tell? You're not even really looking at it."

"I can tell because the watch has two diving chronometers that most flight watches don't, and a world time meter that most diving watches don't. It's also engineered for high-altitude antifogging. And," he offered her a lopsided smile, "the band is cracked."

He held the watch toward her, and she saw the thin crack in the metal next to the case. "Ari had a new one on order. It arrived three days after he was lost at sea."

Lauren stared at him. "Do you think those men—those men saw Ari? Knew him? Maybe they helped him out of the water or saw where he, I mean—" She broke off, clearly unsure of how ready he was to deal with the concept of Ari being finally gone.

He wasn't sure himself, and the need resurfaced to go and interrogate the men. Lauren apparently felt the same way. "We should go back! You should ask them directly now, before they leave."

"No." With welcome clarity, his training reasserted itself. No. He'd waited too long to do this wrong now. He would make his report and let the royal family follow up. Their need to find out what happened to Ari was every bit as great as his own. And their need to do it with ultimate secrecy was paramount. They didn't want to look weak or foolish to either their allies or their enemies.

He shook his head. "We'll go in town to make the full report and ensure I have a strong enough signal to send pictures. But we'll stop first at home to radio it in with the sat phone. I don't want to wait."

"Well, I should say not."

They raced across the sand, Lauren practically bouncing in her seat. She was almost out of the rover before it stopped in front of the villa, running around to tug him out as well. "I can't believe you can't video call. Can you even take a picture with this thing?"

"No, which is why we're going into town. King Jasen will also want the watch secured, so our timetable has probably moved up as well."

That stopped her, and she turned back to him. She'd made it as far as the porch, and as he mounted the stairs, her manner seemed suddenly far too tense. "Moved up as in—"

"As in I expect I'll be recalled back to the mainland immediately, with you as well." He frowned at her as her expression flickered between disappointment, loss, and finally resolve. "What is it?" he asked. "What's wrong?"

Thirty-One

Lauren looked up, blinking as Dimitri loomed over her. They were on the porch, the porch where the day before she'd sat, clutching her beer, wondering if she was reading Dimitri's signals wrong, and practically desperate to have sex with the man, if only once. Her time on the island had been a remarkable, a time-out-of-time experience, and she was already losing the memory of it, her mind already moving forward, everything happening too fast.

Now she felt as if she had to memorize everything around her, because it was all ending. Everything would be going back to normal, and she wasn't ready for normal yet, though she knew that was selfish, knew that that wasn't her place. She didn't care.

"Lauren." Dimitri's large hands came up to her upper arms, and he gently steadied her as if she were a filly about to bolt, or a skittish child about to have a meltdown. Was that what he thought of her, she wondered? And what did it matter if he did?

But it did matter. It mattered a lot. And if she wasn't careful, she'd betray how much it mattered, and then the big hulking possibly demigod-bodyguard would have a better story to tell his military buddies for the rest of his life, however long it lasted, about how he swooped an American heiress off her feet without so much as lifting a hand, and then she turned into a blubbering mess at the prospect of him leaving her. They'd all have a good laugh about that, probably, or at least they should.

"Lauren," Dimitri said again, more sharply this time. "I'm serious. What's wrong with you?"

"Nothing," she snapped, smiling to soften the harshness of her tone. She glanced away to compose herself. How many times had she done that over the years? A simple pause to center on what was important, what counted. A resetting of her expression to ensure that she conveyed exactly what she wanted to convey—and only what she wanted to convey.

But when she looked back to Dimitri, it all fell apart again. She prayed she sounded artful when she spoke, that he couldn't tell how much he affected her, but her heart was in her words too much to her own ears, and there was nothing she could do about it. "It's just that—once you make that call, we're done here, right? We'll pack up and leave this house, this beach, and head back to the mainland on the earliest possible boat."

"Well…yes. But that's better for you anyway. You didn't plan on staying hidden for any longer than a few days, remember?" He smiled, and suddenly he seemed larger, more powerful than she wanted him to. Definitely more in control. Where had all that predictable confusion gone? "Unless you simply can't imagine life without me?"

His tease let her recenter herself, far more than any of her training could have. See? He didn't consider this any big deal. Why should she?

"Ha, no. Of course not." She straightened with a bright smile as Dimitri lounged back against the railing, watching her. She drew in a deep, steadying breath. "What will your role be anyway, after you give up the watch? Are they going to let you take part in the search?"

He shrugged, apparently unconcerned. "I'll go where they order me to go," he said. But he wasn't looking at the watch; he was looking at her. "That's what you do when you commit to serve."

"Whatever." She looked out to the ocean. "Sounds kind of mindless to me."

He chuckled, clearly way too happy about the idea of getting rid of her. "Not really. The military doesn't want you to stop thinking, princess. They want you to think very hard about the right things." He didn't move, but she still sensed him shifting toward her, somehow, like a net that was closing in too quickly. "You aren't paid to counteract your orders, you're paid to be creative in the pursuit of your orders."

"Creativity, right," she muttered, stung to the quick though he hadn't said anything offensive. Once again, he simply seemed so...blasé. So matter-of-fact. As if none of this mattered. As if she didn't matter. "I don't remember creativity being a key attribute of a good soldier."

"I suspect you probably haven't gotten your hands dirty with too many soldiers, good or otherwise."

The fact that he was right didn't make the comment any less annoying. "You have no idea what kind of men I've been with."

"I think I have some idea." He moved toward her then, easy and relaxed, and she took a sharp step back, forgetting how near she'd already been to the wall. The cool, rough plaster pressed against her as Dimitri rested a hand on the wall above her, leaning in to stare down at her, his expression smug. "I suspect you're the kind of women who likes her men pretty but weak. Easily controlled. Fit enough to look good jogging beside you or playing tennis, but not someone you actually expect to get any real work done. And certainly no one that would qualify as *creative.*"

"And you are?"

"We're not talking about me." A hot surge of embarrassment flared through Lauren at Dimitri's chiding tone, but when she would have moved away, he put his other hand against the wall, effectively caging her. "We'll get to me in a second. First I want you to describe the last man you allowed to make love to you."

Lauren's eyes widened at the rude question, but she couldn't stop her brain from jumping to the man in question—not even a man, just some guy she knew from college, someone who was tall, lean, good-looking in a Ralph Lauren model kind of way. His hair had always been neatly trimmed, she found herself thinking now. His face always smooth. His manners always careful, precise. Even in bed.

"On second thought, never mind," Dimitri said. "You've told me everything you need simply with that disappointed look on your face."

She scowled up at him, taking in his hot, hooded eyes, his skin bristling with a two-day beard, his lips curved into a mocking smirk.

She pushed against his chest, not expecting to move him. She didn't. "Well, at least he had manners," she snapped, pushing him harder. Instead of shifting back, Dimitri leaned closer, tilting his hips until they connected with hers, the pressure of his hard shaft shocking though she expected it. It was rough, almost crude, and she wanted to spit out a rebuke. But it was also exactly what she wanted, what she needed. And there was no way she could think of words as her knees wobbled beneath her, her belly swimming with a damp heat that she could no more articulate than ignore.

"Manners," Dimitri murmured, and he dipped his head down to her ear, as if to whisper a confidence to her.

Instead, she felt the cool slide of his tongue as it traced the rim of her ear, his teeth then closing lightly around the lobe. Unable to stop herself, she clenched her hand in his shirt, half grabbing it, half bracing herself against Dimitri's body, unsure of anything but the heady sensation as he kissed his way down her neck and into the curve of her shoulder. His right hand came away from the wall and cupped her breast, hard, as his gaze reconnected with hers. "I've never been a big fan of manners in bed. Perhaps you'll have to explain to me how that works."

"You'd never pick it up," she managed, and then his other hand was massaging her breast as well, practically steaming through her clothes.

"You've got my attention now," he murmured. "Believe me, I'm all ears."

His words were calm and measured, but she could feel the heat beginning to roll off him as his body reacted to hers. His hands moved again to her bare arms, and the touch of him electrified her. She tilted her head up, searching his gaze.

"Do we really need to leave yet?" She broke off at the embarrassment of what she was asking. But suddenly, the world outside this villa seemed a big and lonely place, whereas standing in the circle of Dimitri's arms felt totally safe, impossibly right.

Dimitri leaned closer to her. "Something you want, princess?" he said gruffly, his lips skimming her cheek before barely brushing against her mouth. "Because I'm more than happy to give it to you. But this time, we have to do it my way."

Thirty-Two

Dimitri grinned hard as Lauren's startled gaze met his. She acted like she was this remote, untouchable woman, unwilling and unable to be moved by any man. But he knew differently, had known it since the first time he'd seen her. She wasn't made for the neat little men in their tidy suits and expensive cologne that he suspected adorned all of her boyfriends in the past. She wasn't made for someone willing to toady to her and give into her every imperious request.

She was made to be met halfway—more than halfway. And then taken completely over the cliff.

And he was just the demigod to do it.

Beneath him, Lauren trembled, but only a little bit. He was kissing her face, her mouth, barely willing to let her breathe, to let her talk, but he heard the "yes" she managed as she tangled up her hands in his shirt. Heard the sigh of relief as he pulled her roughly into his body, scooping her up in his arms and carrying her inside. She wanted him to take control. He was more than happy to oblige.

Dimitri didn't stop this time at the living room. His long strides ate up the distance to the stairs, and when Lauren made to regain her own feet at the steps, he growled, bending down to find her mouth again with his. His kiss was fierce and brooked no argument. She didn't give any. He bounded up the rest of the stairs to the room—*his* room. The room she'd slept in two nights before, the bed now hotel-neat, the place spotless, as if no one had been in there. But she had. And now she would be again.

Dimitri hit the bed in three more steps, dropping her on it and immediately covering her body with his. Lauren wrapped her arms around him and pulled him to her fiercely, her legs going around his hips and her hand at the back of his neck, as if she could crawl inside his body. Sounded good to him. He kissed her roughly, tasting, demanding, and the harsh, desperate breath of her response drove him to higher and higher need.

He pulled away from her, then reached over his shoulder to pull off his shirt. Her eyes widened as she stared at him, then out the window. Dimitri knew what she'd noticed, but it couldn't be helped.

"What's happening outside?" she asked, lifting up on one elbow as the room darkened with the sudden onrush of heavy clouds. "Was there supposed to be a storm today?"

"It happens. You have other clothes?"

"Clothes? What—yes." She frowned as his hand moved to the neckline of her loose tank. "These are—they weren't expensive, they're just—"

"Good." He dipped his hand into the neckline and yanked, the thin material giving way, exposing the lace of her bra. It buckled in front, and he snapped the clasp easily. With a guttural growl, he leaned forward to take her bared breast in his mouth, reveling in the way Lauren shifted and writhed beneath him, her hands now in his hair, her body arched. She was made for sex, but now he decided it was more than that. She was made for sex with him.

The crack of thunder boomed across the sky, loud enough to shake the house.

"Seriously?" Lauren gasped, but he didn't hesitate as rain started pelting the villa. Instead, he lifted again long enough to shred the rest of her shirt open, the soft curve of her belly begging for his mouth, his hands, and he gave into the compulsion. Curling his hands beneath her ass, he scorched a trail of kisses down her stomach and over the thin linen of her pants, quieting her squirming as he felt the heat swell up from her and envelope him. The rush was intense, and when she struggled to reach her waistband with her own hands, he batted her hands away, instead ripping open the cheap placket and revealing the soft cotton panties beneath.

"You lie there," he ordered, his voice a harsh rasp.

He ripped down Lauren's trousers and her panties with it, then licked and kissed his way down to the most intimate part of her, the soft folds already full and ready for him. Lauren hissed out a curse as he drew his tongue down the very center of her sex, teasing and tasting, pressing into her while she buried her hands in his hair, asking him things incoherently, to stop, to not stop, to go, to keep going. Her body trembled with adrenaline and desire, and he could feel her climax building by the raggedness of her breath, the looseness of her thighs, the way she pressed his head first one way, then another, unconscious that she was doing it but unable to stop, unable to do anything but lose herself in the pleasure he was giving her.

His own cock throbbed so hard, he thought it was going to burst, but he pulled away from Lauren, hesitated briefly as she cried out in alarm, then lowered his head again and returned to the most sensitive part of her, the nub he had been teasing and brushing. Now he licked into her like a starving man granted a meal, and she clamped her hands on his shoulders, arching back as she convulsed with a gasp of surprise and pleasure. That cry turned to confusion as he lifted himself off her, ridding himself of his own cargo pants in a quick jerk and reaching for the condom to sheathe himself.

A crack of lightning illuminated Lauren instinctively curling away from him, lost in her own reaction, but he wasn't going to let her evade him now. He reached for her wrists, pinning her to the bed, and pressed himself into her body again, her legs falling open naturally to accept the intrusion of him.

Her eyes fluttered open as he slid his cock along her already sensitized skin, setting off another wave of involuntary shudders.

"Yes—now," she gasped. "I want you inside me."

"I want that too, princess," he gritted out. He slipped his shaft into her without hesitation, and she drew in a sharp breath as her body clamped down on him. "I'd say I want that more than you do."

He thrust once, twice, filling her to the brim before pulling out again, then burying himself inside her once more. His own need to explode was pulling him apart at the seams, but he was enjoying watching her too much. Her mouth open, her breath coming fitfully between her lips. Her eyes half-lidded, unseeing. Her hair wild around her head, ground into the covers in a helpless tumble. Her clothes hanging off her, exposing her full breasts, her pink, smooth skin. As the wind howled around the villa, he leaned forward and inhaled the essence of her, his face in the crook of her neck, his lips tracing a line up the curve above her collarbone to rest beside her ear. He nipped at her earlobe, then traced along the delicate arc of her ear, reveling in the way she shuddered.

"You're—a demigod." Her words were little more than a groan. "You really are."

He grinned against her neck. If she hadn't been sure before, this little display would've convinced her.

"You knew that the moment we met, princess."

She laughed deep in her throat, the sound powerful and free, and for another few mindless minutes, they made love beneath the crashing storm. For right this second, in each other's arms, they needed nothing more than that.

But when Lauren cried out again in unrestrained pleasure, Dimitri knew he still wanted more. He suspected he would never get enough of this beautiful, vibrant woman, so like a goddess in every way but real—vital—human.

Another roaring boom of thunder rocked the villa around them.

"I want to fuck you every way there is," he hissed into her ear, and if anything, she went more liquid in his arms. "Till there's nothing else you can imagine but me inside you, making you wet with need, making you come."

"Yes," Lauren said, and the broken desire in her voice cranked him up another notch.

He pulled all the way out, leaving her gasping. "Turn over."

Surprise flared in her eyes, and he held up a hand, grinning into her face. "My way, remember."

She didn't need much convincing. She turned over, and the sight of her made any other action moot. Grabbing her waist, he slid into her again, the unfamiliar angle and pressure drawing her up short, making it that much easier to shift his hands up to cup her beautiful breasts as he pressed farther into her, spreading her wide, his questing fingers then dropping from her breasts to the sensitive vee—

"Oh!" she gasped as her body bucked. "I can't—"

"You can. My way." He placed his fingers over her quivering sex and seated himself inside her again. He pulsed inside her as he touched her intimately, shifting his fingers and body in tune to the vibrations of her body, the urgency of her sighs, the staccato need of her groans. When she came apart in his arms a second time, he was ready, surging forward as she cried out incoherently until he triggered his own release, and his sight went whiteout blind for a second as the rush of need and desire and possession swept over him, taking him into oblivion. Another maelstrom of pounding rain blasted from the skies, filling up the world and he growled, pulling free of Lauren and rolling away to rid himself of the condom. He returned to the bed immediately, pulling her into his arms, cradling her close, as she shook and trembled, reaching for him, finding him.

Finding them both.

Thirty-Three

Lauren stood in the afternoon sun which had finally broken through the clouds again, a smile fixed on her face as she stared at Dimitri making a call on his satellite phone. Though they were back in town and cell coverage was unexpectedly boosted by the recent storm's low cloud coverage, he'd insisted on using the sat phone to make this call. From the animated way he used his arms to punctuate his words, she couldn't tell if the conversation was going well or not. With Dimitri, animation was a part of the equation.

They hadn't spoken after making love—not about anything real or challenging. Not about his status or hers. They had to— she knew they did. But for this moment, set off from the world of reality, words like "demigod" and "stormbringer" and "what the hell just happened" tumbled away from her to dance on the still churning waves of the Aegean. They would have time to work all that out...later.

She shifted her gaze to her own phone. To her surprise, she'd had no incoming texts or calls in the day or so since she'd checked last, but then again, only her sister had the phone number, and the two of them weren't close, not yet. Maddie was barely fourteen, and while their relationship was good, life was simply too different for them both to fully connect. Even her own friends, Nicki, Emmaline, and Fran seemed a million miles away instead of merely a short boat ride to the mainland.

Lauren typed out a quick text to Maddie, then stole another look at Dimitri. He continued to gesture wildly, and it was impossible to tell if he was happy or peeved. Turning away, she keyed in another number.

Nicki picked up on the first ring. "Girl! What is going *on*—Stefan the powerful demigod of obnoxiousness, won't tell me anything. We were getting worried!"

Lauren smiled, warmed more than she would have imagined by Nicki's voice. Of all the girls, she hadn't expected to get along with Nicki so much on this trip. She was Emmaline's friend more so than Lauren's, the two of them having roomed together in college while Lauren had shared a dorm room with Fran. Nicki had always been so outsized and bold, despite her small frame...and Lauren had always thought it was that small frame that had made her so obnoxiously "extreme-sports girl."

Until she'd seen the bottle of meds Nicki had waved at her so casually this past week and realized the deeper truth. Such a simple thing, but it had changed everything.

Nicki wasn't sick, not really. But her big heart that beat so fiercely as she pounded up mountains and down trails was threatened by a disease she refused to acknowledge beyond a precautionary regimen of beta blockers. Her brother and father had both been diagnosed with familial hypertrophic cardiomy-opathy, a condition that could stop the woman in her tracks at any moment...or never strike at all. Testing was required to know for sure if she was going to develop the disease, and even that wasn't foolproof.

So Nicki had decided not to be tested. And instead to go after life as if it could be swept away from her at any moment.

As a result, Lauren didn't look at Nicki any more as some sort of daredevil. She looked at her as a kind of miracle. Or an idiot. Or a ticking time bomb, take your pick. Either way, she was who she was, and Lauren was glad to count her as a friend.

"So what has Stefan said, actually?" Lauren asked. "He told you I was still with Dimitri, right? We had a storm hit—did you guys get it too?"

"Storm? Not hardly," Nicki said, surprising her. "It's been blue skies and beautiful forever. But Stefan totally said you were with Dimitri, and *then* tried to give us some bullshit about you needing a holiday from your parents, which we both know is not true. He's figured out that I know what he is, that we all know what he is, and I think he's pissed."

She sounded far too happy about that. "He knows that Emmaline told us, right?" Lauren asked.

"Oh, yeah. Seriously, how else would we know? But he keeps acting like he doesn't have to dish all the details on every-thing. Have you talked to Dimitri about it?"

"Actually—no. I haven't."

Nicki sighed. "I mean, I guess it's none of our business. I totally get that we all have secrets, but most secrets aren't this *amazing*. Anyway—what he *is* telling us is total bullshit. You're not avoiding your parents. It's that creeper Henry, right? He's your supposed chosen one? Gross. He's a million years too old for you."

Lauren laughed in spite of herself at Nicki's barrage of words, her gaze drifting along the rain-slicked streets. "He's not that old."

"Oh, please. He's pushing forty. That's old when you're twenty-three. I checked." Nicki didn't let her respond to that. "You know, he seemed super pissed when he couldn't find you the other night, and then he got super...not pissed. It was weird."

Lauren's brows went up. "What do you mean?" she asked. Though she knew the answer. Nicki supplied it for her anyway.

"Like, all this was a game to him, and you'd simply surprised him with an unexpected move. He seemed, I don't know, delighted. Almost giddy." She could almost hear Nicki shrug. "Like I said, creeper. I'm glad he split."

That made her hand spasm on the phone. "He split? I thought he was part of the search party or whatever."

"Jeez, do they tell you nothing? That's why you're coming home, I thought. Henry took off last night, back aboard his floating glitter palace, and sailed off into the sunset. Your parents are still freaking out, but creeper man apparently doesn't give a damn about finding you one way or another."

Lauren's throat closed up. She was glad now for time passing quickly. She needed to get back into the open, back into a place where she would be seen, tracked, surrounded by her security people. If Henry had decamped, that didn't mean he'd given up on her, far from it. That meant he was planning something else. Something new.

Probably something bad.

Nicki said something else, and Lauren's attention flicked back to the phone. "I'm sorry, what?"

"I said, when specifically are you coming home? Tonight yet? Tomorrow? I think the queen wants to have another party. Because, you know, we're staying in a freaking castle with the gatekeepers of the flippin' Greek gods, and that's what one does."

"Tonight," Lauren said. "I'm pretty sure it's all going to happen tonight." Her eyes strayed to Dimitri. He'd finished his phone call and had turned back to her, his grin so wide she thought it would take up her whole world. "I've gotta go, Nicki," she said, feeling her heart lighten at last. "See you guys soon?"

"You better! I'm sure they'll be killing the fatted calf in

anticipation of your triumphant return. Only, please, for the love, don't make me wear another ball gown."

Lauren was still laughing as she clicked off the phone, and Dimitri bounded up to her. Before she could ask him what had happened, he grabbed her arm and pulled her into the sidewalk café she'd been loitering next to. "Food!" he shouted. "We're celebrating." The server closest to the door laughed and gestured to one of the tables. Dimitri was electric with energy as they sat.

"So it was good news?" Lauren said, drinking in the image of him. He seemed so completely relaxed and unfeigned around her. Back at the villa, they'd lain together for a half hour as the rain finally died down, dozing in the bed before getting up to shower and head into town. Except for the big human-demigod conversation they both were carefully avoiding, everything felt completely natural with Dimitri, like they'd been dating for years. Now, the sight of him filled with genuine joy and excitement was a balm to her nerves. A balm she hadn't realized she needed so much.

"It was good news," Dimitri said, grinning. "They believe me and want us back on the mainland immediately, of course, so they can inspect the watch themselves. I'm happy to oblige them. There's no boat on the island now that is secure, however, so we'll wait until we can have one outfitted and sent over. Should be later tonight."

Lauren glanced out to the water. The sun was beginning to drop through the still heavy clouds already, so that cut down their time on the island to—what, mere hours? She forced herself not to think about that. "And then what?" she asked. "Will they track down the fisherman?"

"Already underway. He'll be picked up at his next port and questioned. Most likely, he didn't pull the watch off Ari's wrist himself. He wouldn't be so bold with showing it off otherwise. I expect he bought it off some beachcomber, but if there is any lead—anything at all to indicate what happened to Ari…" He spread his hands, his good mood dimming somewhat. "Well. That would be a blessing for the family. For me."

"You'll find something." Lauren reached out and grasped Dimitri's hand. That too seemed natural, as did the roughness of his palm as he closed his other hand around hers. He pulled her close and kissed her, laughing again as they were interrupted by the server bringing hummus and bread and olives.

They had eaten about half the meal before Dimitri leaned back, and she tensed as his gaze moved over her. He was about to shift tactics, she was certain.

She was right.

"So tell me, what will you do when we return? Stefan said Henry has left, probably to plot another day. How will you stop him completely?"

Lauren sighed "I think he'll eventually stop himself," she said, staring at the glass in her hand to avoid looking at him directly. "He's, above all, a seriously proud man. Though I'm sure the story was controlled, the idea of me fleeing the scene to avoid him probably has leaked out in the communities he actually cares about. Eventually, he'll start feeling like the rejected suitor if he keeps after me without success, and that won't sit well with him. Better for him to go on to other conquests and decide if he still wants me." She glanced up again. "If he does, well, I'll deal with that then."

Even as she spoke the words, she was surprised at how sane they sounded. How smart, even. Henry Smithson could arguably have any woman in the world. They were probably lining up for him. He was also, as Nicki so helpfully pointed out, pushing forty. If he truly was ready to settle down, chasing her around the globe had to be getting a little boring, or galling, or both.

Dimitri seemed to agree. "I can understand him not wanting to let you go," he said, with so much bold declaration to the words that it caught her off guard. "But you're right. Eventually, a man wants to draw in his nets and return to port, and not fish all day. I haven't asked Stefan about the media spin. We will determine that and see if what you suspect is true." He grinned at her, rolling his glass in his hand. "And then what? Say this man marries another, no longer worries about you. What will you do? You have the whole world at your feet."

Lauren laughed. "I'll work," she said, waving off Dimitri's startled scowl. "Hey, I enjoy working, and I haven't been able to focus recently as much as I have needed to do."

"Work!" he scoffed. "There will always be work to do. You should *live*." He slapped the table. "What do you do for fun? Besides playing drinking games in countries where you should know better. You go dancing, yes? Meet with friends?"

Lauren smiled ruefully. For as long as she could remember, her social life had been carefully monitored to ensure maximum visibility with minimal effort. And always—always, with a tight crowd of friends and hangers-on. To keep her insulated, protected. Protected from Henry. What would it be like to not have that as a concern anymore? "I go out with friends all the time," she said, hedging.

"What else? What do you do that you enjoy?" Dimitri was grinning at her, disarming her further.

"I have charity work, and social engagements, and—"

"Those are with other people. Say it is you, on your own, and you have the whole world to yourself. What would you do? Where would you go? To Paris? London?" He gestured with his glass. "There must be somewhere."

"What are you hounding me for?" She laughed. "Someplace like this, I guess. But with Wi-Fi. Someplace beautiful and near the sea. That's where I would go."

Thirty-Four

"Then you're very wise." Dimitri waved at the server, then turned to Lauren, fighting hard not to let her see the intensity of his gaze. "There are many beautiful places by the sea you should visit."

"Well, I'd want to see every one of them." Her full lips twisted, and he did his best not to stare at them. "I actually thought about focusing my work on something to do with resort cities, beachside hamlets—something. But the tourism market is already played out. Starting something new in that sector would take someone with a lot more experience than I have."

"Experience means nothing in the face of passion." Dimitri shrugged. "You want something, you do it. You should know that more than anyone. I cannot think you have let anything stand in your way for long, with the life you lead?"

He watched her closely as she tilted her head and laughed. There, it was happening again. A precision to her movements and words since he'd started asking her questions about the future. She didn't believe she would have a future, at least not one that didn't involve the threat of Smithson if she should ever be alone. Which meant she was still running scared.

She hadn't been precise when he'd been with her at the beach last night. Or when she'd been in his arms in his room today. She'd been lopsided and messy and glorious, the abandon with which she'd thrown herself into him a marvel to see. He yearned to see that expression on her face again, or perhaps the casual confidence and open-eyed wonder he'd seen when she was at the cove, pushing her way through all the hanging items of ocean debris. It was as if she was on vacation from her own life, but she would never admit that her life was one she needed to escape. No one was more aware than Lauren Grant of exactly how lucky Lauren Grant was.

But how lucky was anyone when they couldn't imagine a life that didn't include working in some godforsaken office some-where, always in the center of a crowd, if only to avoid a bogeyman that no one else feared? That was no way to exist.

The silence between them had apparently gone on too long, so she went on the offensive. Something else she did with grace and precision, and long years of practice, he suspected. "What about you? You'll be heading back into service, won't you, once your babysitting detail is over?"

He lifted both brows. "I wouldn't call what I've done here babysitting."

"You know what I mean." She smiled. Perfectly. "What is your next assignment, or whatever—or is your military more of a reactionary model, called into action only if needed?"

"There is always a need, whether on our own borders or for our allies." Dimitri shook his head. "We've had trouble with insurgents from Turkey of late, but that's nothing new. Refugees are a constant challenge for a country of our size and limited resources as well. There is a fine line between humanitarian aid and being overrun. So I'll review the status of our current mili-tary outposts, and see what needs are greatest. Cyril may have assignments in the works as well. He usually does." He eyed her. "There's also already talk of how to protect Emmaline when she returns to the US."

"If she returns." Lauren's smile was wistful for the barest moment before she modulated it again. "Who's to say Kristos won't marry her before the week is out?"

"The queen, for one." Dimitri grimaced. "She's obsessed with Emmaline's musical abilities, and if I know the woman at all, she will not rest until she sees her officially installed in an American orchestra. Emmaline seems to think that will require additional schooling?" Lauren nodded, and he curled his lip. "You Americans should do more without asking."

She laughed. "The music program she got into is very prestigious! She would learn a lot and get back into the practice of playing on a regular basis. And be near her family. Nearer, anyway."

Dimitri nodded. "The queen thought the same. But where Emmaline goes, Kristos will want to follow, and that gets more complicated. So there are decisions to be made there."

"Uh-huh." Lauren eyed him with speculation. "Queen Catherine isn't considering the possibility that their infatuation will play out, is she? Because I know Emmaline pretty well. And I don't see that happening."

"No one's more dedicated to romance than Queen Catherine, or enamored of the idea of a royal wedding within the next year." Dimitri grimaced. "But she's also fully aware that decisions made in haste must be lived with for a time to ensure that they are the right course. So anything that builds time into the equation for Kristos and Emmaline, she will embrace."

"Hmm, maybe." Lauren sat back, her eyes alight with mischief that for once wasn't carefully vetted. "Kristos in America would certainly cause a stir."

"Not only him." Dimitri shook his head. "He'd have a security detail—and not me." He cut her off before she asked the obvious question. "Someone has to actually *be* the military, not simply talk about it."

"Uh-huh." Her laughter was once again sincere, direct and refreshing. "And your dedication to home and country has nothing to do with your desire to stay close to the ongoing investigation into Ari's disappearance, I'm sure."

"I will, of course, be on hand for however the Crown needs me." He kept the words light, but he didn't miss Lauren's use of the word disappearance instead of death. He wasn't sure when she'd changed her characterization of Ari's plane crash, or if she was conscious of it. But he appreciated it no matter how it came to be.

Now she was looking at him with open frankness. "Is there really a chance? In all truth? For Ari to be alive after so long?"

Dimitri blew out a long breath. "In all truth? There's very little chance," he said. The words, so long unspoken, didn't hurt him as much as he thought they would. "Ari was as fiercely loyal to his family and country as any man ever was. He wouldn't rest but would be struggling to return. Where there is struggle, there is always a story." He shook his head. "There have been no stories about a man fighting to find his way home."

"There've been no stories about one dying in a fiery wreck either," Lauren said, her words staunch.

"And that's why my hope remains alive," Dimitri conceded. "Finding evidence of Ari's death will reopen the wound, yes. But it will be able to heal more cleanly then. And finding evidence of his life..." He spread his hands. "It would change everything."

"But how?" Lauren frowned, a new worry suddenly clouding her eyes. "If Ari returns, what happens to Kristos? Does that mean he's no longer the crown prince?"

Dimitri grinned. He'd wondered when or if that possibility would hit Lauren, with her tendency to want to stay in control of every life she came into contact with, most especially her friends'. "That's why we have councils and chief advisors, princess," he said. "All that is important is life and love. Kristos and Emmaline have both. Whether he is the head of the military or the head of the royal family, do you truly think she'll mind?"

Lauren's eyes flared, and Dimitri felt something hard shift in his chest, not a good feeling. "No-oo," Lauren said at length, and then she smiled one of her practiced smiles. "She wouldn't."

But Dimitri knew the truth. Emmaline wouldn't, not for a moment. Kristos would be a prince to her whether he was shoveling rocks for the Crown or attending gala parties dressed in his military finest, as long as she could be by his side. But Lauren was a different story. Lauren had spent her entire life categorizing people, judging them, putting them into boxes based upon their parents, the amount of money they had, their position in society. To her, it *would* matter.

Which meant he needed to end this farce between them before it became any more awkward for either of them.

He straightened, suddenly irritated, impatient, and desperate to move again, but he was too late. Lauren lifted a hand, her gaze trapping his. "Dimitri—wait."

He waited, not willing to give her any quarter. If she had questions to ask, she could damn well ask them herself. At his stubborn silence, her cheeks flared a soft pink beneath her new tan, and her eyes shifted slightly. Going harder, more resolute. This woman shifted more swiftly than stormclouds in springtime, and Dimitri knew in that moment he wanted to be there for every pivot, every fresh tack.

He was a fool.

"Okay, we'll do this your way too," Lauren said. She leaned forward as he blinked, recalling his words from just a few short hours before. "You're a demigod." Her words were low, flat, and unhurried. "What does that mean? In short, simple words your basic twenty-first century mortal can understand? And before you think about saying something stupid or flip, know that I'm not willingly moving from this table until you tell me. I will scream, I will burst into tears, I will create a story that will last however long your lifetime is. So talk and put us both out of our misery."

Dimitri curled his lip, but her bald address of the question between them was probably for the best. It didn't mean he had to like it. "I'm a demigod, descended of Zeus." He watched the questions surge in her eyes and felt marginal relief as she lashed down her curiosity. Lauren Grant knew when to keep quiet in an interrogation, he'd give her that.

"Not all descendants qualify," he explained further. "It takes a certain mix of genetics. But I had that mix, and that meant I had two potential life paths before me. I could take the advantage of my distant parentage and live a life of strength and agility, power and health, abundance—all the rest. Or I could go further. I could take on the mantle of protection for the Crown of Oûros, and serve their needs. If I chose to do that, I would have everything that any ordinary descendent with my genetic makeup had—just more of it. More strength, more vitality, keener eyesight and hearing, stronger intuition, longer life. At the age of twenty, I was given a choice."

"So young," she murmured, but the way she was staring at him, he didn't think she realized she'd spoken.

He shrugged. "I'd served two years in the military by then. I was old enough to know where my heart and loyalties rested. I was ready to serve my king and country, and to accept the challenge. That was sixty years ago."

"Sixty!" Lauren's beautiful eyes flared wide, and he could see the calculation in them, the assessments, arguments and rejection of said arguments, the realization...and the dismay. Another wave of anger swamped him.

"Sixty," he agreed. "For every ten years of a mortal's life, I age one, and will until I am killed in service to the Crown or eventually die a normal death many, many decades from now. And now you know everything you need to."

He leaned forward again, his urgency to move returning. "Do you have anything back at the villa that you need, should we have to leave quickly?"

She blinked at him, whether at the sudden shift in his question or in his tone. But she recovered a moment later, the smile she offered him gracious, carefully even. Once again protecting herself, he thought. But from what? He was no threat to her. And he damned well would protect her from Henry. She had to still know that—even if she now regarded him as some sort of freak.

"Not really," she said. "I'm, ah, happy to go clean up your place, though. I kind of left it a mess—"

He cut off her words with a lifted hand. "There's no need for that." He wouldn't mind his villa filled with small remembrances of the American, for a few days anyway. He didn't want to consider the reasons why too closely, but then again, he didn't have to. "I'll check in with Cyril and see about that boat."

As he pulled out his phone, she pushed back her chair. "There are restrooms here, yes?" she asked, her expression grateful as he pointed to the far corner of the restaurant. "Great. I'll be right back."

He watched her go for a moment, memorizing her walk, her grace, the swing of her hips. He would have an unusually long lifetime to revisit those images after she left him for good, so he needed all he could tuck away.

Get a hold of yourself. Growling, he punched the buttons on the phone and turned once more toward the sea.

Thirty-Five

Lauren pulled her phone out of her purse as she walked through the restaurant, the movement so rote that she allowed her smile to turn from fixed to rueful.

It didn't matter now if anyone caught a glimpse of her face. Dimitri had seen right through her back there, regardless of how quickly she'd recovered from the idea of Kristos being supplanted as future king by his brother. A brother who was quite possibly dead anyway, so that made the entire conversation a moot point.

It wasn't moot, though. The practical ramifications of Ari's return had tripped her up, her natural competitiveness and class rules surging forth at the idea that Emmaline might somehow get less than the prince she deserved.

"What is *wrong* with you?" she muttered.

And then she'd made things even worse, pushing him on the whole demigod thing, questioning his life choices, undoubtedly expressing her surprise and even chagrin that he wasn't the vibrant twenty-seven-year-old man he looked like but a damned-near immortal who'd been rolling around this earth for eighty years. *Eighty!* She couldn't even wrap her head around that.

And if he was eighty, then the old woman she'd met...and his supposed "sister"...

"Leave it alone," she ordered herself fiercely, biting out the words as she reached the back of the restaurant. She should leave it alone. It was none of her business. She was an interloper in Dimitri's life, an assignment he didn't want, even if he wanted her body and the lovemaking they'd shared. That hadn't been an act, she knew it hadn't.

She twisted her lips. Nothing about Dimitri was an act. That was her specialty. He was a long-lived warrior of a fairy-tale kingdom, and she was just a mess.

Instead of leading only to a bathroom, the corridor angled sharply, emptying into a small outdoor courtyard open on one side to a cobbled lane. Lauren stepped out into the shadowy space. It was lovely, but only a few diners were out here—the views from the front of the restaurant kept most inside or on the front sidewalk.

She thumbed on her phone, almost dropping it when it buzzed unexpectedly in her hand.

Texts. A lot of texts. More than should have been possible in the short while since she'd last checked.

The reality of the situation quickly dawned on her. There'd been some sort of lag between reaching cell phone reception or Wi-Fi access and her phone loading up with the texts that she'd received. And though she'd talked to her sister yesterday, apparently that had been time enough for some new drama to strike.

Lauren clicked on the text icon, which flipped over to a white screen, the information slowly loading. She moved to the edge of the courtyard and slipped through the gate to the cobbled walk. Dimitri was going to be tied up awhile with his own phone call, and he'd doubtless figure out where she went and come collect her soon enough. And besides, if she was right, this walk would intersect with the main street in a few steps.

She could make the full circuit and be back to him before he knew she was gone.

The last text of seven popped up, and Lauren froze.

OMG, it's a diamond necklace!

There was a picture embedded in the text that made her blood run cold. She clicked on it, her heart in her throat. The image showed a beautiful white diamond necklace on black velvet, something far more sophisticated than anything a four-teen-year-old girl would normally wear, but it wasn't the neck-lace that brought her up short.

She enlarged the photo to see the package more clearly, the crisp paper folded away—stark and lovely...

And black-and-white.

With shaking hands, Lauren went back to Maddie's first text. She had started texting her, though this wasn't Lauren's actual phone. She was fourteen: she hadn't cared. And her initial text was bright and breezy, and from all of twenty-four hours ago. *Mom and Dad called me three times... Haven't asked about you again... Boarding school sucks...*

The second and third were more of the same, but the fourth was markedly different. *"OMG I have a secret admirer! I bet it's William. He sent me this!"* Lauren didn't realize she'd stopped in the street again until a flood of concerned Oûrois pulled her attention away, and she quickly sidestepped the couple she'd almost knocked off their feet.

"Excuse me, excuse me—" she murmured, turning away from the restaurant and heading in the opposite direction. The glow of her screen showed a beautiful collection of black-and-white roses. The next text was more happy speculation. *William? Joe? Mom & Dad being weird and worried?*

Lauren's heart thudded painfully. It was almost verbatim what she'd said to her own friends when she was Maddie's age. That was when the presents from Henry had become more personal, less a kind family friend remembering her on her birthday and at Christmas. That was when the flowers had first shown up, and the jewelry too. She'd kept all of it at the beginning. She hadn't known for sure they were from Henry, and she'd made up elaborate possibilities of who they could really be from. It had taken her a full two years to actually accept for sure that everything was coming from Henry, a man fifteen years her senior. Which for a teenager was—gross.

And now he was starting the cycle all over again with her little sister. Only Maddie wouldn't be prepared for it. She'd been completely sheltered from the world, at Lauren's insistence. Which meant that now she was completely unprotected. Assuming he wasn't just doing this to lure Lauren into his trap.

"No, no, no..." Lauren moaned as she clicked through the fifth text, then the sixth, where Maddie was sharing the excitement of receiving the message on her phone that a present would be arriving soon. Her personal phone—which was a *private* number, available *only* to the family. To Maddie, this was, of course, the coolest thing ever, since the guy had to be smart, some kind of hacker, as well as rich and sweet and...

Lauren lifted her head and stared into the distance, clutching the phone to her chest. She had to call Maddie now. She had to report Henry and protect her sister. This wasn't about her anymore, wasn't something she could manage, something she could explain away or hope would go away on its own. She had to finally get her parents to see what was going on.

Even as she thought the words, her mind ran through a million scenarios, none of them good. Her parents were wrapped around Henry's finger—so was the media, so were the cops. It'd been the same when she'd first tried to explain her misgivings back when she was a teen. Her mom hadn't believed her, hadn't wanted to believe her. Henry was a family friend.

He only wanted the best for her. Lauren should be flattered, not freaked out.

And as to these new gifts for Maddie, she could hear the excuses in her head: Henry probably felt bad—probably wanted Lauren to realize he was a good guy, a caring guy, to give such a lovely present to the innocent, sweet Maddie, who was gracious enough to accept beautiful things with a happy, open heart. Unlike Lauren, so ungrateful, unreasonable, un—

The phone buzzed in her hand.

Lauren wrenched the phone from her chest, her hands trembling so badly, it took her three times to thumb on the phone. When the text screen flared to life once more, her adrenaline jacked.

Got you.

She whirled around, but the street was unchanged. No one was there. The darkness suddenly seemed oppressive, though. And when the phone buzzed again, she knew why.

I appreciate a good chase as much as the next person, but we both know how this one is going to end.

All the blood drained out of Lauren's head, and she swayed a little on her feet. Instantly, automatically, she mapped out her best plan of action. She should go to Dimitri. Intellectually, she knew that. She should go to Dimitri and the authorities and her parents and...

What? Tell them Henry Smithson had given a lovely spray of roses and a diamond necklace to her little sister and that was wrong somehow? Who would believe her, beyond Dimitri? And what would he do? He was a demigod... did that mean he'd just break heads first, ask questions later? Knowing Dimitri, he'd make some sort of scene, and that was no good. Right now, Henry had no idea that she knew Dimitri as anything more than a bodyguard. Based on what he'd done to her last boyfriend, if he knew the truth, Henry would probably...

Her phone buzzed again.

There is a small fisherman's port on the south side of Mira-nos, west of the main town, which I assume is where you are. Be there in an hour, or I will happily send another gift to your sister. She's not you. She might not enjoy it as much.

Lauren's eyes flared wide. She turned back to the water. It was too far to go to on foot. She'd never make it, and she didn't have time to waste.

Would he hurt Maddie? Was he actually even sending her things? He'd gotten Alexi's number, after all. Had he somehow gotten hold of Maddie's as well? Could you fake texts and photos? Probably. But that wasn't the point. The point was it would be easy for him to *start* harassing Maddie, as easy as it had been for him to harass her. Her parents wouldn't stop it, might not even see the problem. In the end, only she could stop it.

And she would stop it, one way or the other. It was long past time for that.

She keyed back a response, clear and concise. She did have a way to stop this, of course. And in the end, it was so simple. It'd always been the simplest course. Just not the easiest. But there was nothing she could do about that now.

She started moving up the street again, her hand shaking as she clutched her phone. Dimitri was making his call, but how long would that last? If he went looking for her, he'd start with the bathroom, then go outside to the courtyard. Only then would he circle around, so if she moved fast...

The rover was right where they'd left it when they'd bounced into town, both of them so full of passion and possibility, it had made her heart hurt.

Oh, what a difference a few hours made.

She got into the rover and turned the key.

Thirty-Six

Dimitri leaned back in his chair. The ONSF speedboat was almost at the main marina, and there were no signs of it being followed, according to Cyril. The Smithson yacht was almost to the southern tip of Greece at this point, with no indication of putting in at port anytime soon. They hadn't confirmed that Henry was aboard his yacht, however, which didn't sit well with him. There were literally dozens of privately owned yachts in the area, and Smithson could easily have commandeered any one of them, while his yacht sailed merrily along to some other port of call.

But that wasn't going to be an issue. The speedboat was heavily armed and boldly marked with the ONSF letters. If it was delayed or attacked in any way, Smithson would have a battle on his hands.

"Where's Lauren?" It wasn't Cyril on the line, but Stefan. "We've been monitoring unusual call activity into her phone."

"Calls?" Dimitri frowned, his gaze skating to the back of the restaurant, registering how long Lauren had been gone. "Her phone hasn't rung since we arrived here. She spoke with Nicki and Emmaline, texted her sister, but that was yesterday." He stood, throwing money down on the table. "What kind of calls?"

A few quick strides took him to the back of the restaurant, where the bathroom door stood slightly ajar—the room empty inside.

"The number has been scrambled, that's why the concern. You say she's had text communication with her sister?"

Dimitri opened his mouth to reply, but a different voice sounded on the other end of the phone. The no-nonsense snap of Nicki Clark. "I'm sure she has. What's wrong?"

"That was well handled."

"Focus on your own American," Stefan said coolly. "Can you access the phone?"

Dimitri stepped outside and swept the courtyard with his gaze. Shit. "I can't access the woman right now." He turned back into the restaurant as a familiar rumble caught his attention. His attention sprang to the cobblestoned alley that led to the street. *Shit!*

"She's on the move." He bolted through the courtyard and into the alley, but he knew it was too late. He scanned the street, identifying two dozen people he knew. "What was in those texts? Her sister texted her?"

"We're confirming that now. Secure Ms. Grant."

"Working on it. Call me when you can say something useful."

Dimitri stowed the phone and stalked up to the first table he could spot, men and women he'd known since birth. Not a minute later, he was racing toward their rover. He tossed his phone on the seat and reached in his pocket for another device, a cell phone not unlike Lauren's but keyed to the same feed as his sat phone. It had only one function.

A small screen flared to life, a green dot in its center, moving fast. Based on her trajectory, there could be only one place

Lauren was heading. But what was she doing going to the fisherman's pier?

The phone beside him buzzed three minutes later. By this point, he'd cleared the town limits, and he had Lauren's rover in his sight. He also had a pistol and knife on his body, but no other weapons. There was a locked gun case in Lauren's rover, but it held only the one weapon, and he didn't have time to stop at his house.

He picked up the phone. "Report."

Stefan launched in. "No texts from the sister. She's on the phone with Nicki, said the last she heard from Lauren was yesterday. No communication since then. Nicki confirms Lauren's assertion that Maddie's phone number was private, used by her and the sister alone, but it's not unreasonable that Smithson discovered and cloned it at some point, as close as he positioned himself to the family. Once Lauren pinged that number, tracking it back to her on Miranos would have been simple enough."

"Son of a bitch." Dimitri squinted toward the water, following the lights of the beach rovers. Only one was moving at speed, but there were enough machines on the beach that he might not be immediately noticed. He wasn't sure how well versed Lauren was in evading pursuit, but he didn't get the impression she cared so much right now. She was moving too quickly, with too much focus. She was meeting someone who was already in place.

"Where's Smithson?"

"Still no sighting.

"Lauren's heading somewhere fast, I think to meet him. How far away is the ONSF boat?"

"Not far. Redivert to where she's heading?"

Dimitri considered it. "Where would the bastard be if he's not aboard his own boat? How many likely options?"

It took Stefan only a minute to respond. "Three options, one of which hasn't radioed in the last twenty-four hours. Pleasure cruiser now anchored close enough to Miranos to be a possibility, if they have a speedboat. Getting the data."

"Nationality?"

"Turkish."

Dimitri blew out a breath. Better if it was Oûrois, but the Turks didn't take appropriation of their nationals' property lightly. If Smithson had boarded the boat without the owners' permission.... "Can you get a man on that boat, make him look like he's not official ONSF? If Smithson is still there, I don't want to startle him into doing something stupid if we can help it."

"Of course. How much time?"

"Sooner the better." Dimitri cut the wheel and headed out onto the sand. He'd let Lauren get far enough ahead now that he knew where he was going. Hopefully, she'd slow down as well, maybe lose her nerve.

He remembered her talking about her sister. Not likely she'd lose her nerve. "I need those texts."

"Working on it."

"Ready the speedboat, but don't move it. Again, I don't want Smithson spooked, if that's who's behind Lauren's flight, which it almost has to be."

Stefan paused. "He could be picking up Ms. Grant as a point of mutual concession. She could want to go with him for some reason."

Dimitri grimaced. "That's what I'm afraid of."

He cut the line and roared ahead, cursing Lauren and her stupidity. For once, she'd overthought the problem from all the angles but one. She should have trusted him to at least go with her. Smithson was dangerous, probably even crazy. But setting aside his natural dominance as a demigod, Dimitri was a trained professional, used to risking his life for his country.

And he was more than willing to risk it for her.

He ditched the rover when he was an eighth of a mile out, and continued on foot to the dock. The place was quiet now, save for a few diehards at the bar. Easy for a boat to sneak into one of the unoccupied slips, especially if they weren't staying long. Miranos was too small a concern, especially in this secondary port, to be sticklers about short-termers. Sooner or later, everyone needed a place to land.

But as soon as Dimitri reached the port, he realized his mistake. He saw the rover, but Lauren wasn't standing on the dock, and she wasn't in the lighted area of the bar either. More importantly, there weren't any boats with Turkish lettering that he could see nosing up to the dock. The dock itself was more deserted than usual, and the boats looked as if they belonged there, all of them fishing craft. Probably anyone out to sea had stayed out, weathering the storm and putting in elsewhere now that the sun had set.

Still, where had Lauren gone? The small cove they'd visited earlier today was too tricky for any large boat to enter, though a dinghy could certainly navigate the shallow waters. But why take the extra chance? What had Lauren offered that had made it worth Smithson's while to play the game...unless it was the game itself that had attracted him? She knew the man better than probably anyone did. What was she thinking?

Then his eyes returned to his rover. There was that spare gun locked beneath the seat—had she taken it?

He moved swiftly over to the side of the rover, leaning into the back of it. The box was there, apparently locked, but when he lifted it, he frowned—it was heavy. The gun remained inside. As he flipped the box on its side, though, he noticed the paper fluttering in the breeze.

Using his phone as a flashlight, he pointed it at the paper. Lauren's script handwriting showed in the dim glow, stark and sure.

Please don't worry about me. I've got this.

There was only one place she could've gone on foot. He headed for the cove at a dead run.

Thirty-Seven

Lauren stepped past the last swaying piece of sea junk, her gaze on the far ocean. She could see a small yacht far enough out to miss the reef, though she had no idea if it was Henry's. Had he really come this close, or did he have friends on the high seas? Or, yet more likely, had he commandeered someone's boat for his own use?

The dinghy pulled up on the beach was a different story. It was large enough to hold six people, yet only three men stood next to it. Two of them with guns, the other apparently unarmed, staring off to sea. Henry.

She didn't have long to wait for the others. Two men appeared on either side of her, walking her out to where Smithson stood. She was glad for the full moon that had come out now that the heavy storm clouds had scudded away, glad for the white sand beach. But mostly glad that she hadn't given in to her impulse to bring Dimitri's gun with her. She wasn't a bad shot, but this wasn't a paper target. It was a man. And there were better ways to kill a man than with a gun you'd never tried to shoot before. She simply had to be patient, go with him. She'd have her chance.

Eventually.

Smithson turned as she moved up to him. "Lauren," he said, opening his arms to her. It took every ounce of practice and restraint for her to stop with a small gasp and stiffen. Henry was no idiot. He'd be expecting her to be afraid of him.

She *was* afraid of him, but she was also so furious that it overrode her panic. She wanted to throttle this man, but more importantly, she wanted to keep Maddie safe. So she needed to play this right on the razor's edge. Afraid but not mute, angry but not stupid. Always aware that he held the upper hand, until she found a way to change that.

Henry's hard smile showed her that she'd executed her first move well. When she would have backed up, the two men flanking her held her steady, allowing Henry to approach her. "Your vacation has done you well, Lauren. You had to know I'd find you."

"I didn't think you'd look." It was a gamble, but it paid off. Henry visibly relaxed, shaking his head as if she were an enigma.

"You say that, and yet when have I given any indication that I wouldn't be here when the time was right? You always seem surprised to hear from me. Why is that, Lauren?"

Lauren swallowed, then voiced the words that had so long run through her head. "I'm one woman, Henry. Like any other woman. I have no idea why you find me so interesting when you could have anyone in the world—anyone." *Anyone except Maddie, you slimy son of a bitch.*

"But that's the wonder of it, isn't it? I chose you. I vetted you before you were out of the cradle, planned for this day. Watched you grow, develop. I was the one who suggested the dancing lessons, do you know that?"

Lauren blinked at him, her lip curling in instinctive disgust. "I hated those classes."

"I know," Henry said, satisfaction thick in his voice. "That made it infinitely better, the idea that I could direct you, force you and your parents into activities you would never willingly have taken on otherwise. But I directed your lessons, your food, your friends. It was...exhilarating. And then when you started reaching your teen years and I saw the beauty you would become, it was as if an entire new vista of opportunity opened up to me. I *made* you, Lauren Grant."

"You didn't make anything about me." Lauren's rage boiled out of control. She wanted to spit Henry's words back at him, and she hated that she recognized the defensiveness within herself. She always reacted most strongly when the accuser was right. Could Henry be *right*? Had she changed who she was in reaction to him? The very thought revolted her, and she forced herself to open her eyes wider, her voice breaking. "You didn't."

"I did." He turned to speak to his men. "You two, stay here. You," he indicated the pair that had flanked her. "Come along. I find I'm not done with the chase yet."

"What do you mean?" Lauren watched nervously as the men took their positions by the boat. "Where are we going?"

"Don't look so frightened." Henry's laugh betrayed his enjoyment of the moment. "I merely thought it would be invigorating to take advantage of the lovely evening on a Greek island and take a tour around the beach. The men told me that there were some unusual sculptures hanging from the trees, and I know you've already seen them. We should have a look at them together."

"It's just a bunch of junk washed up from the sea."

"But junk someone has seen fit to hang. That makes it art, don't you agree?" He curved her arm into his, and she didn't give him the satisfaction of making him tug her across the sand. She moved with him easily, her head high. Why hadn't she taken Dimitri's gun? The men hadn't frisked her when she'd come out of the trees. Then again, they hadn't needed to. Her shift was thin. A gun would've been immediately obvious.

"I never would have picked you to run away, you know," Henry said. "Not in an obvious way like that. It proved an invigorating diversion."

"I'm not ready to get married."

"But I am, and as my wife, you need to get more in the habit of thinking of what is best for the two of us, and not simply for yourself."

Lauren steadied herself, willing her skin to stop crawling. Maybe that's why he'd sent her so many bugs over the years. To prepare her for this moment. "I hadn't thought of it that way," she said at length, since Henry was clearly waiting for some sort of response.

He chuckled. "You see? It's a matter of perspective. And I've waited so long for this. Your father proved a hard man to convince, but he had his leverage points. Everyone does." He drew in a deep, satisfied breath. "He taught me that himself."

Leverage points? What was he talking about?

In the end, though, it didn't matter. Nothing mattered now that Maddie was at risk. "If I come with you, you'll stop bothering my sister?"

"My dear Lauren, your sister is of no real interest to me. You've coddled her from the time she was born. She isn't strong enough." But as Lauren allowed a tiny breath of relief to escape, Henry squeezed her arm. "Though she is useful, I must admit. So no, I can't say I won't draw upon her influence once again. Though only for something I really, really want."

Lauren closed her eyes, sending out a silent plea that Dimitri was somewhere in the forest around them, that he'd completely ignored her hurried note to him. Would he know this was where she'd headed? Had he even noticed she'd left?

She must have betrayed her hopes somehow. Henry leaned

close. "And lest you be concerned about your bodyguard following you, I have additional men in the trees in case he should be that foolish. We're quite safe."

Additional men? She knew Dimitri was trained military on top of being a demigod, and that he wasn't an idiot. She also knew that he was far more familiar with this cluster of sea junk than Henry's men moving through the shadows. That said, they were *expecting* him. They were prepared. While he didn't know they were out there...because she hadn't told him what she was doing. *Stupid!*

She slanted Henry a glance. They were moving among the waving bits of boat and airplane, driftwood and shells. "Well, if you think he's going to come after you, shouldn't we be getting out of here?"

"Not yet."

Henry stopped in the center of the hanging sculptures and drew her close. She tilted her head up to him, forcing herself to play the role, to keep her cool. It wasn't easy as Henry leaned forward and kissed her forehead, then trembled himself in reaction to the movement. He drew his mouth over to her ear, and she held completely still, unsure of what he wanted. Should she hug him? Stay limp in his arms? Things had never progressed between them beyond dancing and formal embraces. He'd never so much as kissed her. How awful would that be?

Henry's mouth blew hot breath against her ear, and she did sway then, moving forward to lay her hands on his chest. "You've done such a good job so far, Lauren," he murmured in her ear. "You've learned so much. I truly don't believe you've done anything inappropriate with that hulking bodyguard, if only because your tender heart couldn't abide another man being harmed because of you. It's unfortunate that your discretion won't matter, in this case."

Lauren's eyes went wide as her brain registered Henry's

words. She reared back, her lips curling into a startled sneer. "The *bodyguard?*" she said loudly, too loudly, so she dropped her tone to more of a growl. "You can't think I did anything with him, Henry. Give me some credit."

Her heart hammered as he studied her, but whatever was in her face must have convinced him, at least somewhat. "Oh, I don't. But he couldn't be in your presence this long without lusting after you. And he *did* defy me, taking you. So he's going to have to go."

"No." Lauren pressed her hands against Henry's chest, so soft and narrow compared to Dimitri's. "You don't want to cause an international incident, not over this. It isn't worth it, and the royal family sets great store by that man. If we're to be invited to Kristos and Emmaline's wedding, you can't do anything to harm him, I'm serious."

Henry's teeth flashed. "Now that's what I mean by couple thinking." And he leaned forward to kiss her.

Thirty-Eight

Dimitri held himself in place, allowing the rage to boil off him. He didn't know what Henry and Lauren were arguing about, but he'd heard Lauren's rejection of him. Hell, half the island could have heard her shocked indignation regarding "the bodyguard." What had Henry asked her? Why had she reacted so strongly?

There was a chance she'd done it so he could hear her, and he held on to that idea as he tracked the two men moving stealthily through the trees. Scratch that, more than a chance.

The information that Stefan had finally radioed him about the text messages had been easy to understand. An excited teenager babbling about gifts and flowers from an unknown admirer. They hadn't gotten the pictures locked down yet, but they didn't need to. Lauren would have taken the bait completely, believed that Smithson had sent her little sister something—good or bad, it didn't matter. She'd clearly understood the message for what it was: a threat.

And now she was here, thinking that she could solve everything by sacrificing herself. She wasn't Emmaline, for whom that kind of sacrifice was second nature. Lauren had made it her business to avoid sacrifices. The fact that she was giving herself up so easily was probably the best indicator of how desperate she was.

Did she know he was out here, closing in on her? She had to. She'd written the note.

Regardless, he needed to focus on the task at hand. The men skulking around the perimeter of the sculpture garden were on the watch for him. They wouldn't be as easy to take out as the men by the boat—those two had been on the ground and out cold before they'd known he was there. These two men had night-vision goggles, however, doubtless with a heat sensor. Which ordinarily would give them the distinct advantage.

But Dimitri had worked a long, long time in the ranks of the ONSF before getting anything close to proper equipment. He'd learned how to evade nearly every military enhancement out there, using his wits and guile if he had nothing more reliable.

Now he perched motionless on a tree branch, watching the men beneath him. A quiet kill probably wasn't going to happen tonight. A kill of any sort would be against ONSF protocol, because kills meant explanations and explanations invited attention the royal family never wanted or needed. Besides, there wasn't any official threat here. Lauren had come to this grotto of her own free will. Henry wasn't binding her, he was.... Dimitri shifted his gaze back to Henry. And froze.

The bastard was making out with Lauren.

A new flood of anger suffused him as he watched Lauren tilt her head back at a precise angle, accepting Henry's attentions as if she hadn't just made love to Dimitri mere hours before. Her body sagged as if in sensual abandon, and she lifted one hand to Smithson's bicep—a bicep that barely filled out the loose suit jacket that encased it. And who wore a suit to an island?

A snap beneath Dimitri drew his attention back, and he scowled. Henry's bodyguards weren't bad, but they also weren't trained in jungle recon. They were much too far apart from each other. An animal could easily come between them, and neither would be able to defend the other while keeping himself protected. The two were doubtless in contact via headset, though. So one of them dropping flat would raise an alarm.

He lifted his head and scanned the forest. The other man was nearing the sea sculptures, which were swaying in the light breeze, near where Henry and Lauren stood. The moment the guard stepped into the mass of shifting metal, however, Dimitri could hear the sudden crackle of the other man's headset beneath him. The guy shook his head, tapping his ear, and Dimitri's gaze leapt back to the man in the sculpture garden. Interference. From the airplane wreckage? He had no idea. He'd never tried radio communications out on this point.

He leaned forward, and the branch beneath him creaked. Just a little, barely a breath of a sigh. But it was enough to draw the attention of the guard below him.

By the time that man looked up, however, Dimitri had dropped down on him, heavy and sure. He didn't want to kill the guy, so he struck him forcefully on the side of his head. The guard fell like a sack of potatoes, and Dimitri fell with him, cradling his body and going flat as he searched the man and divested him of gun, knife—and headset.

"Can't fucking hear anything." He could hear the exasperated English words coming through the headset in scratchy confusion. Dimitri rubbed his thumb against the microphone and murmured nonsense, then tucked the thing in his pants pocket and headed out as the man on the other end hissed a response. Now that he was on the ground, Dimitri was vulnerable again to the night-vision goggles, but as long as the other guy stayed in the sculpture garden, he was safe.

He moved forward carefully until he could find another blind. A break in the moving panels afforded him a clear view into the center of the sculpture garden, where Smithson was now holding Lauren in his arms, gazing down at her as if she was the answer to all his prayers.

Dimitri watched her too, drinking in the view. She smiled up at Smithson with perfect ease, as if she wasn't in fear for her sister's and probably her own life. He could have stared at her all night, if there wasn't the feeling of impending doom closing in. What would Henry do to Lauren once he got her aboard the Turkish yacht that Dimitri had already spied off the coast? What had he already done to the owners of that craft? He'd broken laws without any concern about paybacks, and his every action was that of a spoiled and entitled multibillionaire, too powerful to worry about the niceties of international law.

This was the man who Lauren was handing herself over to. Willingly. Eagerly even. Rather than waiting for Dimitri to devise a better plan. She was so certain that a psychopath like Smithson was someone that she could get through with merely the proper head tilt and studied smile. That she could handle him better than anyone else.

Dimitri tightened his hand on his gun. *The hell with that.*

Affixing the night-vision goggles to his head, he swept the space for the other of Smithson's men and moved through the trees. He'd need to find that guard, but he'd taken his measure already. He simply needed to take out guy number two, then get the jump on Henry and—

The small scream coming from the center of the sculpture garden caught him up short.

So did the gun at his temple.

A third man. He should have expected that.

Swiftly, expertly, while he held the gun pressed up against Dimitri's head, the man lifted his other hand. A knife flashed in the moonlight, and a searing pain exploded in Dimitri's left shoulder before he could block the blow. The guard ripped the knife down and out, and blood immediately welled in the wound. Dimitri staggered but straightened as the man leaned close, the gun never leaving Dimitri's temple.

"I took out the last guard myself, so he's no longer a problem for either of us." The man spoke the low words in English, but his accent was Greek. "I assume you handled the two at the boat?" At Dimitri's nod, the man continued. "Smithson wants you delivered alive. It suits my purposes for the moment. But don't tempt me, eh?"

The man quickly and cleanly divested Dimitri of all his weapons and electronics. This wasn't an amateur. This man had been the real threat all along, which was why Dimitri hadn't seen him. The other two had been a distraction...and had probably never known it.

There was something else about the man, too. Something in the salty scratch of his voice, his wild eyes, the sun-baked skin visible around the mask. Something in the way he carried himself...and the hint of an bold lightning bolt tattoo at his neck.

But why would a fellow demigod of Zeus betray him like this?

"I suggest that you come out now, Mr. Korba," Henry's voice rang out. "Unless you want to see Ms. Grant's pretty throat get sliced open."

Thirty-Nine

Lauren froze as the bushes crashed, feeling the bite of the blade at her neck. Henry had moved more quickly than she thought he could. He'd palmed the knife easily after a whir of static had buzzed between them, apparently from some sort of headset she hadn't noticed in his ear. A second later, his hand was around her throat, gripping her hard enough to bruise. That hand had been replaced with the flat of a thick blade, which now cut into her with cold threat. A thin stream of blood trickled down her neck.

She hated herself for trembling, for the rush of adrenaline and fear that jolted through her system, sending her up on her toes. She wasn't going to make a run for it, and she wasn't going to fight. Not here. Not like this. Not with Dimitri so close. She'd seen what Henry could do to people from afar. She had no idea what he was capable of up close.

Henry, in contrast, seemed relaxed, at ease. Uncaring or unmoved she bled. She didn't say a word, and when the brush moved again and Dimitri stepped out with another man beside him, gun to his temple, she schooled her response to one of average, run of the mill terror. Never mind that when she saw him, she wanted to press against the knife and wound herself more, if only to distract Henry.

"Lose the knife," Dimitri said gruffly.

"I don't think you're in a position to make demands," Henry said, and then Lauren saw something more, the blood blooming on Dimitri's shoulder from what looked like a heavily bleeding gash. Had he been shot? Wouldn't she have heard that? No—no. His clothes were rent with a thick slash. That wound had been made by a knife. He was a demigod, but he could be hurt. He could be killed. She stared in horror, and Henry leaned down to nuzzle her ear.

"There, there, darling. I know this must be alarming. But you must understand the power you have over men. This might make you understand why it is so important that we marry now, before someone like this begins to think he has a chance with you."

"He never—" Lauren said hotly, but Henry only laughed.

"Oh, believe me, I know, my Echidna. You wouldn't waste your time or your body on some bootlicking bodyguard stinking of fish and filth. But that doesn't mean he didn't entertain *aspirations*. And it's that insult that I cannot abide. Among so many other things."

"He didn't insult me, Henry." Lauren's voice was clear and high, and she could only hope it sounded imperious, but reasonable. The name Henry had called her was his pet joke—emphasis on pet. She'd looked that up, too, years ago—and then only the barest minimum. The goddess wasn't some ethereal beauty, but a half-woman, half-snake monster stuck in some horrible cave. She hadn't cared enough to raise a fuss over it, but it seemed especially abhorrent for him to call her that there, now, when she could barely focus on anything but Dimitri's shoulder. "He barely spoke to me. He was here to protect me and make sure I didn't go anywhere else. That's all."

"Is that all, *Dimitri?*" Henry's words were a taunt. "Then you wouldn't mind this, I suppose." Lauren felt Henry's hands shift, felt him grip the thin cloth of her sundress. Before she could draw another breath, Henry ripped it ruthlessly down and away, exposing her bra and the curve of her breast.

"Henry!" she protested with a gasp.

But Henry wasn't looking at her. He was looking at Dimitri, who stared at them from across the clearing with murder in his eyes. Beside him, Henry's bodyguard never wavered from his ready position, the gun point-blank at Dimitri's head.

"That's right, isn't it," Henry said, and she tensed as his hand moved to palm the weight of her breast in his hand, rubbing it coarsely. "You can see, can't you darling? See the fury and possession in his gaze? He's a disgusting, rutting bull. If I hadn't come today, God only knows what he would have done to you."

"Let go of her," Dimitri growled. He sounded like he was going to rip Henry limb from limb. Henry clearly noticed it too.

"Insufferable, isn't it?" he murmured. "He has to go."

"What?" Lauren did pull away from Henry now. "Are you insane? You can't kill him. You don't need to kill anyone. I'm going with you, Henry, and the bodyguard is going home. Home," she said more clearly when Henry didn't move and Dimitri didn't either. She tried again. "I'm not going to start our married life with the blood of an innocent man on my hands. Let him go now, and let's get out of here."

Henry looked at her a long minute. "You know I'd do anything for you, darling," he said, sighing heavily. "Why don't you go and say good-bye to him personally? I know he'll appreciate that. Here." He tucked her dress up beneath her strap, rendering her slightly more presentable. "That should help."

"I don't want to say good-bye to him." The quick jerk of Henry's gaze to her eyes sent a surge of satisfaction rushing through Lauren. *Insufferable prick.* He'd been testing her, wanting to watch her with Dimitri. It wasn't a bad move. The bloodstain was only gathering in intensity at Dimitri's shoulder. If he didn't get out of there soon and back to the rover, would he have the strength to get to a hospital? Or whatever passed for a hospital on this island? She straightened under Henry's shrewd gaze. "I want to leave."

Henry's smile was affectionate again, truly affectionate. Then he pulled her roughly into his body, his hand around her neck, smearing the blood from where he'd sliced her neck. She winced but didn't stop him from pressing against her, because if that got them out of there more quickly, she was all for it.

Henry laughed against her, the sound low and unhinged.

"I want to make love to you," he all but groaned into her ear. "Here, now. With that beast watching."

"What? No!" Lauren went rigid as Henry stepped away from her. He took off his jacket and tossed it over one of the hanging pieces of plane sculpture, and shot out his cuffs. That was when she saw the gun stuck into his waistband.

"Henry, you can't be serious," she said, not needing to fake her desperation. "I'm not going to make love to you here in front of *strangers.* It will be our first time! Surely we can come up with something more romantic."

"You're my wife, or you will be. You need to start acting like it."

Lauren couldn't help it—she curled her lip. Henry laughed at her expression. "You'll learn soon enough. I think your first lesson should be now."

"*No.*" As Henry pulled the gun out of his waistband, Lauren rushed forward, pushing his arm to the side. He smacked her, hard, the force of the blow cracking against her cheek, and she faltered. Then an unearthly roar of rage erupted from the far edge of the garden.

"Lauren!"

Forty

Dimitri was done with waiting. Turning to the side, ignoring the pain in his left shoulder, he cracked his right elbow down hard against the throat of the soldier standing next to him, driving him to his knees. With another roundhouse punch, he leveled the demigod flat. Then he turned and bounded toward Lauren and Smithson.

The two of them were in a battle for Smithson's gun. Lauren, in her ridiculous shift, torn and hanging from her shoulder, was fighting the man as fiercely as anyone he'd ever seen. But Smithson was clearly no stranger to a fight. With another resounding crack, he struck Lauren in a body blow that caught her across the shoulder, and she went flying as he whipped around. He stopped Dimitri cold with his raised pistol.

Dimitri raised his hands, his attention torn between Lauren and Smithson. "Take it easy, Mr. Smithson," he bit out. "This is a misunderstanding."

"Yes, it is. Yours." Smithson drew himself up. "This is how it's going to work. You're going to die like the good little bodyguard that you are, and I'm going to collect my fiancée and return to my yacht. I'll express my condolences to the king and queen, maybe settle a nice cash amount on your family—assuming you have a family—and wash my hands of the whole affair."

Lauren was pulling herself to her feet, and Smithson flicked a glance to her. "I didn't strike her that hard, and my doctors will pronounce her fit and competent. And, fortunately, you won't be around long enough to complain."

She wobbled a little, and Dimitri fought to keep himself from clenching his hands into fists. His standing orders from the Crown were good ones, solid ones. He couldn't kill Smithson, had to take him alive or not at all. He sure as hell wasn't planning to die by the idiot's hand either, of course, but Lauren didn't know that apparently.

"Henry—no," she said, her voice so ravaged and broken, it distracted both Dimitri and Smithson. Slowly, as they watched, she dropped to her knees, her hands up in supplication.

She was begging. This woman, this proud, defiant, spoiled woman who had every advantage handed to her and never needed anything in her life, was begging for his life.

"Don't kill him, Henry," she said, knowing instinctively not to give Dimitri a name, a face. "He's nothing to you, the merest inconvenience. His words don't have the weight of yours—or of mine. And I will be your wife, your Echidna, dedicated to you in all things."

His *what?* Dimitri's lip curled as he glared at Smithson. The fact that Lauren even knew the name of Typhon's consort, that Smithson clearly had assigned it to her as some sort of term of endearment, still didn't give them solid proof that Typhon gave one shit about this scumball. But it definitely gave the Crown plenty of reason to interrogate Smithson within an inch of his life. Even if he might be roughed up a bit by the time Dimitri delivered him for questioning.

But Lauren kept going. "I will do whatever you want, be

whatever you want. All for this one favor. Don't take a life as we set forth to embark on ours."

"Why shouldn't I?" Smithson's gun never wavered, but he seemed transfixed by Lauren, marveling at her. Her torn clothing and disheveled hair somehow didn't stack up to the strength of her face, her eyes. The rigidity of her body as she kept kneeling in a position of devout prayer. Beseeching Smithson, who appeared to be enjoying being beseeched. *Bastard.*

"Because you have everything, Henry. You don't need to add an insignificant death to the ledger. You more than anyone know the value of having someone be in your debt. I will be in your debt, for this as in so many things. I will owe you so much more than I can ever repay. I will be yours, without murmur, without opposition. What you want, I'll want. What you crave, I'll give you. Give you or find for you. And I will never leave you."

Henry's focus sharpened. Something seemed off about that, and Dimitri thought again about the documents on Smithson's boat. The marriage contracts, binding and final. Why was he so fixated on securing Lauren Grant to him, forever and always? It couldn't be her money. He had that in spades. So what...?

Lauren wobbled, fell, scrambling up to her knees again as Smithson watched her struggle, a smile playing over his lips. "He may not live the night anyway, Henry. Look at his shoulder. That's a lot of blood. Why do the work of nature if that's what's in store for him?"

She pulled herself upright then and edged closer, and Dimitri blinked. She wasn't moving toward Smithson; she was moving in a direct line—toward him. Not toward him precisely, but *between* Smithson and him. As if despite everything, she could still regain control of the situation somehow.

"And if he does live, who would take the word of a critically injured man against yours?" Lauren continued. "He'll have no supporters alive. But if you kill him, he's a martyr."

That seemed to get Smithson's attention, and Dimitri fought another surge of outrage at Lauren's intervention. She was playing a dangerous game here. No, he wasn't planning on taking a bullet from Smithson's gun—one wound was enough for tonight—but he could tell by everything in Lauren's body, her words, the tone of her voice that she'd already made up her mind to take that bullet for him. As if that would change anything, as if that wasn't the dumbest damned thing he'd ever heard in his life.

As if that didn't make his heart want to stop, right there in the middle of the clearing.

"Threaten him, Henry," Lauren said quietly. She'd almost dragged herself into the direct line of sight between the two men, but she stopped, smart enough to know that capturing Smithson's attention alone was better than having that attention split between two focal points. But she was speaking so softly now that Dimitri had to strain to hear her. "You have the power of the world in your hands. You know that. You've always known that. Because it's true. Tell him now what will happen to him if he tries to cross you. Make him understand."

Smithson's lips twisted, but his expression was supremely smug. "That's the Lauren Grant I have come to know and love," he said, waving the gun at her. "You tell him." He watched her hungrily as Lauren pivoted, reaching out to Dimitri, her face resolute.

"If you do leave this place alive, you must never go after Henry. He will always win." Her words were deliberately cold. She didn't look at Dimitri. Couldn't look at him, he realized, whether to protect him from Smithson or because she would falter, he didn't know.

But he found he yearned for the feel of her gaze upon him

once more. Wanted nothing more than to drink in her beautiful eyes, her smile.

She continued in a wooden tone. "Whatever your weak point is, he'll find it. Your childhood friends you had lost complete contact with, until a pattern forms that you can't ignore. Former lovers. Current lovers. Family members. Coworkers. Pets. Your bank accounts. Your treasures. Your mementos. Things you didn't know you cared about desperately, until they were taken away from you. He applies the right pressure, and he applies it quickly and assuredly, so that he doesn't have to reapply the pressure again. Because with the first touch, he's already broken you."

"You're making me seem quite frightening," Smithson drawled, clearly enjoying the moment.

Lauren didn't turn to him. "And when he grants you some sort of reprieve, it isn't over. It's never over. That's his genius. He'll remind you in ways you can't imagine that he is always out there watching, always waiting for you to make a misstep, say or sometimes merely think the wrong thing. He's everywhere."

"Why, Lauren, I'm flattered."

Dimitri's lip curled. He couldn't abide allowing this man to live another second. Just as he couldn't abide the fear that rolled through Lauren like a sickness, the incredible hopelessness. That she was consigned to a future without rest, without escape. No one should feel that way.

"And yet," Smithson continued, "I think the lesson isn't quite over yet. You should never try to talk me out of something that gives me so much pleasure, Lauren. Remember that."

He lifted his gun, and Lauren screamed.

But the shot that came was fast—too *fast!*

Everything seemed to happen in slow motion. Dimitri reacted to Smithson lifting his gun to surge forward and away, to get himself and Lauren out of the trajectory of the bullet, but

Lauren jumped sideways, her arms outstretched, as if in a single leap, she could cover his body with hers.

But it was Smithson who staggered back at an unexpected angle, Smithson who fell as Dimitri lurched toward him, the blood bursting from Smithson's head irrefutable proof that he wouldn't get up again. Dimitri turned, bracing himself to launch at the soldier who stood at the edge of the clearing, the soldier he'd dropped to the ground but hadn't—quite—knocked out.

The man who threw his gun down as they watched and rubbed his face with a grimace.

"My thanks. I've been waiting for a chance to take him out cleanly for over a year," he said, his accent once again placing him as Greek, though he spoke clear English. "The owners of the yacht Smithson commandeered are dead, you should know, dumped into the sea. You won't find them. However, there's a brace of his men left aboard who I'm sure would turn on him in an instant. He wasn't well liked."

"I can see why. He claimed to be a follower of Typhon. You have any intel on that? Is Typhon on the move?"

The man shrugged. "Not through this asshole, not from what I could ever tell. If he had a direct link to Typhon, he would have been better protected. You'll still want to check the gates, though. Always pays to be prepared."

Dimitri snorted, though he was relieved to know that the monster god's grasp hadn't extended so far. At least not yet. "Agreed."

"I'll leave you to that then. My work here is done." The soldier of Zeus stared up at the night sky. "The official story circulated to the criminal syndicates will be that Smithson cheated my employer. My employer took offense. But he is a patient soul, and now he will be a happy soul."

"Your...employer," Dimitri drawled. "I feel I may know this employer."

"You could know him a lot better, if you choose to do so." The man favored him with a wry gaze, his wild blue eyes fierce with unexpected joy. "He knows of you, is proud of you. He's honored by what you've already given. But a man must make the decision to serve him twice. Once when he doesn't understand what he's giving up, and once when he does. Your time is coming and..." he slid his gaze to Lauren, then back to Dimitri, and smiled. "I know you'll make the right choice."

Dimitri stared at him, but the man merely turned to scan the dark forest again. "Unfortunately, if Smithson's men see me, I get shot—and as you well know, I can die as easily as the next soldier, no matter who I work for or how long I've done so. I don't suppose there's another way off this rock?"

Dimitri pointed. "Path to the secondary port. The bartender will set you up if you have money."

The man's teeth flashed in the darkness. "Money, I have. Sorry about your shoulder. I cut for show. Smithson liked blood. A lot of it. With you injured, he relaxed his guard just enough."

It was Dimitri's turn to smile. "It's the only reason you're still alive. You should have told me who you were earlier or I wouldn't have hit you so hard."

The demigod of Zeus snorted, teeth gleaming in the darkness. "And where's the fun in that?"

Forty-One

Lauren couldn't stop shaking. It all happened so quickly, and yet at the same time, she couldn't stop seeing everything as if it was in slow motion. Dimitri lurching forward, the sound of the gun, her turning in time to see Henry falling back and collapsing to the ground. His eyes were open the whole way, but he wasn't looking at her anymore. He wasn't looking at anyone.

Vaguely she was aware of Dimitri talking with the guard who'd obviously shot Smithson, but she couldn't hear them over the roaring in her ears.

Then Dimitri was at her side again. "Lauren—Lauren, easy now. How bad are you hurt? Is it only your neck?" he asked, his voice brusque and firm. He placed a balled-up wad of cloth against her collarbone where Henry had sliced the deepest, and it took her a second to realize where it came from.

She stared at Dimitri's bare chest, fully coming back to the moment. "You just couldn't wait to get naked again in front of me, could you?"

Dimitri laughed gruffly, then he pulled her against him, lifting her in one swift move.

"Wait—your shoulder!" she protested. "You're injured worse than I am."

"Bloody but not deep," he dismissed her concern. "Henry apparently needed to vet his bodyguards more closely, but there was no faulting the man's aim."

He reached the edge of the swaying trees, then set her on her feet and dropped to a crouch. He picked up a small pile of weapons and equipment, stowing his gun and knife efficiently. He waved the phone at her. "He didn't hurt me badly. He also didn't destroy my equipment right away, the way he should have. So I had a suspicion he might prove useful in the end. As I proved useful to him."

She swayed a little but stepped back from Dimitri when he stood. "Where is he now? Are you going to let Stefan and Cyril know?"

Dimitri grinned in the glow of his phone as he powered it back on. "Not yet, I don't think. He deserves a head start."

"But Henry...his other men—"

"That we'll need to address. But first, let's get you out of here."

The flight back through the trees was swift. She refused to let Dimitri carry her, because the wound at his shoulder still seeped blood, despite his clamped hand on it. Her own wound was far shallower, but he wouldn't accept his shirt back until they reached the rover.

"Dimitri, you have to go to a doctor," she said, trying to force her words to remain steady.

"Not necessary for either of us, though you'll get the full workup when we get back to shore, so brace yourself for that." As he spoke, he half-ripped, half-knifed his shirt into long, rough strips, quickly and competently instructing her on how to wrap his wound. The remaining cloth he used to form a neat pad, which he handed to her. "Pressure is key. I don't have tape, but they will on the boat."

"Why do I get the feeling you've bound up a lot of wounds?"

"Not as many as you might think." He flashed a smile. "The ONSF are too fast for most of our enemies." He looked up and squinted to the port, nodding once. "The speedboat's here. Let's head out." The phone was at his ear as he turned, leaving Lauren to trail behind him as he connected a phone call. They spoke in rapid Oûrois, and she found she didn't have the heart to translate. She hadn't lost that much blood, but suddenly— nothing seemed to matter anymore.

A curious melancholy settled over her, impossible to shake. She managed to keep her feet until they reached the boat, and with quick dispatch, her wound was reviewed, her vitals checked, and she was pronounced not likely to go into imminent shock. Dimitri left her side the moment she had the blanket around her, and the boat turned toward open water. She stared through the narrow windows as the boat picked up speed, and found herself drifting...drifting...

Seemingly seconds later, Lauren woke up with a start, blinking owlishly.

This wasn't the boat.

This wasn't a hospital either.

In the semidarkness, which was punctuated by glowing monitors, the room seemed lavish yet vaguely clinical, with a cart at her bedside set up with blinking monitors. Where was she?

Then she woke up more fully and jerked to attention as she recognized Dimitri by her bedside.

He was sleeping in a chair. The seat should have seemed too small for him, as large as he was. But he seemed to occupy the space perfectly, not ungainly at all, more poised, ready for action...even in his sleep. His shoulder was heavily bandaged—she could see the trailing edge of the white gauze beneath the collar of his loose button-down shirt. But he appeared healthy. Whole. As if he'd already healed.

Was that possible? She watched the rise and fall of his chest, and her mind was suddenly filled with too many images, too many impossible truths.

And is Henry really...gone?

She jerked her attention to the front of the room as a door opened quietly. She squinted as she recognized Nicki, who strode into her room without making a sound, her weight on her toes in that uniquely athletic way she had, always ready to dash off in another direction at a moment's notice. Lauren waited until she was all the way up to her, then pointed to Dimitri and held a finger to her lips.

Nicole nodded, leaning down to keep her voice low.

"Hey. I figured out where they were keeping you as soon as I could." Her eyes widened as she eyed Lauren's bandage. "Girl, you know how to have a good time. They told me Dimitri was *knifed.*"

Lauren glanced hurriedly at Dimitri, but he didn't stir. "Did they tell you anything else?" Self-consciously, she gripped the sheets hard, ignoring the dull ache in her shoulder. "Do you know what happened to Henry?"

"I know he threatened Maddie, and so you went after him. After that, they completely shut down about the whole thing, and I toyed with trying to get more information but decided I would rather see you instead." She met Lauren's gaze. "Is Henry dead? Did you guys get in some sort of actual *fight* fight?"

"I..." Lauren sighed heavily, trying to get used to the idea. "I think so, yeah. Henry's dead."

"Oh my God, girl." Nicki reached for her hand and gripped it tight, the simple act of friendship nearly undoing Lauren's control. As if sensing that, Nicki kept talking. "They all blew up when Dimitri's call came through, everyone talking fast. I couldn't understand them. They spoke only Oûrois, of course, which was pretty annoying even if it is their native language." She grimaced. "I plan to be on hand when they meet with your parents, because they're totally going to have to speak English then."

"My parents? Where are they?" Lauren endured an entirely new rush of anxiety. Did they know? Had they guessed? And what would their reaction be to Henry's death? Surely they wouldn't blame her.... She tried to remember the sequence of events on the island, but her mind slipped and slid over the facts, unwilling to focus. "Do they know I'm here?"

"In the castle, but not aware of your presence, no. Apparently you're allowed to get a full night's rest before you're put through the gauntlet." Nicki made a face. "Of course, here I am, ruining that. Well, me and the bodyguard anyway. Though at least he has the grace to stay quiet."

Lauren's gaze strayed to Dimitri. He remained asleep. "I tried to warn him away, but I also hoped he'd follow me when I went to meet Henry," she said, unable to speak louder than a whisper. "I didn't know if he would."

"Well, of course he would. That was kind of his job."

"True." Lauren frowned, her appreciation turning into speculation. How much of the past few days had been a duty to the Oûrois captain? How much simply a distraction? And why was he here, now, dozing by her bed, when there would be no way that anyone could get this deep inside the castle to attack her? Why was he with her at all? "Do you know anything about the watch Dimitri found? The one he thought was Ari's? Did Stefan talk to you about that?"

"You're so cute that you think Stefan talks to me. About

anything. He's the most closemouthed demigod I've ever met, no matter how much I want to get him naked. Again."

Lauren blinked at her, focusing on the important part of the sentence. "Again?"

"Well, nearly. I *might* have challenged him to a swim-off in the castle pool once when he decided to read me the riot act about swimming in the ocean. I almost beat him too. But either way, totally worth it. You have never seen anyone so gorgeous undressed in all your entire life, I'm telling you."

Lauren let her gaze shift back to Dimitri. "Well, I think I could give you a run for your money on that."

"Totally different type of hot." Nicki rocked forward on her heels. "So what's going to happen now between you two, anyway?"

"Between us?" Lauren frowned, her heart twisting. "There is no us, Nicki. He's a military captain of a country I don't belong to."

"And a demigod. And your bodyguard."

"Well, that last part was a short-term assignment, one he executed very well. But now he'll go back to his life. I'll go back to my life." The words curdled in her stomach. She hadn't considered what life would be like without Dimitri. Which was stupid. She barely knew the man—demigod—whatever. And she knew only one version of him at that, the version that was designed to keep her in place on a tiny island by whatever means he had at his disposal. He'd chosen a very effective means.

But now that assignment was over, and they both had to get on with their lives. Him to serve his country and the royal family, and her to...do whatever it was she was supposed to do.

What was that again?

"Well, if you ask me, and—" But Nicki didn't get to finish her sentence. The door opened with a sharp click, and Lauren's gaze swung to see Dimitri now standing at attention while Stefan entered the room along with Cyril and the king and queen. When had Dimitri woken up? How much had he heard of her conversation with Nicki?

She watched Stefan take in the room, zeroing in on Nicki. A pulse jumped in his jaw, but he said nothing as Queen Catherine stepped forward quickly. "You're awake, oh good. I told Stefan that you would hardly sleep the night away. You're going to be fine," she said, taking Lauren's uninjured hand in hers. "We have the best doctors on the continent, though Dimitri tells me your wound should be sufficiently tended for the moment, as long as there's no infection."

"There won't be." Dimitri said the words gruffly. Queen Catherine squeezed her hand.

"Well, there you go, dear. Dr. Korba has spoken, and we should all be at our ease now, right? But how are you truly feeling? How can we help you?"

You can't. No one can.

With those thoughts ringing in her head, Lauren removed her hand as quickly as she could from the queen's without being awkward. She turned her face to Dimitri, her chin tilted to the right, her expression serene, though she felt like she'd lost all her tools and tricks. She was completely alone again, her shields torn away.

She'd gotten through worse conversations, however. She would get through this one too. The way she always did.

By distracting everyone.

Forty-Two

"So, is the watch truly Ari's?"

Dimitri heard the question like a pistol shot, only it wasn't aimed at him. Not directly, anyway. It was a flare that Lauren was firing off as a diversion to turn their focus away from herself, and by God, it worked exactly as she'd intended it to.

The queen froze. The king grimaced with the kind of weariness of a man whose secrets are always discovered by the one he loves the most. Stefan bristled with irritation, and Cyril went red. Just another day in paradise.

Catherine recovered first, as Catherine always did. "You found Ari's watch? Where?" It took only a glance at her husband to confirm the truth, and she poked him in the arm. "When, precisely, were you planning on telling me, Jasen? I mean, for God's sake, what does a woman have to do around here to stay informed?"

"It would appear that's becoming easier and easier." Stefan's gaze was once again on Nicki, boring holes in her temple as she ignored him, her eyes also trained on the king.

Cyril tried to break in. "Your Highness, there's no need to discuss this now."

"Don't you 'Your Highness' me," Catherine said, turning on Cyril hotly. In her eyes, Dimitri could see the hope that bolstered him and broke his heart at the same time, the one thing he'd guarded against but hated to see die these past long months. "I asked you if the watch—why am I asking you? Give it to me!" She held out her hand imperiously, as if Cyril had the piece on him.

The adviser lifted both hands. "The watch is currently being examined, Your Majesty."

"It's his." Dimitri was surprised to hear his own voice cut across Cyril's. As everyone pivoted to stare at him, he fought back his own flush at speaking out of turn. But this was Ari they were talking about. Ari, who'd been gone for far too long. "Or if it's not his, it's a close enough fake that it would raise questions all on its own."

"You found it?" the queen demanded. "Of course you found it. Where? How?"

Dimitri glanced at Lauren, who was watching him with eyes too big for her face, as if she couldn't absorb the image of him all at once. Anger surged anew, and he fought it with his own brand of offense. "Lauren did."

That took Lauren off guard as the queen swiveled back to her.

"I didn't intend to!" Lauren said hurriedly, and now it was her turn to lift her hands in unconscious protection against the queen's intensity. "I noticed it as odd, is all. It was being worn by a man who didn't seem to be the type to have such an expensive watch. When I brought Dimitri's attention to it, he thought he recognized it."

"Who is this man?" the queen pressed, and King Jasen gripped her shoulder when she would have wheeled again on Dimitri.

"Catherine, we don't have those answers. Why do you think

I haven't told you yet? There is far too much that we don't know." He squeezed her arm to forestall her next question. "And yes, we are going to question the man who had the watch. As Ms. Grant said, it's clear that he wouldn't have been able to purchase the watch at anything near its real value, and yet he was wearing it openly and without any attempt to hide it, at a port where he knew Dimitri had put out calls for scavenged or discarded wreckage."

There was no way he could miss the queen's wince, but Jasen continued. "We have men in place to intercept his boat at the next port. We'll learn what we can then."

"But where is he from?" Catherine turned again to Dimitri. "His boat—is he Oûrois? Surely not. Greek, then?"

"Turkish." Dimitri fought a weary smile at her expression. He recognized that look as well. Ari had worn it far too many times to count. "But we must first find out how long ago he took ownership of the watch."

"We have to go there—to Turkey. But..." She frowned, her hands coming up to her brows. "We sent so many envoys, requests for assistance. We scoured that coast!"

"We didn't scour it, in fact." Surprisingly, it was Cyril who spoke, almost as if the words were being dragged out of him. "We sent out search parties, of course. But the plane didn't carry enough fuel to fly to a Turkish airstrip, and it was unlikely that Ari would drift so far off his trajectory as to crash-land on a hostile coast. He wasn't an idiot."

"Still, we have to go there," Catherine said again. "We need to find out where he might have been. If he's holed up somewhere, sick or injured or—"

"Catherine." Jasen's words were quelling, but to his credit, he didn't touch the queen or gather her into his arms. Queen Catherine was a woman of strength in her own right. Her emotional outburst might have seemed a sign of weakness in another person, but with her, it simply overlaid a steel core. "If he's still alive, don't you think he would have moved heaven and earth to find us?"

"What if he *couldn't*?" she snapped back. "They could have him in some prison, Jasen, until they figure out what to do with him. Our relations are not all they should be. You know this. What better way to torment us?"

"Not torment." Once again, it was Cyril's voice of reason blanketing the room with its matter-of-fact practicality. "If we don't know, how can we suffer? A year is too long for men with political agendas. Such people are not careful statisticians; they are devious and cunning strategists. If some faction of the Turkish government, recognized or otherwise, had Aristotle, we would have known about it already."

"He could be hiding." Nicki was up on her toes, balancing her weight. "If he's injured, can't get out, he could be trying to hide his identity." She tilted her head. "You know, I was toying around with that windsurfing competition coming up in Alacati, but I bailed for this trip. I could totally try to sign up anyway and poke around—"

"Absolutely not." Unsurprisingly, it was Stefan who snapped the response, but Nicki barreled on.

"Seriously, I'm really good at windsurfing. And I'd be the perfect cover. If there's somewhere you want to check out on the down low, and it's near anything at all remotely coastal, not only would it make sense for me to go it would make sense for you to send some of your strapping ONSF types to protect me. Being the fragile flower and all that I am."

"Nicki—" This was Lauren, now, her face set in unexpected lines of worry. Dimitri caught the wrongness of that look, the tension, but Nicki scowled back at Lauren.

"I can do this," she said resolutely, then brightened and shrugged. "If there's anything to be done, that is. You find something on that boat that makes sense to explore, then I'm your girl. If not, then no harm, no foul."

The men in the room exchanged a glance so obvious it was laughable. No matter what was found on the boat, Nicki wouldn't hear of it.

Queen Catherine apparently didn't get the memo. "Excellent. It's an ideal subterfuge, and completely reasonable. Half the hemisphere knows we have the Americans under our roof, and Nicole's expertise in adventure travel and extreme sports is well documented. With the proper escort, she would be quite safe." Her gaze traveled meaningfully to Stefan, who looked ready to burst a blood vessel.

"Your Highness, it is not advisable in any situation to embroil a civilian in the affairs of the Crown, let alone an *untrained* civilian—"

Nicki scoffed. "You're just mad because I beat you in rock climbing."

"Who doesn't know when to keep her mouth shut."

The comment was so rude coming from Stefan that it was almost breathtaking, but Nicki defused the situation immediately with her bright, bold laugh. "Seems to me having a loud, obnoxious American who doesn't know her place would cause about as much distraction as you could hope for, letting you, and whoever you have tagging along, skulk about while everyone's eyes are on me. I know the Turks aren't big on Western women acting foolishly, so I won't be an idiot, but a little bit of brash can go a long way, I'm telling you."

The queen lifted a hand. "It's an excellent idea if we discover anything of merit from the boat of this man who had Ari's watch. A watch I now want to see." She turned to Dimitri. "Take me to wherever Cyril has sent the thing, Dimitri. I refuse to wait another minute."

She glanced back to Lauren as Dimitri stood at attention.

"You focus on getting well, dear. Your parents will be informed of your miraculous return early tomorrow morning, and you'll want to look your best."

"Of course." Lauren wasn't looking at the queen anymore; she was looking at Dimitri. But he wouldn't—couldn't—meet her eyes. Not and maintain his control. Instead, he focused on the queen.

"Your Majesty?" he said, gesturing to the door.

The queen's sharp eyes traveled between them. "Thank you," she said primly, and exited the room. He fell into step beside her.

She wasn't three steps down the corridor, however, when she turned on him. "Right after you show me where Ari's watch is, get your head out of your ass and go to that girl. You people are so young and foolish, you make my bones hurt."

He looked at her hard. "I'm eighty-two years old, your highness."

"*Exactly* my point," she snapped, looking fiercer than he'd seen her in a long time—maybe ever. "By now you should be old enough to know that love is a gift from the gods, and it should be treated with honor and care. You've given your life in service to the crown, Dimitri. You were a legend in Jasen's father's time. He never would speak of it, but I've seen the reports, seen the paintings. Then you left, returned and became a legend for Jasen. Then you disappeared again, returning only when the crown needed you to protect and guide a new set of princes. You've done that."

"I haven't." Dimitri's fists clenched. "Ari—"

"Is out there, and we'll find him," she said, resting a light hand on his arm. "And when he returns, you will be here for him. I know you will. But the royal family isn't the only reason worth living, Dimitri. Love is, too. Especially the kind of love that comes on the wings of Eros, to strike you unawares. Not even Zeus can deny a love like that."

Dimitri scowled at her. "I committed myself to Zeus and to Oûros a long time ago. It was an honor and a privilege. I have no regrets about that."

"Nor should you. But you were a boy then. It's a different choice now."

He stiffened. How was it possible she was saying the same things as Zeus's agent on the island? What was going on here? "I wasn't a boy. I knew exactly who I was, and I made my choices honorably."

"You did, yes. But this is the first time in all your long life that you've fallen in love. We are all made new in that moment, if we choose to be." She leaned forward and poked a long finger into his chest. "Choose it. Choose love. Don't just protect that girl, grow old with her. That's the biggest gift any soul could give another."

Then she turned and sailed down the corridor.

Forty-Three

Lauren barely waited for the room to clear before turning on Nicki. "Are you *insane*?"

Nicki bounced on her toes. "So I maybe got ahead of myself. But it's not my fault. Stefan has that smirk on his face that I want to rip off him every time he looks my way. I haven't been so universally disapproved of since Mrs. Matusek in the third grade."

"Nicki, that's not what I'm talking about. This is a nonstandard experience if ever I've heard of one. What if you..." She pointed at Nicki's chest. "Collapse or whatever?"

"I won't," Nicki scoffed. "I only told you about my situation because we were zip-lining, but before that, you had no idea—none. I've never gone into cardiac arrest, and I probably won't, no matter what my family history."

Lauren closed her eyes. On the day that Emmaline had met Prince Kristos, the two of them had gone zip-lining in the middle of the Oûros mountains while Fran and Emmaline had toured the royal palace. Before they'd reached the base where they'd begin their expedition, Nicole had measured out a cocktail of beta blockers, which she downed with the practiced ease of someone long used to medication. She'd explained the bare minimum of the risk she took on a daily basis regarding her heart condition and had refused to say anything more.

Lauren had gotten the rest out of Emmaline, and it wasn't good. It wasn't bad, hopefully, probably, but Nicki would never know for sure until she consented to get fully tested. Which she was dead set against. And that meant that every time Nicki pushed herself too far, she ran the ultimate risk.

So, of course, she pushed herself too far on an almost daily basis.

"They have to know, right? Stefan and the others. They worked up a file on you."

"They did." Nicki grinned. "But my heart data wasn't in it."

Lauren narrowed her eyes. "Why not?"

"Because I haven't been tested for hypertrophic cardiomy-opathy. Not officially." She waved off Lauren's glance. "I got the beta blockers due to migraines I had, and I take them because hey, they might keep anything worse at bay. And though I'm sure our families all got a full financial workup once the whole Emmaline thing hit here to make sure none of us needed the royal family's cash reserves, apparently our medical conditions weren't considered a potential threat to Oûros national security."

"But they should know."

"Why?" Nikki shook her head. "Worst case, I get dizzy and sit down. If it's worse than that, well, I'll deal with it. If I can find a way to bring along an AED, I will. But I told you before, I'm *fine*. I would have collapsed by now if I was going to."

"You don't know that."

"I don't not know it either." She shrugged. "It's kind of a moot point anyway. If the Oûros Powers That Be decide Ari is in the middle of some sort of danger zone or somewhere super public and official, they won't let me go anywhere near Turkey.

They'll handle it with their brass and flash. But if he's some-where kinda remote, you gotta admit I'm great cover."

"More like you're a menace."

"Well, don't let anyone know about my heart thing, okay?" Nicki's eyes widened, and she looked more earnest than Lauren had ever seen her. "Promise? If I get the chance to go and do this —it would mean a lot. I can't go through life half-assed, you know? I need to actually *live* it, every day, every moment that I have. Promise me you'll let me try."

Lauren sighed, her own heart twisting. And, as Nicki said, she was probably fine. Familial cardiomyopathy didn't neces-sarily affect everyone in the gene pool. Nicki might have been lucky. She *was* lucky, Lauren was sure. "Promise," she whis-pered. Though it required all her long years of practice to keep the tears at bay.

Nicki's grin was quick and full. "I don't care what Emma-line said about you. You're good people." She was still laughing as she moved toward the door, and only then did Lauren realize that the door wasn't closed.

Hadn't the king shut it when they'd retired from the room? Or Cyril?

As Nicki reached for the door, however, it was pushed open. Dimitri stood there, looking larger than life. He nodded to Nicki and stood aside to let her pass, murmuring something to her that made her laugh.

Then he was in the bedroom again, and this time, he made sure the door was closed. Trapping Lauren in with him, the movement was at once too intimate, almost dangerous.

Suddenly, Lauren's covers didn't feel substantial enough. "Is anything wrong?" she asked as he paced toward her. "Is it my parents?"

"No." He wasn't thrown by her question. Instead, his atten-tion remained focused on her. "Your parents remain unaware that you're here. Your other friends are also unaware—I suspect Kristos may have told Emmaline, but not if he's been overseeing the analysis of Ari's watch."

"Oh." Lauren's eyes rounded. "Have you spoken to Kristos, then? Is he okay?"

"Of course." He took another step toward her, then another. "Finding a piece of Ari's personal effects is a step toward closure, one way or another. It's only a good thing."

"Oh. Well, um, good." She furrowed her brow at him as he finally stopped in front of her bed. "So...what are you doing here?"

"I'm supposed to be here."

"Dimitri, bodyguard duty is officially over, okay? I'm fine. Everything is fine."

Suddenly too nervous to stay in the bed, Lauren threw the covers to the side and exited to the far side of the bed, the large piece of furniture now between them. Was Dimitri smiling? She straightened and reached for her robe to cover up her nightshirt.

"Are you cold?" The low rumble of his voice caught her up short. Before she could process what he was doing, he had moved around the bed and all the way to her side. He lifted his hand to press it against her forehead, as if she was a child with the sniffles.

"What? Of course not."

"Then don't dress. In fact..." He drew his finger down the neckline of her gown, feeling her heart quicken beneath his hand. "I think you might be overdressed."

"Um." Lauren glanced at the still-shut doorway. "What are you doing?"

"This," he murmured, leaning down to her. With a movement as natural as breathing, she leaned up toward him as well, then caught herself, putting her hand on his chest to stop him.

"Dimitri. Seriously, you don't need to do this anymore. Your assignment with me is done."

His laughter rumbled in his chest. "I'm not here on assignment."

"Sure you are." She pushed him away. "You're going to honestly say to me that the queen didn't send you back here?"

The moment he blinked at her she knew she was right, and a sudden, unreasonable outrage took hold of her. More than that, she couldn't bear to be in the same room as Dimitri until she figured out what she wanted—what she needed. And she'd never be able to do that with him looming over her. "You know what, I'm tired of being herded around by you people, and I'm tired of hiding. I want to be taken to my parents. Now."

He scowled. "They're not awake."

"Oh, bullshit. Henry's dead—and even if they don't know *that* yet, they know he's gone missing." She shook her head. "If you think they're casually sleeping while that's hanging over their heads, you're nuts."

Dimitri sighed, clearly exasperated—but also clearly distracted, which worked for her. "You should rest," he said finally. "They can survive until morning."

"No." She pulled back from him, equally resolute. "My parents should know. I have to tell them. Now." She put her hand on his arm when he would have protested. "Please, Dimitri."

He spoke not another word, simply nodded, then waited for her to dress. He also didn't speak as they moved through the long corridors, and she got the feeling that he was angry with her, but she couldn't care about that. Henry was gone. Her sister was safe. She was safe. Dimitri's job was finished. It was time for her to move on with her life.

Her parents were not only awake, as it happened, they were drinking some of the Crown's finest *tsipouro*. When Lauren walked in with her bandaged neck obvious above the tank top sleeve of her shift, they cried out in alarm.

"What happened to you?" her mother managed first, but her father was up on his feet and hustling toward her as well. Both of them looked different. A little desperate, but Lauren accepted their embraces easily enough. It was only when they pulled back that she realized what was strange about them.

Henry. He wasn't with them, when he'd always been with them, every time she'd seen her parents for the last several years. He'd hung around like a specter for so long, coloring everything he touched, that it was exceptionally strange not to have him at her parents' side. Strange...and wonderful.

"Mom, Dad," Lauren said, drawing in a deep breath. "There's something you need to know."

Forty-Four

Dimitri watched the get-together with as much cool dispassion as he could muster, a distant part of his mind acknowledging Lauren's skill at managing the announcement of Henry's death. Her parents were startled—then outraged, especially when she explained how Henry had come to the island searching for her, and how he'd used a threat to Maddie to close the net. Dimitri sensed the grim undertone to her father's reaction, though. He wasn't shocked, not entirely. On some level, he'd known the truth about Smithson, Dimitri was certain. Known it and turned a blind eye.

No wonder Lauren had distanced herself from them.

Dimitri observed their interaction keenly, knowing that he'd be called on to report this incident, to detail the reactions, the words, the protestations. To identify any potential risk to the Crown, even now, when the trouble was past. He did all this work with detached, intense focus.

But inside, he was fighting his own losing battle with his temper.

He'd seen the truth in Lauren's eyes, there in her chamber. He'd heard what she'd said to Nicki, when she thought he was still asleep. Despite what the queen might believe, Lauren was already withdrawing from him. And why shouldn't she?

Lauren didn't understand—couldn't understand—that when his queen commanded his action, he acted. But the queen's order to return to Lauren was only half the equation here. The American remained convinced that his interest was some sort of duty to her, some obligation that she could sweep aside with her checkbook or the promise that she'd take care of herself, when that wasn't remotely the issue.

It was her choice to accept or deny his protection, yes. But it was his choice to offer it to her. Even knowing...knowing what that would mean to his life, his service to the crown. His promise to the gods. She may not choose him, in the end. He might make this sacrifice, give up everything—for nothing.

But seeing her now, so strong and steady...

How could he not promise her everything?

"I feared something like this was going on. But I didn't act, not fast enough." The crack of Mr. Grant's voice recalled him, and he realized Lauren's father was looking at him now, his eyes hard as diamonds. In that moment, Dimitri was reminded that this man was a tycoon in his own right, a savvy businessman. And the ashen cast to his cheeks betrayed his guilt. He was correct. He hadn't acted. Not quickly or well enough. And that was his own burden to bear.

Mr. Grant cleared his throat when Dimitri didn't respond. "You saved her, didn't you? You took her over to that island. You protected her."

"Dad, it was his job—" Lauren began, but though anger flared quick and hot through Dimitri, he didn't need to speak.

Her father did it for him.

"It probably was his job, Lauren," Mr. Grant said, his voice now gruff with emotion. His gaze never left Dimitri's face. "We all have our jobs. If we're smart, we do them really well. But it's not anyone's job to make it personal. That's what he did, made it personal. And that's probably why you're alive now. Alive and safe. Both you and your sister."

Lauren drew herself up stiffly. "You knew Henry had targeted Maddie?"

"No." Her father grimaced. "But I suspected she was the next likely pawn in his game. A pawn like you were, for far too long. I had plans in motion to take Henry down—finally—but the marriage documents...I didn't expect that." He shook his head. "He said you wanted it as much as he did, and I didn't know how to respond. Not until I spoke to you, and I didn't have the chance."

Lauren stared at him. "Wait. What are you talking about? What plans to take him down?"

Her father shook his head, and when he spoke, he sounded as if he was coming from a far distance, his voice remote, stark. "When Henry Smithson showed up in my office twenty-three years ago, he was the most extraordinary young man I'd ever met. He was quick and smart and above all, hungry. I wanted him to be my protégé, my pride and joy, and he was. He so was. I wanted to show off a young newcomer in business who could be as successful as I was, and he exceeded my every expectation. He was perfect."

He sighed. "There was only one time that I doubted him, one time that I saw beneath the façade. A business deal we closed unexpectedly, due to Henry. It was only after the papers were signed that he revealed the sort of leverage he'd placed on our business partners. Leverage that wasn't legal, let alone ethical. But no one complained, and the deal was the biggest of my career to date. Still, I was shocked—and distanced myself for a time. I truly did. But all too soon, I'd forgiven him."

Mr. Grant's gaze was fixed on the far wall, as if he tried to remember how that had happened. "It was as if nothing had ever turned sour between us. And then, later, when he expressed an interest in you, well...it seemed that he was eager for approval. Our relationship stabilized. His business grew apart from mine, and I allowed myself not to watch him too closely. But neither would he let me stray too far." He winced. "He needed me, you see. For legitimacy. For acceptance. Me, and by extension you. I saw that, in the end. I couldn't see how to extract myself from the situation and keep my family safe. He'd grown so powerful by then. I'd begun working with the authorities, but I was too slow."

He shifted his gaze to Dimitri. "You have my thanks, Captain Korba. More than that, you have my gratitude. Thank you for returning my child to me, my family." He sighed heavily. "Thank you for returning my life to me."

"Sir." Dimitri bowed as Mr. Grant turned and frowned down at Lauren's mother, who was weeping quietly, having sunk down to the couch, her head in her hands. "Shall I call for assistance with your wife?"

"What?" He looked up again, then his mouth creased into a tired smile. "No. I have a feeling everything's going to feel a little lighter now." Leaning over, he helped his wife to her feet. The two of them turned to Lauren then, and Mr. Grant's face betrayed his expectation of her rebuke, her disdain.

"Lauren, I have no right to ask for you to forgive me. Henry Smithson was everything I'd ever wanted to be in business, but younger, stronger. And he seemed to look up to me, which played to my vanity and pride. He took what I gave him and grew it fourfold. When I questioned his success, he had all the right answers, and I took those answers at face value. I wanted to believe him. I needed to believe him."

He straightened further, as if he was facing a firing squad for a crime he fully accepted committing. "When he showed attention to you—even affection, eventually—I'm ashamed to admit I was relieved. I felt certain that with a family bond I could control Henry, ensure that all my work with him would make him an honorable man. Surely, softened by his feelings for you, he would take the higher road. When you—your mother—suggested that he was stalking you, causing you distress, all my old doubts resurfaced. But I confess I didn't want to believe you for a very long time. Too long." He shook his head. "And when I finally did, I couldn't tell you. I couldn't risk Henry catching on. Everything I did was in the background, weighing, watching, hoping I would be quick enough to spare you any more danger. I wasn't."

His face looked hollow now, his words barely a whisper. "I should have trusted you, though, trusted your strength. Your skill. Perhaps if I had, you would have been spared this trial. Of all the things I have done, not trusting you to be the extraordinary young woman you are is my greatest regret. I'm sorry, Lauren. I have no right to ask your forgiveness, but I hope one day you can give it."

Dimitri's gaze riveted on Lauren. She had no reason to forgive her father, in truth, no reason to accept his halting, stilted explanation.

The Lauren of a few days ago might not have.

This one, however, stepped forward, enveloping both her parents in a sure embrace. "We'll be okay, Dad," she said, her voice cracking. "Take care of Mom now. You and I—we'll talk. We will." She hugged him tighter. "We'll be okay."

"Lauren." Her father seemed to collapse a little into himself, accepting his daughter's embrace with a racking sob. Dimitri watched, marveling at the scene. The child comforting the parents, when they had never been there for her when she'd needed them most. Her mother might not have understood the importance of Lauren's gesture, but from the look on her father's face, he did.

Both parents were crying by the time they left the room.

Lauren watched them go, and when she spoke, her voice was strained. "I didn't expect that," she said shakily. "I assumed... I mean, all this time. He was working with Henry. They were friends. Since the time I was very small, they'd been friends. He was always at our house, at Dad's work. He was simply... *present*. It never occurred to me that Dad doubted Henry. Not once."

Dimitri nodded, though she hadn't turned to him. "And now? How does that change things?"

"I don't know," she murmured, finally turning to him. "He's gone, Dimitri. I chose to confront him and now he's gone."

He held her gaze. "You've done everything you needed to do to protect your family. Your sister."

"I have," she said, as if trying to convince herself. She seemed lost in the middle of the sumptuous room, drawing her confidence and style around her like a cloak. But her eyes were stark and empty as she glanced away, unsure of where to look next, unsure of what she'd see when she did.

He could help her with that.

He moved closer, then closer still, reclaiming her attention. "I'd be honored if you would make another choice, Lauren," he said. "About the role you want me to play in your life."

Forty-Five

Dimitri seemed to be speaking from a million miles away, and Lauren tried to focus, tried to speak. But it was all—too much. Not only her father's words, but the way he'd looked at her, looked at her mother. This man who had been invincible in her eyes had been reduced to unfeigned, heartbreaking tears. And then he'd left with her mother, the two of them locked in the circle of their mutual love.

Which left her the last woman standing. Exactly the way she'd planned to be.

And that made her feel unbelievably alone.

Dimitri spoke again, and she came back to the room in a rush, her mind suddenly jolting back online. "What?" She blinked up at him. Had he gotten taller? Somehow, he seemed...taller. "I'm sorry, what did you say?"

"I asked you, what role do you want me to play in your life?"

Lauren tried to understand him, but he was saying words that made no sense. "You don't have to play any role in my life, Dimitri. You've done more than anyone could possibly ask."

"That's not what I asked. What role would you *want* me to play? Would you prefer for me to remain your bodyguard?" He smiled as he watched her, as if he was enjoying some private joke. "Your lover?"

Embarrassment flared through Lauren. Why was he saying this? What game was he playing? "You don't have to do anything."

"Again, not what I asked." He leaned down and lifted her chin with his fingers, then brushed his lips across her mouth. The taste of him, honey and heat and Mediterranean spices, speared through her pain, her loss. "What do you *want* of me?"

Lauren closed her eyes to compose herself. Dimitri's job was finished, and so was hers. They both needed to move on to what came next. She knew that.

And yet, she couldn't face the reality of that "next" quite yet. Her parents were handled; her friends were asleep. The future was on hold for everyone else in the stillness of the night. Why couldn't it be on hold for her, too? Why couldn't she simply imagine a future with this man, an impossible, ridiculous future that she could wake up from in the morning? The morning was so far away, after all.

"Why?" she blinked her eyes open again and managed a smile, trying to match her tone to his. She could do "light." She could do "fun." "What do you want to give me?"

"Everything." Dimitri's intensity wiped the smile from her face and she straightened, startled. "Anything, all of it. What-ever you will allow me to give. You're the reason I was born into this life, Lauren. The only reason. And I want you, however you are willing to be in my life. I'll take you as your bodyguard, as your lover, or as your friend—or all of them. As long as I can be near you, protect you. Because though Henry's gone, there is no denying the light that shines from you, a light that only grows brighter as you draw near. There will always be someone who will want to dim that light. Who will want to make you feel less than what you are. And I want to always be there to ensure that doesn't happen."

What is he saying? "You can't mean that." Lauren didn't recognize her own voice. "You barely know me."

"Then it will be my pleasure to get to know you better. Starting now."

"But this is impossible."

"No."

He took her hands, which she hadn't realized were flapping in front of her, and held them between his rough palms. The raw vitality of him radiated through her, and she held still, transfixed by the fierceness of his gaze.

"Flying to the moon and back in a single night is impossible. Loving you is not. You're mine to protect, now. You might not understand that, might not know how to handle it, but that doesn't change its truth."

"Dimitri—"

"You're mine to defend, Lauren. However, and whenever I can." Dimitri's words were low and intense and impossible to ignore. "Mine to cherish in my heart, whether you're a breath or a lifetime away. Mine to honor, whether you're by my side or you never let me see you again. Mine to love."

"Love? Who said anything about love?" There were tears in her eyes. Why were there tears? This was a conversation like any conversation. A negotiation, even. Nothing more. She should hold her face just so, tilt her body slightly to an angle, fix this particular expression on her face...

Except the tears were ruining everything.

"Why are you crying?" Dimitri rumbled, drifting a calloused thumb across her cheek.

"I don't know! You're doing this all wrong. You're doing everything all wrong!" She shook her head, trying to make sense of his words. "You can't love me, Dimitri, you can't be with me.

You have a life. A service to the military, to your people—to Ari. I can't take that from you. I won't take that from you."

"Then you can have a home here."

"Yes, I—what?"

He smiled, so gorgeously full of life that it was breathtaking. "You'll have a home here, in the beautiful lush land of Oûros, a home that flows down to the sea. Where the skies are endless and the water is the blue and green of a million jewels trapped beneath its waves."

"I have work to do..." Her voice faltered. *Is he really offering this?*

"And I have time, Lauren Grant. However you want me in your life, I'll be there. I will keep you safe. I will help you reach whatever goals you fix your heart upon, and I will love you more with every passing day. It's as simple as that."

"But..." She searched his face, struggling to understand. "You can't mean any of this."

"I'm pretty sure I can." He smiled. "There will be some things I need to attend to. Some contracts to honor and others I must break. But if you don't mind, I feel there's some better use of our time than negotiating the terms of this deal you believe is so impossible."

And he kissed her.

Forty-Six

It was as if he had never truly breathed before that moment. Standing in the middle of the palace of Oûros, with this beautiful, infuriating woman in his arms, the woman who was his purpose and his future—even if she had no idea what that meant quite yet—Dimitri felt beyond perfect. He felt vindicated. He felt healed. He dragged Lauren closer to him and kissed her more deeply, reveling as she relaxed against him, her tears streaming down her face. They made her, if possible, lovelier, her careful veneer cracking because of him. Because of the emotions he was making her feel.

"Dimitri," she gasped at length, drawing away from him far enough to rest her head against his chest. His arms slipped naturally around her, the rock that she would always have, as long as she wanted it. As long as she wanted him. And whether that was a moment or the rest of her life—a life he would spend growing old with her—it would be enough. "Truly. You can't mean all this."

He rumbled a laugh, drifting a soft kiss over her hair. "You keep saying that," he murmured. "You are smart, resourceful, caring, determined. These are all things that are easy to love in a woman."

"But..." Lauren blew out a long breath, struggling for composure. She won it after another moment. "Okay," she said. "Let's say for the sake of argument we, um, date." Lauren shook her head at the word. "And let's say I finally start working in earnest, and I'm in Dubai or something and you're here. How is that going to work?"

He shrugged. "Perhaps I will go to Dubai to meet you. It is not so far as that. Or you shall come here to meet me. And we shall have that house to find for you, remember. That will take some time."

"But your work—and Ari. You'll be assigned to go find him, won't you?"

"No. I'm a visible part of the ONSF. I'm not the man ever chosen for covert work. First, I'm too handsome. Second, I'm too big. Very noticeable, especially around the Turks. It would be foolish to send me."

Lauren's tension cracked a little as she smiled, her gaze searching his face. "You want to go, though."

He sighed. "I want to go. However, for the good of Oûros, for the good of Ari, I will stay. I have my men to train, and Cyril will not rest easy unless he is giving someone orders. With Kristos embracing his role as prince, he has no one but me to yell at."

"And what about Kristos? If Ari is actually alive—if he comes back—what happens to him?"

"This is a problem worth having, no? Kristos would be the first to say so. Before this week, I would've said he'd have returned to the military in a heartbeat. Now, with Emmaline in his life and constantly on his mind, he may find a different role to play."

Lauren's lips turned down. "But he won't be able to be crown prince? That's off the table?"

Dimitri rumbled a laugh. "You make it sound like he is being kicked out of the country. There are many roles for royals in Oûros—there need to be. We have noble blood coming out our ears."

She frowned at him. "You do?"

"Ceremonial, mostly, but yes, we do. A long line of fighting princes, spread over every rock and ravine. The royal family may be the gatekeepers, as Emmaline has apparently shared with you, but everyone has a role to play." He heaved a long sigh. "You see, there's much for you to learn about our country. It's good that you'll have a few more days here now."

He watched her face. "Unless you'd rather be traveling in Paris than here while decisions are being made about the search for Ari? It would appear that Nicki seems intent on her ability to assist with the investigation. Which she won't be allowed to do, I've gotta tell you. Stefan would sooner eat his own tongue than go on a mission with an American civilian. Especially an American civilian who gets under his skin. No." Dimitri shook his head. "She would be at best a distraction, and at worst a liability."

"Well, she's not so useless as all that," Lauren protested. "She can run and shoot and fight as well as any man—even with her smaller size. She can swim. And she's fierce."

Dimitri laughed. "So are you when it comes to defending your friends. I can assure you, we will have no reason to bring a civilian into Ari's rescue, if he is truly alive. You Americans have done enough rescuing already."

As if she sensed the changing, more intimate tone in his voice, Lauren dropped her gaze, focusing on his chest. "You make everything seem so easy. You don't know me, Dimitri, not really. This is a vacation, not real life."

"It is real life, Lauren. My life, anyway." He knew, eventually, he would have to explain what he was promising her, what he specifically was giving up to be with her. He knew, eventually, he'd tell her everything. But he also knew that if he did it too quickly, she'd protest. She'd deny. She'd insist she wasn't worth it. And he wanted time to convince her otherwise.

He'd take that time. Take as long as she needed. Even if it was the rest of his life. "I have already decided that my lot is to be by your side. It's up to you to do all the deciding now."

Forty-Seven

Lauren fought not to burst into tears again. Instead, she closed her eyes, willing herself toward calm. Which was why she didn't see Dimitri as he leaned toward her, didn't know he was doing that until he brushed his lips against her brow. "You don't need to compose your face into a camera-worthy smile, Lauren," he murmured. "There's no one to see you but me, and I have already seen the truth."

"You haven't," she said, shaking her head. But she opened her eyes again, struggling to see him clearly. "You don't know anything about the truth of how I feel."

Dimitri's own smile was infinitely tender. "I do. You were on your knees and pleading for my life not six hours ago, princess. You don't do that for a mere bodyguard, not that convincingly."

She sniffed. "I'm a very good actress."

"You're a very good actress to someone who hasn't held you in his arms and watched you sleep. You're a very good actress to someone who hasn't sat across from you as you tried to lie your way out of a conversation time after time after time. You're a very good actress to someone who hasn't seen you defend your friends—whether in public or in the bedroom of a castle, or to someone who hasn't seen your face when you thought all was lost."

"Really." She scowled up at him. "And what are you seeing now?"

"I see a woman who's in love but not sure she should let herself be, a woman so used to disappointment in life—in her precisely arranged and beautifully decorated life—that she pushes away the possibility of great joy if only to avoid the potential of pain or mediocrity. And I see a woman who hasn't stopped touching me since we met. Who's been unable to stop looking at me since we met."

"That's not true!" Embarrassment flooded her cheeks, but Dimitri picked her up bodily and held her to him, bending her back as he kissed her lips, the unbandaged portion of her neck, every inch of her skin that he could reach.

"It's not only true, it's a good thing," he said, his breath hot against her skin. "Because since the moment you strode into the prince's circle on the beach just a few weeks ago, I've not been able to stop looking at you, touching you, tasting you. And I don't plan on giving that up anytime soon." He held her close. "So what'll it be? Will you give this future a try, or will you return to your pale walls and pale men and pale life?"

"It has to be on my terms," Lauren said, sounding desperate to her own ears. Desperate—and strangely right too. "My world. My terms."

"Of course," he said. "And what are your terms, Lauren Grant, so that I'm sure to get them straight?"

"I'm working on that." She stared at him, disbelieving but unable to deny the fierce resolve in his gaze, in his body, in his strength. He was giving her...everything. If only she could take it. If only she would. "I do know I want you in my life, though. Here, wherever. Until I change my mind—or you do—or—"

"We will handle any changes as they come," he allowed. "But until then..."

"Until then..." She met his gaze head-on, pouring everything she couldn't say into the only words she could. "Please don't let go of me, Dimitri. Please don't ever let me go."

His sigh of relief was so deep that it sounded like it came from bottom of the ocean, then he grinned and drew her close again. "Your wish is my command, princess."

Thank you for reading CAPTURED! Lauren's and Dimitri's story was too big to be completely wrapped up in one story, but we'll leave them to learning about each other a bit more and catch up with them in a future epilogue! For now, the adventures of Oûros continue as a demigod spy with ice in his veins reluctantly teams up with a hot-blooded adventure girl in **CLAIMED**, where Stefan and Nicki lock horns...

I'VE GIVEN the gods everything. They're not getting her, too.

As the chief diplomatic ambassador of Oûros, there's no challenge I won't accept from the crown. No task too dirty, no op too dangerous. After all, I was committed to serving this country by Hermes himself—and as a demigod of trickery, subterfuge and adventure, I know life is the ultimate game.

Then the crown asks me to team up with a daredevil American who sets my blood boiling and my teeth on edge, the two of us assigned a dangerous mission to find the long-lost royal son. How can I protect this woman who tempts the fates so blatantly, always taking the most dangerous course, the riskiest leaps, and never seeming to care if the next adventure will be her last?

I'll just have to give her something to live for.

Keep the romance going! Sign up for my mailing list at www.jenniferchance.com to learn about upcoming books, giveaways and more. Other places you can find me online include my website, or on Facebook.

I appreciate your help in spreading the word about my books, including telling a friend. Reviews help readers find books! Please leave a review on your favorite book site.

Turn the page for an excerpt from CLAIMED!

Excerpt: Claimed

Nicki Clark inched her fingers along the thick ridge of the stone wall, grateful as always that the kingdom of Oûros had a deep and abiding love for ornamental frescoes over every door, window and empty roofline in the city. She hadn't tried escaping the palace at this particular point before, but the descent so far had been easy.

Getting down the last several feet would be more of a trick.

"One...two..." she muttered, planting her right foot solidly as she eased her way down. She didn't have to jump the entire distance, not yet. The wall was smoother below this point, but it was nevertheless hewn out of thousand-year-old chunks of stone. She could get purchase for at least another yard, then drop. Her shoes were sturdy and her grip strong. Besides, she'd already done this a dozen times in the weeks she'd been trapped inside the gilded palace like a caged lion.

She shimmied downward, her heart rate picking up. She'd not scouted out this specific four feet of wall, she'd merely glimpsed it in passing from down the alley when she'd been out shopping the day before with her three friends. It'd looked promising, but the space below her was currently hung with early morning shadows, and she couldn't see beyond the next small jut of stone.

She swung a foot out experimentally—

And nearly fell off the wall when it was forcibly stopped by someone's hard grasp. A grasp that was infuriatingly familiar.

Nicki gave her foot a hard shake. "Back off, Stefan."

The diplomatic ambassador of the royal family of Oûros held fast.

"If you insist on clambering over walls to escape the confines of the royal palace, you should at least do a better job of picking your locations," Stefan said in his cool, superior voice. When he wanted, like now, he could speak English without so much as a trace of the thick accent she'd heard him use when he spoke his native tongue. As usual, she wished he would stick to Oûrois so she didn't have to listen to his complaints about every detail of her existence.

"So far as I can tell, there's nothing beneath me but you. And if you have your hand on my foot, it's not a far drop. So go away."

"I'll catch you."

Nicki took a moment to rest her head against the cool stone. Solid rock was more reasonable than Stefan when he got that tone. But she couldn't give in to him—not on this, not on anything. And she definitely couldn't let the drop-dead gorgeous demigod know how he made her feel.

Purchase CLAIMED now!

Acknowledgments

A huge thanks is due to my original editor, Linda Ingmanson, and proofreader, Toni Lee, as well as my new editor Holly Thompson. Any remaining errors after their careful work are definitely my own. To Liz Bemis, thank you for everything you do to make the internet—and my site—a more beautiful place! To Sabra Harp, thank you for being with me on this crazy journey—I couldn't do it without you! To Jennifer Dickey and Laurie Clark, thank you for your thoughts and suggestions on some of the factual elements in this tale. I won't share what, so as not to incriminate you in the inevitable event that I have gotten anything (everything!) wrong.

And to those readers who have continued the journey with the gatekeeper royals of Oûros, *thank you*. And keep on dreaming.

Also by Jennifer Chance

Gatekeepers of the Gods

Courted

Captured

Claimed

Crowned

Boston Magic Academies

Touch of the Mage

Blood of the Mage

Heart of the Mage

Soul of the Mage

The Hunter's Call

The Hunter's Curse

The Hunter's Snare

The Hunter's Vow

Teaching the King

Tempting the King

Taming the King

About the Author

Jennifer Chance is an award-winning author of magical modern romance and romantic fantasy. She is also the urban fantasy and paranormal romance author Jenn Stark. For free reads, news, and a magical escape from the ordinary, connect with her at jenniferchance.com.

link: https://www.jenniferchance.com

fb: https://www.facebook.com/authorJenniferChance/